THREE BULLETS TO
THE WIND

ALSO BY NICHOLAS OSBORN

Bullets Trilogy

A Day Late and a Bullet Short

THREE BULLETS TO THE WIND

BULLETS TRILOGY BOOK TWO

NICHOLAS OSBORN

WOLFPACK
PUBLISHING
— EST 2013 —

Three Bullets to the Wind
Paperback Edition
Copyright © 2025 by Nicholas Osborn

Wolfpack Publishing
1707 E. Diana Street
Tampa, Florida 33610

www.wolfpackpublishing.com

Paperback ISBN 979-8-89567-300-3
Ebook ISBN 979-8-89567-299-0
LCCN 2024951292

Dedicated to those protecting the pages of history we may never read.

THREE BULLETS TO
THE WIND

CHAPTER 1

For most, a blank check is a ticket to do just about anything they damn well please, but for a man aiming to do something as downright ruthless as what Cannon Hunter was after—it amounted to nothing more than a hasty means to a violent end.

All the money and resources Cannon could muster led him to face down the drunken mess of a man in front of him. His sniveling, bloodied nose from a brawl that had turned deadly in a hurry looked worse against swollen, bloodshot eyes. Cannon stood like a grizzled, stoic sheriff of a forgotten town, staring down the poor excuse of a man who'd pushed his luck too far. A shock went down his arm, building up in his shoulder before shooting down through his wrist. It was an all too familiar feeling for Cannon that concentrated as it always did in just a single point on his body—his trigger finger.

"You know good and well what you done back

there was bullshit," the frenzied man shouted in Cannon's direction.

"You don't have a clue what I know. If you did, you sure as shit wouldn't be doing all this. All it's gonna do is get you killed."

"I did what I had to. And I don't regret it none either."

"I'm sure you don't," Cannon admitted, tugging at a leather strap on his hip that snapped open to reveal a S&W.45 blackened carbon steel revolver clung to his hip. "Assholes like you don't tend to regret much. Not until y'all see what it's like to get caught staring down the wrong end of a barrel."

Their untimely standoff had broken out beneath the shining stars hanging in the East Texas sky. They blanketed the horizon, shining as if each one existed only to cast a glorious light down on their feud unfolding in the middle of the night. The sweltering humidity had caused enough sweat to form on their faces to reflect that very same light back at one another. Pine needles and dead oak leaves crunched beneath their boots with every shift of their weight, signaling the kind of all-too-quick movement that, more often than not, ended with someone dead.

A dirt road stretched out behind the men in both directions. Its presence snaked through the hills and trees like it was placed by a hand that wasn't man's. For Cannon and the unlucky SOB that stood across from him, it was the road that brought them to confront an inevitable truth of existence. It was the truth that all men must face, one way or another. It was a reckoning.

There was only one pickup truck parked in the ditch. It was a 2000s model Chevy that looked like it hadn't been washed since it was driven off the lot. No matter what happened, only one of the men would be cranking up the old V8 motor to leave with air still in his lungs. It sat off the road with its headlights left on, sending a dingy tint of light into the man's eyes as he watched Cannon closely.

"I ain't gonna take much more of this," the man sputtered through a bloody mouth.

"I don't think you're gonna take much of anything ever again once I'm through with you."

"Sure hope you can do more than all that talkin'."

Cannon let loose a smirk that would piss off a wasps' nest if they caught sight of it on the wrong day, but the man was none the wiser. He was too focused on Cannon's left hand, which had moved ever so slightly to hover above his hip with fingers refusing to tremble.

"You yank out that piece on your hip and ain't either of us is gonna walk away from here. We're just gonna bleed out into this godforsaken dirt in the middle of nowhere. That ain't possibly what you want, right?"

"What do you suggest then, you thievin', murderin' piece of—"

"You turn around and go on that way," the man cut in, flicking his hand toward Cannon nonchalantly, trying to hide the quiver in his voice. "I'll go the other way, and I won't ever come back. That'll be that."

"That might've been an option at one point. It ain't now."

"This wasn't supposed to happen."

"You can still get out of it, you know," Cannon coaxed the man. "All you gotta do is tell me the name of whoever the hell thought it would be a good idea to make you cross paths with me."

The man stopped his blubbering just long enough to consider what Cannon had told him. He was starting to understand the likelihood of surviving a shootout wasn't in his favor and it was long past time to escape. His eyes surrendered first as he painfully came to terms with what was about to happen. The realization he was about to die was setting in. Defiance soon revealed its true self—cowardice. The man could only hope Cannon didn't see his pant leg turn dark.

"Must be a real prick if you'd rather die than give him up," said Cannon, holding a fiery gaze straight ahead. "Or maybe there is no other guy. Maybe you just decided to take the lives of a couple kids and their parents for no other reason than because you could."

An unwelcome silence hung between the two like a delayed pause between two sad country songs on the radio.

"What did you get out of killing that family, by the way?"

"I ain't saying one more damn word to you."

Cannon took his time to study the man across from him. He ignored the burning sensation that spread out across his knuckles, caused from the fight that had taken place before coming to this destitute spot. Although he couldn't see the murderer's pearly whites, he knew the man had one less tooth in that twisted head of his. The gash on his own knuckle was all the proof he needed.

They'd started brawling outside of a liquor store a couple miles outside of Mooringsport, Louisiana. Cannon showed up without saying a word and hurled a haymaker right at the mouth of a burly man buying a case of cheap beer. The man he'd attacked had a week-long beard grown out to hide his weak chin and rotted teeth from decades of spitting snuff into any bottle he could find. A curled-up baseball cap sat haphazardly on top of his balding head and his clothes looked like they were about two sizes too big. After Cannon had grown tired of using his fists to pound the man's face into the concrete for what he'd done, he dragged him inside his own beat-to-shit pickup and found the closest back road he could. With a tightening grip on the steering wheel, Cannon told him that he'd learned about a father of two and his wife who'd gotten killed recently in a random attack not too far away. He told him that he knew who'd done it and he had an idea as to why. The only part he wasn't so sure about was how someone could be so stupid.

The attack hadn't lasted more than an hour up to this point, but for the man Cannon happened upon, it was dragging on without end. A warm stream of his own blood filled his nostrils, leaving a metallic tingle that matched the taste in his mouth. He wanted to think about escaping, but all he could do was try not to piss himself in fear. Pure terror was written plain as day across his face. Their drive soon took them across the state border into Texas where Cannon wasted no time in pulling over onto the side of the road.

"The family you killed inside their own home, they were working for a man named Hugh Mason. He's a private collector who has spent his whole life dragging up just about everything he could find at the bottom of Caddo Lake," said Cannon. "It was the family's job to tag and archive anything that'd been found."

"The hell are you talking about?"

"I want you to listen to this. Hugh wasn't there when you showed up with that shitty pistol stashed in your glove box, lucky as he is, but he sure does want to know who exactly did all that shooting. You starting to get my point?"

"How many times do I gotta tell you? Ain't no one put me up to anything," the man begged, trying to defend his own actions before his outlook soured. "I have my reasons. If you ain't fit to see 'em, then I think we better just get on with whatever it is that needs to be done here."

His tone shifted as he spoke. The battered man tried to find his footing once again. With a shaky hand, he pushed back his jacket to show a rusty 1911 pistol tucked inside his waistband, half hanging out for anyone to see. It was the kind of carelessness that represented just about everything the man attempted in his life.

"If you insist."

Cannon held his hand steady above his hip, no more than an inch above the walnut-handled six-shooter. The gun had seen him through a tough time or two and had earned its way to becoming the extension of his arm that it was today. He wasn't the type to name a tool like some others, but if there was one that was worth a name, it would've been that S&W.45 emblazoned with gunpowder blasts that carried him through fight after fight. His fingers itched to grip the familiar wooden handle again in search of answers that always seemed to elude him. This time they wouldn't.

The man had at long last swallowed his fear and scrounged up just enough stupidity to face down his attacker. There was nothing else left for him to do. His trembling hand wavered, but nothing happened. The liquor that dried his mouth out and left him numb was taking its toll. He swayed amid the dead leaves at his feet, and still nothing happened. The grace he'd been given in drawing the gun at his waist gave him a sense of confidence that he wasn't owed by any means. An inkling of unfounded hope began to swirl in his belly.

The two men—deadly in their own right—stared each other down, basked in the yellow headlights of the pickup. Mosquitos danced in their beams against a dull hum of the internal battery. The power would time out any second, leaving nothing but darkness between them. It was an unspoken agreement that would last until the last light of the headlights.

That agreement wouldn't last long though.

The hand of each man hovered with deadly intent, waiting until just the right moment to make their move. With the sudden echo of a short clicking sound from under the hood of the pickup parked in the ditch, the headlights flicked off and darkness immediately swallowed up everything around them.

Bam!

A muzzle blast of flame and light burst out

between the two, mimicking the stars above them with a blinding flash. A visceral grunt followed soon after. Just a few seconds later, the hard thump of a body collapsing to the ground signaled the end of the fight.

The man could've sworn he saw the Big Dipper right above him in the skyline, or maybe it was the little one. He looked up and let himself become lost for just a moment in the final sight of beauty that his eyes would ever take in. The approaching boots stole the last good thing he'd experience in this world sooner than he wanted. Cannon leaned over the bloodied man and watched him clutching his torso through ragged breaths, eyes darting wildly from side to side. Before death could creep its way across his body, Cannon said something to him.

"You might've hocked away my last chance at finding him," Cannon said through his teeth. "After all I've been through, to think a waste of a man like you might've cost me so much is just about more than I can stomach."

"Please…" the man tried to let out in between short gasps.

"No use."

"Please…don't…"

Cannon kneeled down and flicked at a lighter a couple of times before it struck. Its warm glow illuminated the man's face and reflected against his dying eyes. His expression was frantic, but he was motionless. Cannon extended the lighter closer to his face and leaned in.

"Give me something and I'll make it quick."

The flame of the lighter danced in the fading pupils

of the man. Within the fire, he saw the stars from above once again. He could hear Cannon's words, but they were meaningless. They passed through him without concern. He could see Cannon's lips moving through the shadows of the night, and he thought no more of it than a fly drifting by. A warm sensation began to flow like waves through his trembling body.

"Don't you die yet. Don't you dare do it." Cannon was spewing saliva as he spoke this time. "Not until you tell me where he's at!"

The words that Cannon was shouting down at him no longer seemed to exist to the man losing his grip on reality in the dirt, gazing into the stars surrounded by blackness. That wasn't going to stop him from hollering them anyway though.

"Not yet, you piece of—"

The man stared endlessly into the night sky, unresponsive to the desperate pleading of his own killer.

"Fuck!"

A fist came down on the man's already bruised and bloodied face, then another. Cannon was screaming obscenities as his blows rained down without end. Each strike caused him to raise his voice louder and louder. His hoarse yells turned into the soundtrack of the man's final seconds on Earth. Soon, his face was no longer recognizable. He was lost from this world, along with everything he'd ever known.

Cannon's eyes were as red as his fists as he stared down at what he'd just done. The death that came by his hands had grown as of late. It was becoming him in a way he'd never imagined before. The mess he'd made because of it had cost him this time though. The man wasn't meant to die so soon, and now he'd only become the latest failure in a long line of dead ends. Each one haunted Cannon more than the last.

His frustration had spilled over this time and gotten the better of him—something he wasn't proud of deep inside his bones. Looking down at the lifeless man he'd been bickering with just a few minutes before, he understood this about himself more than ever before.

Sweat ran down into his eyes as he pulled his cowboy hat off to reveal matted black hair against his sunken brow. He wiped his face with a plaid sleeve on his forearm and planted his hat on top of his head once again. Without making eye contact with the results of his work, Cannon walked back to the old musty-green Chevy resting in the ditch without another sound. Fleeting urges of regret and dread swelled in his head. He didn't have many more of these kinds of dead ends left in him.

The engine cranked right up with the first turn of the key and Cannon allowed himself to sink back into the bench seat for just a few seconds. An exhale he knew wasn't earned came next, but he would never afford himself the comfort of closing his eyes. Instead, he focused through the windshield still freshly splattered with bugs from their night drive, and wondered what the man was looking for in the stars. He assumed anything had to be better than what he was going through and didn't blame him for how he reacted, but in some twisted way, he hoped to find the same relief in staring up at them himself one day.

That day would have to wait though, because it

wasn't just a few seconds after he climbed into the pickup that the cell phone buried in his pocket began to vibrate against his leg. He dug it out a few seconds too late and almost missed the call before pushing the phone against his ear.

"What?"

"I take it now isn't a good time." The voice of a woman came through the other end of the line.

"What do you want, Daugherty?"

"You missed your check-in."

"I told you—"

"That you'd call me back. I know. That was three days ago. I think I've been more than patient enough, if you ask me. Then again, that's not really something you ever do."

Cannon let his head fall against the back glass window and tried his best to hide the groan that escaped him at the realization. Time wasn't kind to him these days. Miss Daugherty was always the person to remind him of that cruel truth.

"I got caught up," he started in.

"You always do. That isn't why I'm calling though. You told me to let you know if I ever had anything that might help you find what you were after. And well, I think I might have something here."

Cannon lifted his head and sat up in his seat, plugging one ear with a finger to hear Daugherty's voice a little clearer.

"What is it? Did you find him? Where is he at?"

"Easy, Cannon. I didn't find him, not exactly. You're going to have to come here for me to explain it to you."

"I'm on my way now."

"And Cannon, one other thing. I got another call today."

"From who?"

Daugherty left the line in silence just long enough for Cannon to get the point. He finally allowed himself to close his eyes after all and pushed his fingers into them in frustration.

"Got it."

"She just cares about you. We all do, you know. You don't have to keep up this lone wolf act and damn near dying every night. Your mom is only trying to help. There are other ways to find people in this world that don't involve killing everyone you come across."

"He's my dad. There is no other way," Cannon told her before hanging up and hurling his phone across the cab of the pickup. He jerked down on the shifter to put it in drive, pausing just long enough to click the headlights back on and see their familiar yellow glow —then rolled off into the night to face down one last lead.

CHAPTER 2

"His legal name is Johnathan James Jr., but those who work under him just refer to him as Major James. He says he did a stint with the Navy or something," said Etta Daugherty, longtime operations director for the Nations Heritage & Culture Preservation, more commonly referred to as the NHCP by those who even knew of its existence. "We haven't been able to verify anything like that."

The woman was speaking from the other side of a manila folder that was separating her from Cannon, who sat across from her with his usual frown of disapproval which was impossible to read.

"Major James seems to believe he is a modern-day Buffalo Bill, with a traveling show and all. He's been going from one town to the next like a door-to-door salesman with performances, crowds, animals, and who knows what else. You really do have to see it to believe it. His train carries everything they need to hold their little spectacle, including the staff, horses, supplies, and tech. People pay for a ticket and show up at the train station where he sets up shop for a few hours, only to tear it all down once it comes to an end so they can head to the next show."

A blank stare and static frown were all that met her speech. Etta was an imposing woman on her own. What she lacked in stature was more than made up for with a brazen attitude. Her cropped hair barely touching the reading glasses on her face and upbeat manner belied the intensity that dripped through every word.

"You brought me in for a circus?"

"Not just a circus. You're gonna want to pay attention to this."

Cannon nodded without another word. He stared right through Etta Daugherty, giving all the hints he would ever need as to what she should do next. After taking an awkward second to let it sink in, she continued her explanation.

"I only wish I was exaggerating when I call the man a modern-day Buffalo Bill. It's not only because of the show he is performing for anyone with a spare ten bucks. It's the things he won't show anyone that caught our interest. The man is a purveyor of antiquities where nothing is for sale. I would say he's just an obsessed collector, but that would imply some sort of legitimacy—or sanity."

"So, the man's a common thief."

"Think bigger. Big enough to warrant your attention."

"What do you mean?"

"We think Major James has been rounding up a

trove of just about everything he could get his hands on from the Wild West shows all the way up to the 1920s. In the process, he's said to have the lost records of those employed by Buffalo Bill, birth and family records from Natives that he personally kept, and even documentation on every old cowboy and hand that traveled from convoy to convoy for work."

"You think there's a connection?"

"I think you'd be the best person to find out regardless," Etta told him with her usual bluntness. "If he's got even a sliver of what our sources are telling us, then it's absolutely gotta be you who does this."

"I don't really see how I'm the most qualified guy around to rob a train, but I do appreciate you thinking of me."

As Etta continued the in-depth description of just about everything this Major James had gotten into across a five-year span, a depiction of a relic of a man came to Cannon's mind. The man built the traveling Wild West show in the vein of Buffalo Bill but provided a unique twist for audiences of a more modern sensibility. The NHCP couldn't pin anything technically illegal on him just yet, but if Cannon could verify his possession of stolen artifacts, it would only be a matter of time before the law could catch up to him.

While he half-assed listened to his boss, Cannon couldn't help himself but to notice the room he was forced to return to. Etta Daugherty's office was not at all what someone would expect from such an official agency. It wasn't all worn office furniture with dingy walls and fluorescent lighting. Her office was decorated with ornate wooden trim and uplighting that caused a warm glow throughout the room. The pictures on her walls weren't of trips she'd taken around the world or trophies she's captured in her exploits. They were the last remnants of her own family. A few pictures were framed above her desk, a fringed bag, and a few pieces of jewelry were on a corner shelf behind her desk and a large cowhide rug was stretched out across the floor.

It was something Cannon could relate to. As he sat there taking in what would undoubtedly turn into his next mission for the NHCP, he finally allowed himself to consider what his family must've thought of his most recent exploits. He mostly thought of his mom. Cannon's family had been through so much for so long. Now that they had found their footing at last, he'd been given a sense of the kind of freedom that he'd never experienced before. The only thing he did with this freedom was let himself become obsessed with finding the one missing piece—his father. Cannon Hunter was a man who hailed from an empire that was forged in generational adversity. In her quest to reclaim it, his mom had become the next in line to endure the trauma that such an empire wrought. As much as he hoped to break that cycle, he could do no such thing until he unearthed one last discovery for the family.

Etta Daugherty was one of the only people who was aware of what the business end of his revolver had been up to over the last year. Etta had worked with him over the months to find any leads he could possibly track down and had ruffled enough feathers in the process to get their asses in trouble more than a time or two. She took her position at the NHCP seriously. She believed in the mission to uncover the hidden secrets of rewritten history that were once thought to be lost. Combined with Cannon's own ambition and fervent tenacity, the two found out they made a pretty good team.

"The Major James Out West Show is on tour for the first time and it's already gotten plenty of eyes. People are saying the show is the biggest performance in the last hundred and fifty years. And as luck would have it—"

"Here's where the demands come in." Cannon let out a sigh as he spoke.

"The tour is coming right through Texas with plans to stop at several stations in our neck of the woods."

"There it is."

"You are going to get a couple of good hands, find out where the tour is going to stop in East Texas, and do what you do best. Go get what was taken from us and hidden from the world for so long."

Cannon considered what he was hearing. He thought about the man who was most likely still lying in the ditch off some dirt road still staring up into nothing, and he thought about the countless others that he'd left in his path. He also thought of the envelope that he carried stashed away inside the back pocket of his denim jeans. It was a secret that he'd kept even from Etta, and he thought maybe it had finally become time to let her know about what was inside. It had become a source for so much destruction, leading him to this moment for a reason, but his obsession had become him completely. He refused to return home empty-handed. There was just one more question he couldn't leave alone.

"You learned all of this from someone. Why isn't your source here with us now?"

"About that," Etta started to explain.

"That bad, huh?"

"Well, yes. He's dead."

Cannon sat back in his chair and sighed at what she was trying to hold off on telling him for as long as possible. He hated to think of it, but he had to wonder if she'd left that particular part of the story out on purpose. Even so, he knew all too well the feeling of hiding something out of pure necessity.

"Go on then." He gestured lazily as he spoke, brushing off everything that was going through his head as he did.

"He had standing weekly check-in meetings with us during the show's tour through Tennessee not too long ago. He did good for a few weeks, even got us some other contacts we'd never have found ourselves. Then one day, he stopped showing up. We did what we could to find out what happened to him, but unfortunately, his body turned up last week. He looked almost unrecognizable. We found the rest of his victims over the next few days, spread out down through the path of the train tour."

This time, Cannon sat up in his seat before he spoke.

"Getting the collection in our hands I get, but taking down this asshole based on nothing but a hunch and some dead rat isn't as convincing as you'd like it to sound. We need to be sure."

Etta stood up from behind her desk and turned around without saying anything. She walked over to the shelf in the corner and picked up a necklace that seemed so fragile it might shatter from being lifted. She stared emptily at the jewelry for just a few minutes before Cannon finally spoke up.

"It isn't a hunch, Cannon. He's a murderer, through and through."

"Can I drink on it?"

Etta shook her head and rubbed the back of her neck. "Don't you always?"

Those words were all he needed. Cannon stood up to meet her gaze and finally broke his hard-ass character to let out a smirk. It seemed like the two would have come to the same agreement no matter what was soon to come, and both were aware of it. They instinctively reached out to shake hands for an arbitrary gesture that would get them no closer to finding the lost relics of time hoarded by the showman Major James than the drinks Cannon craved so suddenly.

"You should call her, you know," she told him, pulling him closer without warning while still gripping his hand a little too tightly.

"Yeah, I'm sure that would go real well."

"It's been long enough. She's your mom, and I ran out of excuses three months ago. You won't be able to keep this up forever."

"I shouldn't have to."

"Do you still have that picture? She's asked about

it a few times, I keep telling her I don't know what she's talking about."

Cannon patted the small pocket on his chest and stared at Etta without saying anything else, then stood up, turned his back toward her and never looked back. He made an attempt not to slam the door on his way out as the last bit of goodwill he could scrounge up.

Just as soon as he stepped out of the office and into a small hallway that led to a larger lobby of the NHCP headquarters—which had recently moved from Austin to this side of Jefferson, out in Marion County—he sighed just loud enough to satisfy the uneasy feeling that was building up. The office was empty, so he took his time leaving. Even then, he walked with delicate steps when making his way out to avoid drawing too much attention to himself. The front desk woman sat patiently, clacking away at a keyboard, most likely what she did with every waking second in her life whether at work or not. As he exited the building and was confronted with the blinding sun, he felt for his right-side pocket where he kept the picture Etta had just mentioned.

This time, he reached inside as he kept his stride to the parking lot, and quickly produced a small photograph that still had to be unfolded. He took a quick glance at the woman who graced the picture with an unyielding, piercing stare that went right through anyone who saw it.

Cannon rolled the picture of the young woman over in his hand and saw the one-word note which read a simple name—Rose.

"I'm going to find him, Mom, and then I'll be right to come home," he promised to himself with a whisper no one else could ever hear. "I have to know."

CHAPTER 3

"Round it up! We'll be outta here by nightfall, one way or another." A voice rose from a dull roar of a crowd of people shuffling in every direction. "With or without you!"

The booming voice echoed throughout an entire encampment that had only just been set up the night before in the small town of Hope, Arkansas. They were on their way to Texas at long last, following a six-month trek through the southern United States where they stopped at any station that could wrangle up an audience worthy of performing in front of. So far, the crowds had been enough to sustain them, but Texas was a gold mine waiting to be tapped.

"Round it up, I said!"

The voice belonged to the one and only showman extraordinaire Major James, host, owner, and creator of the Major James Out West traveling show. He was an elderly man of gray, receding hair save a fluffy mustache on his upper lip, a belly that pushed against the buttons of his striped shirt, and a posture that was a little too dependent on the cane at his side. He walked with one leg stiffer than the other but got around otherwise just fine. A history of gathering up crowds simply to take their money in exchange for nothing more than a promise and a little bit of his time had taken its toll. He was a man of experience, of resolution, and insufferable insistence that would carry him through one successful scheme to the next. This had resulted in turning him into a man who'd seen damn near everything at one time or another.

"Mary Anne! You get your ass to the stable cart and help them pack up all those saddles," he hollered. "And don't you forget the bits this time dammit. I ain't paying for another batch again."

A woman scurried off past him as he yelled without making eye contact. Each push of the cane into the dirt carried him just a little further, allowing him to hold a watchful eye on every single thing that happened during the Major James Out West Show. He was too proud to see anything less than the highest standard he could possibly forge.

"And Jesse, I swear to Lord Almighty above, if I see you kick another bovine performer in front of a crowd, I'll start every show from here on out by puttin' my own size eleven shit kicker right where the sun don't shine for everyone to see. You understand me?"

Major James continued his walk through the disappearing encampment that looked like a ransacked rodeo collided with a concert stage, strewing about rope and wire to the point where you couldn't tell the difference between the two. Somehow, just as they had done dozens of times before, the show would be packed up within the next few hours and ready to hit the rails again to their next destination. This was the real performance, and Major James knew it deep down. There were few who could pull off such a feat. It was an artform that was learned in the old Wild West that he knew had to be resurrected for the world to see. The pompous performances, light shows, and trick horseback riding were all a sleight-of-hand distraction to draw attention away from what was really happening each and every night.

"Sir!" a shout came from behind a group of passing men lugging a wooden crate twice their size. They were burly, bearded, and mean-faced men who had grown accustomed to the labor of loading and unloading an entire train worth of equipment day in and day out. They were also the exact opposite of the man who finally broke through their crowded lane, still shouting for Major James.

"Sir, sir!"

Major James watched with a bored look on his face as the man continued to push and shove his way through the crowd, obstructing just about everything he could on his path.

"I have exciting news, sir. I've been looking all over for you," the man continued to shout despite now being close enough for a much lower volume.

"Spit it out, Burwell."

"He told me to tell you he's ready," said the right-hand man and resident scapegoat for anyone and everyone's problems, Ned Burwell.

Major James stood motionless, refusing to respond until Ned caught the hint at what he'd missed out on communicating.

"The gun hand. Pickett, I mean, sir. J.R. Pickett has everything ready to go. He sent me to find you so that you can see for yourself what he's been working on for the grand entrance into Texas."

"Well, why didn't you say so, Burwell! That's just fantastic, and between you and me, it's about dadgum time. We are Texas bound, so we're damn sure gonna need him."

"Yes sir, I agree sir," Burwell stumbled through, still trying to find his footing.

"Come on then, no better time than now."

The two turned to follow the same trail that Major James had just made through the crowd of workers. Ned quickly fell a pace behind so as to not upset his boss. It was a dynamic that had been established between the two the second they had met. Major James had a way of demanding certain things from certain people, and for Burwell, that certain thing was unwavering loyalty in all he did.

"We've finally found a bit of success in this weary old world," Major James spoke up as he threw his cane forward with every staggered step.

"Indeed we have, sir."

"Look at all these people around us. They know their job and they do it well, no different than you.

When everyone accomplishes what they ought to, we all benefit. Does that make sense to a mind like yours?"

"I think so, sir."

"I doubt it, honestly. But can you at least tell me what it is exactly that they *ought* to do?"

Ned took a second to ponder what was being asked of him. He thought so hard about it, in fact, that he stopped walking entirely and let Major James get a few paces further ahead of him in the process. He closed his eyes tight. When an idea finally popped into his head, he speed-walked up to Major James with his arms swinging wildly before he said it aloud, proud as a peacock.

"I can't answer that question because what they ought to do is to be determined by you."

"Took you long enough, but that's why I like you Burwell. You always do what's in your own best interest."

"I do try, sir."

Their stroll through the traveling show gave an idea of what the community at Hope, Arkansas had just been treated to. The horse maze was finding its way back to the stable cart as the wranglers and ropers followed shortly behind. Their backs were piled high with saddles and gear. The dust they all kicked up swirled all around them up into the air, doing its best to obscure any line of sight more than twenty yards ahead. Even that couldn't stop Major James and Ned Burwell from noticing the reenactment crew with a wardrobe that was plucked from museums to show-case the realities of life in the old West, both decadent and desperate all the same. When the crew was backed by the live string orchestra and a light show that'd give any stadium a run for their money, it was easy to see how their performances had become the heart of the Major James Out West Show.

There was no shortage of small-time acts that tagged along as well. Singers and their bands, orators, riders of broncs and bulls—and the teams of behind-the-scenes talent that made it all flow seamlessly for three consecutive hours with each performance—all created the commotion that Major James and Ned had to weave their way through.

On the other side of all of this, the two came into an opening on the backside of the train tracks, out of sight for most continuing to toil away at their work. What they found was far from spectacular, or even impressive. A lone man stood in the center of a circle—dug into the dirt with a stick around him—surrounded halfway with cardboard target. He was holding a mare's leg lever action pointed into the sky and donned a six-shooter strapped to his hip, but it was his smile that drew the most attention.

"The mighty ol' J.R. Pickett has joined us in the twenty-first century!" Major James hollered in a much more lighthearted voice than he used only minutes ago. It was a familiar tone to those who had been sweet-talked by him in the past. "Only, it seems he's brought firearms from the nineteenth century. An interesting twist, but not unexpected. You cowboy types sure do cling to your ways."

"Good to see you too, Major James," J.R. Pickett spoke in a low rumbling voice from behind a bright toothy grin, but loud enough for the two approaching him to see. He gave a simple nod to Ned who puffed out his chest at the slightest acknowledgment.

"I hear that you've something to show me. I can only hope it will be something to impress the entire state of Texas. If there is one thing you should know about me, it's that I'm always on the lookout for my next star attraction."

"My job is to impress you, sir. All I ask for in return is a fair shake. The only thing you need to know about me is that I go where the money goes."

Major James leaned over to Ned and put his opened hand up over his face halfheartedly covering his mouth. "I like this one," he told him. Ned nodded with a crooked smile creeping up onto his face.

"I appreciate the way you think, Mr. Pickett. So, how exactly do you plan on impressing me today?"

"Well, I like to think it's better if I just go ahead and show you."

J.R. knelt down to a small black box at his feet and pushed a button at the top. A couple of seconds later, the cry of a fiddle rang out from its small speakers with lackluster volume accompanied only by a background of white noise. The fiddle played on at an upbeat pace as the man standing in the center of the circle lifted his arms up, hyping up a nonexistent audience.

J.R. Pickett was a black man with a smile that could cause a crowd to burst into applause all on its own. He flashed it for a split second before his face turned serious. The stubble that lined his broad jawline framed the glare in his eye with an approachable look that could catch even the most discernible of folks off guard. It was the ace up his sleeve, and combined with even the slightest smirk, he was able to charm his way into opportunities that had a way of passing others by without notice.

Major James watched him get situated alongside the rhythm of the fiddle, eager to be entertained. He leaned on his cane a bit more than usual as he waited. Ned, however, was almost jumping with joy at the front row show to the newest potential headlining act of the Major James Out West Show.

A familiar cocking sound of the lever action at work seemed to happen harmoniously with the fiddle playing along in the background. J.R. Pickett faced toward Major James with the shortened rifle tossed casually over his shoulder, and with one more flash of a smile, he squeezed the trigger and a target behind him blasted backward to smack the ground behind him. A second later, J.R. flipped the mare's leg in a circle and manipulated the lever action to chamber a new round all in one fluid motion. He followed up with a rapid shot at the second target right from the hip. This set off a chain reaction of three reloads and gunshots that all happened in less than a couple of seconds, each one sending a target flying backward into the dirt.

When he was finished with the rifle, he dropped it to the ground and looked back at Major James. With one hand, he yanked his six-shooter out of the holster on his hip, and with the other, he pulled out five playing cards and splayed them out for each to see. Before either Major James or Ned could predict what would happen next, he tossed the cards into the air and got to slapping the hammer of the revolver. Five shots rang out and each of the five playing cards fell to the ground with a hole in every one of them.

"That's pretty—"

Bam!

The last gunshot from J.R.'s six-shooter fired out with a noticeable muzzle blast from the end of the barrel, but there were no more targets to fall. Instead, it was Major James himself that almost toppled over into the dirt. He stumbled before regaining his composure with a shocked face as he lifted what was left of his cane up into the air. It had been splintered in half by the bullet from damn near thirty-five yards away.

J.R. Pickett stood there with that trademark smile of his and the revolver still aimed straight ahead from his hip. Luckily for the gunslinger, Major James had enough of a sense of humor to see just how impressive each shot truly was, even the one that missed him by merely inches. A smile stretched from ear to ear across his face.

"Say hello to our new headline act, Ned."

"Hello!" Ned let out, obviously confused about why he was doing it.

"That impressive enough?" J.R.'s voice rumbled again as a trail of smoke pouring from the end of the gun barrel reached eye level.

"Moreso. The Texans are sure to love that shit."

"I thought so too."

"I have only one request." Major James settled into his more natural demanding state. He knew when to push his luck all too well. It was a trait that had served him well in the past.

"What do you have in mind?"

"Bigger."

"You said, bigger?"

"That's right. I want the whole town to know what you're doing whether they attend or not, and I want the town next to them to wish we were there instead. You make this act as big and loud as you possibly can, and I'll do everything in my power to make sure everyone sees what you can do."

"You got yourself a deal, mister," J.R. said with a tip of his worn felt cowboy hat. "I've already got ideas."

"Then get to it," Major James said with a cheerful boast. "We're gonna have something mighty special in store for the great lone star state."

When the showman turned to leave with only a slight stumble, Ned assumed it was an invitation to follow him the same way he'd gotten there, but he was wrong. Just as Ned attempted to match his pace, Major James waved him off without another word and left him right where he was standing. Ned Burwell and J.R. Pickett both watched their boss leave them behind, sharing a careless shrug of the shoulders before parting ways.

Major James fought against a noticeable limp without his cane for as long as he could. Though he'd never allow the two he left behind to see him, he was red-faced and furious at the gunshot that took out his cane. He said every cuss word he could think of as he walked, but he kept them all under his breath so nobody got the wrong idea. The only thing he couldn't suppress was the violent cough that surged in his chest. He hacked into his fist with squinted eyes as he pushed himself to get back.

The train he'd gone through so much trouble to get ahold of was the last of its kind still running the rails. A nearly industry-wide monopoly of the railways made a long-term deal almost impossible to accomplish. The key word was *almost*, though. Major James worked with the railroad companies of the future and through mergers, plenty of checks, and even a few more-than-warranted threats to the good people at Amtrak, he secured just what he needed to secure a Union Pacific FEF steam locomotive with a permit to run it. It may have come from up north, but the six-car train looked right at home on tour south of the Mason Dixon Line. When he was all alone with his train, he called her "Big Betty," but that was something only he would ever know.

Major James made his way onto the engine of the train to see the driver with his boots propped up against a ledge and his hat pulled down over his eyes. He would soon be awake for the ride across the border into Texas, so he figured it best to let the man sleep.

The first train car that Major James entered when leaving the engine were the bunks for the crew. They smelled worse than he'd imagined they would at this point in their tour. He pushed forward through the mess and did his best not to think about what he'd seen there ever again. The odor faded into a more welcoming smell of hay and feed as the stable car came next. He once again pushed forward through the car to come out of the other end with a breath of fresh air and a gentle breeze against his face. Facing the flatcar that came in third, he eyed the black steel-enclosed car that was fourth in line and started limping his way to its entrance.

When he slammed the heavy, rattling door closed and spun the lock behind him to ensure he was alone, he exhaled for a few well-earned seconds. With a sudden burst of energy, he hurled the splintered cane across the inside of the car as hard as he could. He listened to it smack everything it could in its flight and only grew more pissed at what had happened outside. If he didn't need the sharpshooter so desperately, that entire situation would've been handled differently, namely with letting the son of a bitch take another breath after what he did.

Locked inside all alone, Major James let his limp settle back in as he continued through the train car that landed right in the middle of the train. This one was only his to enter, though. This was a sacred place for him. It held everything he ever worked for in his life, his pride and joy, and only reason to continue putting up with the shit he dealt with.

He walked short of breath beneath an oversized banner advertisement that read BUFFALO BILL'S WILD WEST AND CONGRESS OF ROUGH RIDERS OF THE WORLD without ever looking up at it. There were saddles strung up by the dozen—with some belonging to the original showman William Cody himself—along with firearms owned by the likes of Annie Oakley and her husband Frank Butler, and an entire wall of belt buckles coming from across the entire United States, given to just about every star of the Wild West shows from over a hundred years ago.

He made his way through the inside of the train car that looked more like the home of a hoarder than a respectable collector or purveyor of fine antiquities. There were stacks of old torn pages that piled up six, sometimes seven feet up into the air, and tilted hard enough to tip over against a faint gust of wind. It was a whimsical chaos that inundated the senses when experiencing Major James's collection car. Plaques and advertisements, rows of dusty old books lining every shelf, century-year-old trophies, and enough pictures and artwork to cover every open spot on the walls made it an impossible feat to focus on only one item.

Major James plopped himself down at a desk hidden behind old documents that littered the floor until forming towers that had become covered in thick layers of dust during their travels. He used his arm to shove aside a few folders before throwing his boots up onto the top of the desk.

He never gave himself much time to admire what he'd collected through the years. That would be a waste of time when he could be growing it instead. When he allowed himself to sit at his small secretary desk and gaze around at what he had acquired in just the short time of their tour, he couldn't help but let out an exhausted smile. There was a feeling of fleeting contentment that he hoped to find surrounded by relics of history that the world knows only to be lost to the passing of time, but he never seemed to hold on to it for long. He was consumed by holding onto more and more of that lost history, and more than that, he yearned to carve his own legacy into history. For that, he would give everything he had or would ever make. Luckily for him, he had the money and the opportunity to chase that dream of making his mark in the history books every single night.

Major James picked up an old rotary phone off the corner of his desk that looked like it hadn't been used in a few decades and pushed it to his ear. The spinning of the dial clanked and grinded, but it still worked after all this time. He listened to a single ring before it stopped. He was the first to speak, as always.

"What do we have tonight, boys?"

The other end of the line came through staticky, but understandable, as someone from his staff answered. "More than last night, if you can believe it. We even have one guy who says he turned down a million-dollar offer from the Smithsonian for an art collection by Frederic Remington that no one has ever seen before. Says he can verify its authenticity and all that."

Major James didn't miss a beat in his response. "Anything else of interest?"

"A couple of gun collectors have called in with a few five-digit serial 1880s engraved Colts, one who has some letters written by his family—the Throckmortons —that go back to the late 1840s, and some guy who claims to have a ten gallon from the real Tom Mix."

"Throckmorton? You're right, I can't believe it. Looks like we have another busy night."

"Yes sir," the voice answered. "We sure do."

"And the checkbook?"

"After these last few shows, I'm starting to think

we could do this every night for the next year and never see a single problem come our way."

"Good to hear," said Major James. "Anything else?"

"Only that we're ready when you are, sir."

"Well, in that case, go ahead and send the first one in."

CHAPTER 4

A dull roar surrounded by the clattering of drinks and screaming of drunks somehow made for the most effective soundtracks to solve a problem that at first, had no answer in sight.

The thinking mind hopped up on liquid courage isn't always the most reliable, however, and Cannon's was no different. Whether or not he could trust the decision he would eventually land on was still up in the air if he was being honest with himself, but he was determined to keep his ass planted in that stool until he came to one regardless.

For a reason that had always escaped Cannon, the bar was a place like that that he typically did his best thinking. He admittedly would have more than his fair share of drinks to help speed the process up, but that was an acceptable consequence more often than not. The particular problem on his mind tonight warranted it. He'd found himself in another steel building with a neon sign hung out front designating it as an official establishment. It was far enough outside of Marion County to keep prying eyes away from him.

Any building in this neck of the woods was bound to be surrounded by pines that looked like spires in the night sky, reaching up perilously in every direction, overtaking everything they towered above. There were few things in nature that could blot out the stars of the Texas sky the way they did. At the very least, the screeching cicadas they housed were drowned out by the noise pollution of the bar nestled right in the middle of it all. Some things in nature still had a unique way of maintaining their beauty.

The interior of the building was every bit as dilapidated as the front. Depending on who you asked, that might be exactly what gave it such a unique charm; the kind of charm that attracted the most unruly, unlikeable type of folk around. These were men who wore boots made more of mud than leather, lived thirty miles from the nearest grocery store, and didn't give a shit what time they started drinking. Although they would most likely turn their angry worldview onto Cannon if he were to say even one disagreeable sentence within earshot, he had no plans of making more enemies with what he had on his mind.

Which brand of cheap whiskey that filled Cannon's glass and how low he should allow it to get was all he focused on. His head swirled with too many thoughts of what he should do next to take any one of them seriously. All he had to do was ignore them until the whiskey did its trick. The only answer worthwhile would undoubtedly linger on. Until then, the only thing he could really do was keep drinking.

"Let's go again." He let out through a deep, burning breath and a slam of the glass, hoping the bartender was paying attention.

The aging man with a belly that hung from the bottom of his shirt and thinning hair that revealed skin on top of his balding head perked up. With a short-stepped waddle which felt more cartoonish than manly for such an establishment, the bartender made his way over to Cannon. He held tight to the bottle in hand as he poured another double. Before he could turn to go back to his stool at the end of the counter, the familiar sound of empty glass hitting the wooden surface set him turning right back around to do it all again.

"This time I'll let you sit down first," said Cannon with a smile on his face and a dazed look creeping up in his eyes

"Sure thing."

The only problem was the place was so loud that Cannon couldn't actually hear the words of the bartender. It was becoming packed with men who were only worried about being louder than the one next to them. The bar swelled from annoying background noise to a place of confined yells and hoots and hollers.

"What the hell is going on tonight?" Cannon asked, now almost unable to hear himself speak.

"County fair. Tonight's rodeo night. These people

here are the locals smart enough to loosen up before gettin' themselves tossed around."

"That makes sense. Looks like I showed up at the wrong time."

"Never a wrong time to be in that stool."

"You're supposed to say that," Cannon smarted off before gesturing to the line of barstools next to him. "How come I don't see you saying it to any of these other fine patrons tonight?"

"Because they're always here. Been here so long they forgot the point of it all."

"There's a point?"

"You don't look like you forgot the point, just like you're trying to figure out what it is. Ain't nothing wrong with that," explained the bartender. "I might be right there with you pretty soon if you keep it up much longer."

"I'll drink to that." Cannon raised his voice as he spoke, lifting his glass that had already been emptied high into the air. Cannon was letting the alcohol do most of the talking at this point, but he didn't mind. Instead of joining him, the bartender saw the underhanded request and started to waddle his way back over to where Cannon was sitting.

The letter that had become as close to him as the revolver he'd known most of his life felt heavier in his back pocket. He dug it out and stared at the folded, stained piece of paper in his hands. He was chasing what it promised, but he also wasn't sure what he would do if he found it. No different than a dog with a squirrel, Cannon had found himself obsessed with the chase, and it stopped him from agreeing to the best chance at finally catching it. Etta had just given the path forward he so desperately needed. He couldn't accept it though. Not even when what he wanted most was staring him right in the face,

Watching the bartender refill his glass yet again, Cannon struggled to consider what taking on the latest assignment from the NHCP would mean for him. The prospect of finding any information that could lead to your dad was too good to pass up. He knew there was no choice. He had to accept it. What he didn't know was why it was so hard just to say yes, much less thank Etta for her hard work in finding such a valuable lead.

Worst case, he could at the very least continue drowning his thoughts with cheap whiskey by himself. He figured he'd give Etta a call once he had too many to drive. Everything else would fall into place after that.

He didn't have long to let his thoughts get lost in the liquor, though. When he lifted his elbow to pour back yet another shot, he was accosted by a man who was further ahead of the night's drinking than he might ever be. His tumbler toppled over into his lap and before Cannon could feel the whiskey seep through his pants, he stood up with a sudden fury and tossed the chair behind him. Everyone's attention quickly turned to him.

"Can't wait to hear the apology for that one," he hissed to the nearest group of guys next to him. Had he seen them before he acted out of a buzz-induced anger, he would have known that it wasn't the type of barflies he should fight all alone. That didn't matter at this point, though.

The tallest of them had no problem talking back. He was still holding half a beer with a crooked elbow when he stepped forward. "You better look somewhere else, asshole,"

Surrounded by three other guys who seemed to all find their Western wear at the same boot store, the one with the quick mouth had just enough confidence to shake off all the eyes that he'd drawn. The men weren't just any typical dumb grunt types. They looked like they were cowboys, lost in time together. Their boots carried thick layers of mud and cow manure that tracked just about everywhere they went. Their mesh back caps were crushed in and worn, with sweat stains that discolored the fronts. Their calloused hands and hardened looks told Cannon just about everything he needed to know about who he was smarting off to. They were rodeo or farm guys, and either way, that meant they were ready to scrap.

None of that changed the fact that someone needed to apologize to Cannon, though.

The twang of a steel guitar leading a sad country song from the jukebox in the corner cried out. The song seemed to inspire the men to huddle around Cannon close enough to make out the snuff filling their drunken smiles. He looked them each in the eye and knew what was about to happen but did nothing to stop it.

"I ain't gonna wait around much longer," he said with a bitter tone finding its way into his voice.

"Who the hell you think you're talking to, little boy?"

"From the looks of it, just a bunch of—"

Those were apparently enough of the words the group were hoping to hear. Though Cannon didn't see where it came from, he felt the bony knuckles of a fist slam into his left cheek and down he went. The next blows came from kicks and jabs as he was down and defenseless. All he needed was one wild swipe with his leg to catch one off guard and turn the tables in his favor.

When one of the denim-clad rodeo men went down, Cannon popped right up in his place with the closest thing to a haymaker as he could throw in such a chaotic scuffle. It had become something of a go-to move in a bind, and yet again, it worked like a charm. His wild strike landed and before he knew it, two of the men were down on the ground.

The next man came charging immediately after, spearing Cannon and shoving him against a nearby table with a loud crack in a spot that shouldn't ever bend in such a way. A guttural grunt escaped him on impact. The table that would undoubtedly leave its mark on his spine for him to discover the next day also stopped the two in their tracks. He'd hope this would provide him with a more than welcome chance at recovering. He pushed back to find out but to no avail. His efforts would be cut short by his opponent's buddy, the one who had only spoken a single sentence to him at this point.

While he became locked in a struggle with one man, the other stepped forward, fist clenched and ready to swing. When he did, Cannon swung his body over and flung himself down to the ground. A loud THUNK followed. The man who'd been clenched tight against Cannon took the blow of his friend right on his chin, sending him straight into unconsciousness.

"Thanks for that, asshole," Cannon quipped while picking himself up off the beer-ridden hardwood floors of the bar.

"You're next."

Standing face to face with the man close to his age yet twice the fighter as him, Cannon had to admit that a senseless bar room brawl was just what he needed to clear his head to get him going on the right path. A good punch to the face had an unexpected way of knocking a certain kind of sense into you. He lifted his fists up to cover the blood that was trailing down his chin from his split bottom lip and did his best to figure how he could make the man across from him bleed even more. With a red spat, Cannon pushed the pain that he was feeling down and used it as fuel to take another swing.

Unfortunately, this wasn't the rodeo man's first scrap, and he saw the strike coming from a mile away. He dipped to the side and planted his fist right into Cannon's nose, sending more blood spewing from his face as it landed.

"Son of a bitch," Cannon let out as he stumbled backward, somehow still on his feet. Through the tunnel vision and hazy focus after the blow, Cannon couldn't help but notice just about every person in the bar had stopped what they were doing to watch the fight unfold. It was a place that no one wanted to be, the source of the spectacle, the downfall that you couldn't look away from no matter how bad it got. Unfortunately for Cannon, it was still only going to get worse.

"We ain't done yet."

The words passed through Cannon's stupor as if they weren't even directed at him. A hand landed on his shoulder to yank him around and he finally realized that his rush to judgment on the group of men had put him on the losing side of a public fight. No matter how sad it got, he had to face the music. He turned to make a final lunge at the last of the men standing against him, putting everything he had in the attack. The result was no different than the rest of the fight.

This time, it was Cannon who could see what was coming for him a mile away. The man's fist found his face once again and this time, with enough force to make him see pitch black mixed with swirling stars. He could feel the blood pouring from his face and pooling at his cheek, which told him he was on the floor for the last time. He couldn't see the man standing over him, celebrating to cheers from the crowd who'd now passed him a new beer, and he was likely better off for it.

For a reason that he couldn't quite come to terms with after getting his ass kicked, he felt a sense of clarity that he'd struggled to grab hold of lately. It was almost as if the answer to why he'd come to drink himself stupid had been beaten into him in the worst way imaginable. Sprawled out on the floor with his cheek smashed against the floor, both eyes already starting to swell, and a pulsating pain right in the middle of his back—Cannon let his thoughts drift to his missing father that he couldn't stop himself from chasing.

He'd told the NHCP he'd consider finding the newest asshole of the month, Major James, and his band of conspirators soon to be traveling into Texas. He never told them just how much he knew about the man, however. Now that it had come down to it, he realized there wasn't all that much to consider. There was nowhere else for him to go. He had no choice but to find the missing piece to his past that made him who he was, especially now that it had been laid at his boots. If there was anything he'd learned growing up in a family like his, it was that persistence was the only thing that truly paid off in the end.

The stars hadn't stopped swirling in his vision when he was dragged off the bar floor by a couple of old drunks who'd taken pity on him. They propped him up against the wall right on the most painful area of his back and left him to deal as best he could.

Blood had yet to stop pouring from his mouth when he reached down into his pocket with a grunt to pull his cell phone out. It hadn't been totally destroyed in the fight, so he stared with blurry vision and tried to dial a call with trembling fingers. The blood smeared on his screen as he dragged his fingertip across it for several seconds before pushing the phone to his swollen cheek. He could barely hear the ringing of the call against the jukebox blaring in the background and men hollering, likely each boasting about the beating they'd all just witnessed.

"NHCP." Etta's voice came through at last.

"Cannon," he forced out through heavy breathing, almost immediately giving away just how bad of shape he'd been left in.

"Let me guess, you need a ride and can't call an ambulance or some shit?"

If his lungs didn't hurt as bad as they did, he might've let out a laugh at her response, but he didn't have it in him.

"I'm in."

"Gotta say, I'm surprised you called so fast. You didn't seem like you wanted much to do with it when you were here. I've already asked around, and I have a couple of potential partners for you to take along that could be useful."

Cannon let out a sigh into the phone that was in response to either what she was telling him or the debilitating pain that was spreading through the rest of his back. He tried his best to spit out the blood in his mouth before speaking again.

"None of your people. I'll do it."

"What do you have in mind? Also, you sound terrible."

Cannon let his eyes focus on the people who were still cheering in the bar. From what he could make out, most of them were still watching videos of him almost getting his back broken and his face beaten to hell on their phones. Sure, they were all having a great night at his expense, but they'd also given him the answer to how he'd pull off what the NHCP had asked. It might be another dead end, another ass kicking to take, but after what he'd just learned—it sure couldn't hurt to have a few rodeo hands on his side.

"Not so sure you want to know," he answered while still struggling to suck in enough air to force words out of his mouth.

"It's going to be hard enough to get all this through as it is, Cannon. Just tell me who you want, and let's get it over with."

"You know of any rodeos in town?"

"You're putting me on. Seriously?"

He wiped another spurt of blood from his mouth and groaned as he tried to sit up just a little more against the wall. "Yes ma'am."

"Why does everything have to be so much harder with you? Why can't you just do something the way it's supposed to be done, just once?"

"I told you I'm in. Is that not enough?"

"No, no," she sighed.

Cannon was starting to get annoyed at the people in the bar stepping over him like he wasn't propped up against the wall in dire pain. He tried to stand up while keeping the phone pushed to his ear. His boots were slick, and the spilled beer everywhere on the floor from the fight didn't help matters. He pushed one hand onto the floor that was still swollen and cracking with every movement to balance himself. While he could still hear Etta chewing him out on the line, he did his best to ignore the prying eyes and tried to stand up with as few grunts as he could manage. It took just a second for his right boot to slip in the beer and send him crashing back down to the floor and slamming his already messed up back against the wall again.

"What the hell are you doing over there?" He heard Etta continue on the phone that was now laying face up on the beer-covered hardwood home he'd been forced onto. His blood-covered hands fumbled to pick it back up before he could finally speak up again.

"I think I'm going to take you up on that ride you offered after all."

CHAPTER 5

There are few vestiges of Western entertainment as revered as the local rodeo in the heart of East Texas. Calf wranglers, ropers, riders, and even the clowns all gather before hundreds—sometimes thousands—of spectators hell-bent on keeping alive a tradition born of a not-yet-lost way of life.

Tipped cowboy hats and pointed boots lined a set of steel stands with men swigging on bottles of beer and women fighting the urge to slap it out of their hands the longer the night went on. Their cheers were loud, but their hollers were ear piercing if you sat too close. The announcer riled them up as best he could too, knowing that he didn't need to do all that much. These were people who took the bait every chance they got. It was a culture of respect for the relationship between men and women with their animals, a competition that had become enshrined throughout time as a testament to that respect, but that damn sure didn't mean everyone there couldn't have a heck of a time.

Dust swirled around the arena as the flag of the United States of America waved to each one standing in solidarity, watching the lone rider hold firm through a single lap for everyone to see. The anthem played along in the background, voiced by the singer of a local student still learning her way through the notes as she went, but not a single person in the stands acted as if it was anything other than the best interpretation they've ever heard.

The anthem came to a close and the announcer's booming voice came out through the old speakers, crackling yet confident. A swell in the response from the crowd only pushed him to be louder and louder as the competitions kicked off. First up was tie-down roping. There was a uniqueness in the air that came in part from a specific mixture of livestock shit and barbeque sandwiches that was impossible not to fall in love with.

"Are you finally going to tell me who we're supposed to be looking for here?" The voice was Etta Daugherty, who'd surprisingly accepted an offer to join Cannon on a trip to the small town of Carthage out in the piney woods for the annual Panola County pro rodeo.

"You'll know, trust me," Cannon answered, sitting next to her on the hard metal bleachers that lined the rodeo arena.

"I never did go to enough of these. Always wanted to."

"This one's been around for over seventy years. If

you want to see who's cuttin' their teeth to make it to the big leagues, this is the kind of place to go to."

"We aren't scouting for a damn rodeo, Cannon."

"I never said we were," he answered nonchalantly. "You saw my eye, right? And that black and purple area on my back too? These are also some of the toughest sons of bitches around. We find the toughest one here, that's going to be as good of a start as we could hope for."

"There's plenty of tough people around. The men I had lined out for you spend half of every day lifting weights the size of those calves running for their lives."

The crowd exploded onto their feet, screaming and lifting their drinks in the air as one of the tie-down ropers earned the top spot with the quickest time of 7.9 seconds. The cowboy was off his horse and slamming a steer to the ground in the blink of an eye. There was little chance to speak to one another during the sporadic cheers between ropers, so Cannon and Etta sat patiently until they could at least hear each other again.

"They ain't like this, though," Cannon finally answered.

The tie-down roping came to a brief end, and the chutes were already lined up ready to go for the bareback broncs up next. The riders straddled the gates and hollered in anticipation. As the first one broke free and the crowd joined in, Cannon stared closely at one chute in particular. The next one rocketed out and the crowd erupted again, but Cannon kept his focus on one man perched confidently above the rest.

He was a brute of a man with a down-turned black felt cowboy hat despite being in the middle of May. His eyes stayed down and his lip stuck out from the snuff tucked inside. His clothes were worn and faded, but his resolve seemed more intact than any man joining the rodeo or even spectating. After a quick spat into the arena ahead of him, he swung one leg over the chute and lowered himself on the back of a bronc with a twisted look in its eyes.

Etta nudged Cannon with her elbow and broke his focus. When he glanced over at her, she smirked and nodded toward the chutes.

"That's him, isn't it?"

"Don't know. Not sure yet."

"Well if tough is what you're looking for, I'm willing to bet he checks the box."

"Sure looks like you're right."

Another bronc rider bolted out of the chutes just ahead of the one that had drawn their attention. The horse bucked wildly into the air, seeming to defy gravity as the man's grasp on the reins of his rigging clenched tighter and tighter. His legs flailed in response and the silhouette of a rider and his horse was lost in a frenzy of fringe. The result looked torn off the walls of an art museum and thrown into a dusty, sweaty, and crowded ring of rusted old cattle panels.

Etta was still coming to terms with what she was seeing, but Cannon knew he'd be hard pressed to find a place more naturally at home for him. Maybe in another life—one free of desperate hunts through history with no end—he could've had a chance to be stupid enough to strap himself to one of those horses.

Cannon would never tell Etta that was the real reason he needed to find a rodeo hand. They were tough, sure, but she was right in what she said earlier. Anyone could be tough. He knew that if they were going to pull off what the NHCP was asking, whether they understood it or not, he was going to need someone just a little more open to being a damn fool in every sense of the word. He considered telling her briefly, until he was interrupted by a question that almost made him fall off the bleachers.

"Did you know you never told me what really happened with your mom so many years ago," asked Etta. "You just showed up one day with a gun in your hand and not a single one of us questioned anything."

"What are you trying to say?"

"I'm saying that I think it's plenty fair if I finally ask what happened."

Cannon took a swig from a bottle of his own and sucked his teeth before nodding halfheartedly.

"Go ahead then."

"Why would you leave them all behind? Your family, I mean. Just about everybody who had a damn phone knew what happened, what y'all had found. No one ever talked about you though."

"I played my part, that was it."

The crowd roared once more as the last bronc rider shot out of the chutes. Their excitement at the prospect of eight seconds had just about driven each of them crazy. Heavy boots pounding on bleachers and alcohol-fueled hollers pushed the rider to the buzzer. He was the first of the night to hold on until the buzzer and the people made their approval known louder than ever. With a toss of his beat-up straw cowboy hat, the rider sprinted to the panels closest to the bleachers and leaped in excitement. Cannon couldn't help but notice a slight turn of a smile on Etta's face next to him as they watched it all unfold.

Once the rider was able to climb down from the fence and make his way back to the chutes, the crowd seemed to decide all at once that it was time for a new drink. They filed out of the bleachers as a tractor came out into the arena to prepare the dirt for the next competition.

"You have all the money you could want, all the opportunity you could possibly hope for, and you're still just floating from one town to the next leaving half-beaten to death men everywhere you go," Etta continued as if they hadn't missed a beat.

"You know what I'm after. There isn't anything deeper than that to share with you. My mom has her life and her family. She found what our ancestors left behind after fighting for it her whole life. Now, she's your boss."

"And yours too, whether you believe it or not."

"You're probably right. I try not to think about it too much."

"Are you ever going to stop looking for him?"

"My mom never stopped looking for what her past hid from her. I got that from her, and I couldn't possibly bring myself to quit now."

As the crowd predictably filed back into their seats just before the barrel racers started up their runs, Cannon and Etta settled into a welcome silence between them. The women rode like madmen on their horses around each of the barrels, garnering screams from the crowd every time. The first woman made the trip in seventeen seconds, the next beat her time by just a single second. The third rider smacked the first barrel for a penalty, before the fourth pushed the time to beat down to just fifteen seconds. Each of the riders seemed to glide through the air in a majestic partnership with their horse, each focused on but a single goal—to hit the fastest time of the night.

"Couldn't hurt to have someone who can ride like that," Etta commented when the fourth rider appeared like a blur through the gates to end her run.

"You know, I was just thinking the same thing."

The barrel racers may have been one of the crowd favorites, but it seemed Cannon was holding out hope for a different kind of competition. When the steer wrestling came up next, Etta was sure they'd found their reason for attending. The men were more than tough, they were crazy. To leap from their horse at such speeds and avoid landing on the horns was an art form that was easily recognizable. Each run looked like a Western painting created from the hands of Charles Marion Russell himself. It was a force of nature with indescribable beauty.

"When I called you a couple days ago to tell you I'd do all this, I'd just gotten my ass handed to me by a group of assholes in a bar I shouldn't have even been in. At the time, I thought it was a sign to just keep going, but that wasn't it at all," said Cannon.

"You think maybe you just finally picked the wrong fight?"

"I figured that much out after the first hit to the chin, but now I see that it's only another example that I just haven't hit the bottom yet. I can't stop. There's too much I just don't know."

"The grass is always greener, I guess." Etta did her best to understand. "As much as I think he might, this Major James guy might not have what you're after. You do know that, right?"

Cannon's thoughts went to the letter still tucked away in his pockets. He even considered telling her this time, but pushed those thoughts away as soon as they entered his head. "Won't know for sure until we see for ourselves," was the best response he could get out.

Just when the breakaway ropers were announced to start lining up beside the chutes, Cannon and Etta took notice of a sudden, strange shift in the tone of the crowd. It was like black clouds rolling in. A thunderous outburst from a single old gray-haired man with a half-buttoned flannel and rolled-up cowboy hat changed everything. When the crowd joined in on the antagonizing chants, Cannon and Etta afforded themselves a passing awkward glance.

The entire rodeo had broken out in boos and expletives aimed at the arena. As the announcer's introductions were lost in the uprising, Cannon could see one of the women riding up to the chutes with a smile as bright as day.

"Ladies and gentlemen, if you continue to harass our contestants, we will be forced to shut down the rodeo for the rest of the year," the announcer's speech was formulaic and rehearsed. "Please be kind and gracious to all rodeo participants."

Cannon turned to the crowd and saw nothing but angry faces chanting and couldn't begin to understand why. There was always a chance of local issues coming to surface at the rodeo, but this was something worse, like something that followed the smiling woman around everywhere she went. Not only did she seem to be expecting the backlash she received, she looked as though she thrived on it.

"Get her the fuck out of here!" A yell came from the top row of the bleachers.

"Holy shit," Etta blurted out. "What the hell did that poor woman do to earn all that?"

Cannon didn't say anything at first. He watched as the only black woman breakaway rider of the night was showered in insults and disdain from just about everyone who showed up to the rodeo. Her chestnut quarter horse was every bit as proud as the woman who sat in the saddle strapped to its back. They were a duo that stood apart from the rest, and they would have done just that even without the vitriol from those in attendance. The woman donned her own fair share of fringe hanging from black leather and a brilliant wide-brimmed white felt cowboy hat. Through her halo of hair tucked neatly around glinting eyes, Cannon saw something else. He saw her hardened hands from years of rope burns, her worn-out spurs, and a sense of determination that exuded from everything that she did.

As they sat and listened to the announcer describe

the woman's place at the top of the world rankings in breakaway roping, Cannon got the idea she was someone that people really did love to hate. Being the best had a way of bringing that out in everyone who was left. It was a rule of thumb all around the world. As the boos continued to rain down without any sign of letting up, the breakaway ropers got in line, prepping their ropes nervously and keeping their horses from moving in the lane too much.

Cannon kept his eye on the woman who'd drawn all of the attention. Although it was too loud to catch any hometown gossip in the bleachers about the woman's reputation, it didn't take much to see it had mostly gone south. The people almost seemed to enjoy rooting against her as she got comfortable in the arena and he wondered if he was missing something about the exuberant woman.

The first breakaway roper burst out of the gate with her lasso in the air, trailing on every step of the calf ahead of her. Their hooves beat the dirt with every step as the horse right behind it seemed to be running on air, catching up with every step. The woman's rope came down hard around the calf's neck and popped off her saddle into the air to stop the clock at a crowd-pleasing 2.9 seconds. The next wasted no time in beating her predecessor's time, coming in at 2.7 seconds to send the crowd into a fit of roaring cheers as they forgot about the woman they seemed to despise for just a moment.

The competition was stiff at a small-town rodeo like this. With trailers spilling out into the lanes of Highway 79 from out front and traffic directors waving every truck in the county down, people just kept spilling into the event no matter how late it got. Cannon looked around to see that the size of the crowd had nearly doubled and there was no more room in the bleachers to be found.

"This place is losing their mind," he heard Etta try to shout in his direction.

"Breakaway roping looks like it's the next best thing, but it's been around forever. Just wait until the bull riders line up."

"Oh god. Is that who we're after here?"

Cannon chose not to respond to that question and continued watching the riders as if he'd never even heard it.

The pasture full of people circled around some cattle panels and an announcer's box was creating a roar that could be felt all throughout town. The breakaway ropers still waiting their turn were all intent on staying focused with pursed lips and furrowed brows —except for one. The woman who'd been cast as the villain of the group, who also just so happened to be catching up to the world leader in the rankings, had a smile from ear to ear as she stepped up in line.

The next rider shot out of the gates quicker than anyone before her, lasso swinging wide over her head like she could wrangle the whole crowd in one toss. The calf broke free, and the crowd started up again with beers raised high, until the announcer broke their hearts with a penalty—she broke the barrier. It would be an added ten seconds to her once-stunning original time of 2.4 seconds, putting her in last place.

The next rider was the one the crowd had been

waiting on. She made her way up to the gate and when she got in place, her bright smile turned into a look of channeled, burning intensity. Another old man tried to get the crowd back to booing her, but another shushed them, bringing the whole rodeo into silence. She fidgeted with her rope a while longer as the bugs danced in the spotlights above and the crowd watched with bated breath. When she was ready, she leaned into her saddle, gripped the reins a little tighter, and gave a quick nod that tilted her white felt hat down over her eyes for a split second.

What happened next almost couldn't be perceived by any human eye. The gates flew open, the woman rocketed out in blinding speed just beyond the barrier and the calf never stood a chance. When the rope popped off and the clock stopped, she came in at an unbelievable time of 1.9 seconds. Before the rope could hit the ground to be dragged through the arena by the calf, the woman had hopped off her horse and tossed her cowboy hat high into the air. The white felt looked like a star shining in the night sky against the flood-lights beaming down onto it. Before it could hit the ground, the woman had two middle fingers raised high at the crowd and a smile once again wrapped from ear to ear.

The crowd had never cheered so loud that entire night. It was like they were playing a game, one where both the rider and the rodeo lovers had each won. Their yells got loud enough to cause static in Cannon's ears, and when he looked over at Etta, he saw she had plugged her own with her fingers.

No one ever did seem to settle down as the woman

dropped her middle fingers and resorted to waving at everyone with her now dirt-stained cowboy hat in hand. Cannon and Etta would have never guessed it, but she turned out to be a crowd favorite and they were letting her know all about it.

Etta couldn't hear shit at the moment, and not only because she was covering her ears. Her eyes darted around at the hordes of people in the bleachers and surrounding the arena as if she was concussed from the noise. When her eyes made it to Cannon sitting next to her, she saw that he was trying to say something. His voice was drowned out, though. She could only make out what he was saying by reading his lips.

"She's the one," he was telling her over and over again.

CHAPTER 6

"You need to let me be the one to talk to her. I'm telling you right now, this just ain't going to go how you want it to if I'm not there," Etta tried to explain to Cannon as they weaved through the crowd leaving the rodeo.

"Don't need to do all that."

"We're going after people who haven't heard from us in a long time. They may not take so kindly to us just showing up."

"It'll be fine." Cannon didn't even bother turning around to make eye contact.

The crowd wasn't nearly as rowdy filing out of the rodeo grounds as when they were crammed into the bleachers just a couple hours ago. The event came to its end after the bull riders managed to not get mangled too hard in front of the audience. It was like everyone there was thrown back into the reality of the world. The cheers and drinking all came to a stop and the phones came back out. Everyone fell back into ignoring one another as best they could, leaving only the polite ones chatting between simple passing gestures, and a few apologies after bumping into others unexpectedly. That left Cannon and Etta as the only ones shoving their way through lines of attendees as they fought to get out behind the arena where the contestants were.

Etta reached out and tugged Cannon's arm, forcing him to turn around and finally make eye contact with her. He saw the intent in her eyes. She was a woman who had earned her place at the table. She wasn't one to sit idly by when she knew what needed to be done. Cannon could respect that, truly, but he wasn't the type to be told what to do. He never had been, and no matter what he thought of Etta, he wasn't about to start now.

"Let me do this," she implored.

"Etta, have I told you that I appreciate you being here? Because I really do. But also, now ain't the time, just trust me."

She sighed and fought the urge to roll her eyes. Cannon turned and continued making his way through the crowd, ignoring her and heading toward the trailers that filled the pasture extending out far beyond the arena. They had already started loading the livestock and cleaning up facilities, so Cannon knew they didn't have much time to find the break-away roper with all the unique qualities he was looking for.

It smelled like manure just about everywhere you went on the rodeo grounds. The grass and dirt had been trampled enough to become the kind of mud you had to stomp off your boots anytime you came across concrete. The night sky held no stars above and the trailers surrounding them in every direction blocked any breeze that might have helped ease the humidity that had settled in.

"How do we know where to find her."

"I can't imagine it'll be too hard. Whole damn rodeo seemed to have an opinion of her."

"I've never seen anything like that. It was like she wanted them to boo her, but the way she reacted to everyone—"

"Let's do this damn thing already, boys," a voice interrupted Etta from behind a row of rusty and shit-covered steel trailers with stained canvas tops. "Let's go!"

Cannon took off running at the sound, desperately looking for a spot between the trailers he could cross through. His boots slid in the torn-up grass. His breathing was wild. Etta had never seen this side of him despite sending him off to situations that caused it time and time again. It didn't take long until he found the right spot and darted between an early 2000s Ram dually truck and its gooseneck trailer.

"You wanna run your mouth up in the stands like some kind of tough guy? Well here I am, assholes," the voice carried on.

"We were sent here by someone, as I'm sure you know by now, not because of anything he did," someone else joined in. "But because of what *you* did. We aren't here to fight you. We're here to send a message."

Cannon turned the corner to see the breakaway

roper he was after staring down two burly, bearded men dressed far too nice to be at such a place willingly. Their boots didn't look like anyone else's at the rodeo and their haircut looked like it cost a heck of a lot more than twenty plus a tip.

"You can tell him the same thing I told all those people out in the arena," the woman responded before holding up the same two middle fingers that had caught Cannon's eye after her ride in the rodeo.

This time, her middle fingers weren't quite the cause for applause like they were then. One of the men took it upon themselves to take a swing at the woman, and before Cannon could do anything about it, his wide, hairy fist landed right on her cheek. Her body was flung to the side at the cheap shot and she slammed against the closest trailer with a harsh *thump*.

"Son of a—"

The other man was right on top of her before she could finish cussing. He reared back, laughing as he stood over her, and attempted to end the scuffle right then and there. Before his fist could come down, a muddy boot came up from the ground and struck the man right between the legs. He absorbed the blow and wheezed in response, but another violent kick in the same spot from the same boot sent him down into the dirt.

His buddy was next, but the woman had already gotten up and spat the blood filling her mouth onto the groaning man rolling around on the ground. The next one figured he'd try his luck charging right at her, but the woman was faster in a fight than she was with a rope. She ducked left and closed her fist to strike back if her first plan didn't work out. The twenty-foot steel trailer did all the work for her. He ran headfirst into a steel bar that made him weak in the knees. He hit the ground with a baseball-sized knot on his forehead, but the woman was on top of him in an instant, raining her own fists down onto his face. He was bloodied and struggling to breathe, but she was just getting started.

"This what you wanted, you stupid assholes? You don't send me a message; you don't send me shit!" Her screams went higher pitched with every strike, until she suddenly remembered the second man lying just a few feet away.

The breakaway roper was standing over the first man, stomping the heel of her boot down on his face when Cannon caught her eye. He was leaning up against another trailer, watching her damn near kill the men who had shown up to threaten her.

"Don't stop on my account," said Cannon.

She didn't, either. She brought her boot down one more time just as the man fell unconscious and sent a stream of blood splattering from his nose into the dirt. Without saying a word, she made sure that each of the men knew exactly what message they had to take back with them.

"Can I help you?" She finally spoke up through ragged breaths. "Or are you with these guys?"

"I sure ain't with them. After what I just saw, even if I was, I'm not so sure I'd tell you. I do think you can help me though. Matter of fact, from where I'm standing—I know you can."

The woman threw her arms up in the air and

shrugged. Then, a familiar smile came back across her face. "The hell do you want?"

"There's a bad man who needs catching. I'm here to make sure that gets done."

"Look man, I appreciate you hoopin' and hollerin' with the rest of them fine patrons of the Carthage pro rodeo, but I ain't doing anything except packing my shit and moving on to the next one."

"You don't understand—"

"No, no," she interrupted. "You don't. You come here saying you ain't with the assholes who just made a pass at me, but you want to do the same thing. Let me guess, you want to make me work for you? Unless you have something worth saying to me, then you might as well climb back in whatever sedan brought you here and find yourself someone else."

"You call that making a pass?"

She scrunched her face and sucked her teeth without thinking about it. The halo of hair that had been rolling in the dirt just minutes ago created a perfect silhouette around her face. Cannon couldn't help but stare. She was steadily chewing him a new one and he didn't seem to mind all that much. One thing was sure though, Etta was probably right when she said she wanted to be the one to talk to her. Cannon was already preparing to eat that crow before the woman stopped talking.

"I'm trying to tell you, I'm with—"

"He's with me, Ms. Cathay Fields," Etta came around from behind one of the trailers to cut off Cannon.

"Get the hell outta here," said Cathay with a big

grin finding its way onto her soured face. "What are you doing here, of all the damn places?"

Etta and Cathay ran up to each other for a long hug between old friends. As they stood there embracing each other between the two unconscious men, Cannon couldn't help but let shock and surprise wash over his face. When they finally broke apart, he was the first to speak.

"You know we're with the NHCP?"

"Do I know? Me and this little badass here have gone out a time or two ourselves, not too long ago either."

Etta turned to Cannon and smiled. "It was actually like three years. Cathay is something of an on-call volunteer."

"So, the whole rodeo we sat through was just you screwin' with me?"

"Not quite," Etta admitted. "I never did get a chance to go to one after Cathay here started up her touring life. It was interesting though, I'll give y'all that."

"Glad you enjoyed it. So, what was this guy just talking about again? I wasn't really paying much attention."

"There is a new kind of rodeo, one mixed with a Western theater and concert, making its way into Texas here pretty soon. The guy who runs it all, Major James, is just the kind of guy who draws our attention."

"Thief, plunderer, murderer," Cathay started listing. "All the usual suspects?"

"The Nations Heritage & Culture Preservation

doesn't stand for those who keep history locked away from our people, and it damn sure doesn't let them go around killing folk to make sure that happens," said Etta.

"I'm going after him." Cannon stepped in. "And I think you can help me do that."

"If this woman here is in, then so am I," Cathay said without missing a beat.

"I've gotta ask though, what was with the crowd back there? We thought they were going to climb down from those bleachers and come get your ass in the arena."

"Oh, they're good people. They just like to give me a hard time, is all. It's turned into something of a game we all play."

"Sure didn't feel like a game when that guy was cussing you out before your ride," Etta chimed in.

"I do better when I've got something to prove. Once I got to chasing the top of the ranks, I also started looking for a little extra motivation. I had one crowd up in Tennessee all riled up one time, booing me, cussing me out, and all that mess. Once they saw how well I rode, I guess word spread and everyone got involved. Now, it seems like every damn rodeo I ride in has a crowd of people all too ready to tear me apart."

"Until you pull a two-second time," Cannon quipped.

"That sure helps."

"I've been to my fair share of rodeos, and I've never seen anything like that."

"Well, you ain't never met me before. But now it's

my turn to ask questions. Why did you come after me? I might scrap a little here and there." Cathay let her eyes drift to the unconscious ones in the dirt. "But I'm a roper now, not a real fighter anymore."

Cannon took a second to think about what he should tell her. He had no choice but to hold back his own reasons for finding his way onboard that forsaken train tour, but he could at least tell her what won him over.

"This fight, it isn't like any others we've done before. This isn't just going in and taking down some guy willing to kill over his possessions. I need more than just a gun hand."

"Don't beat around the bush with me, you need someone dumb enough to run head-on into all that mess."

"That too," Cannon admitted.

"I figured. That doesn't matter though. I'm in. You just gotta tell me how to get started now."

"Well, about that," Etta said, breaking eye contact as she spoke. "Before we get to that, we were hoping you could help us get in contact with someone."

"No, not him, Etta. You know better than that," Cathay said, shaking her head and taking a step back. "Tell me you know better than that."

Silence fell between the three standing behind the trailers. It was the dead of night with nothing but passing headlights dancing across their faces. Mosquitos and gnats swirled in the air around them and the sounds of diesel engines tugging their trailers home faded further into the distance. They were surrounded by the piney woods but standing out in the pasture by the rodeo grounds, it was difficult to escape the night sky swallowing them up everywhere they looked. It was humbling to stand beneath the blanket of darkness stretching out across the East Texas horizon, and they all felt it in their own way.

"Damnit, fine." Cathay finally broke the silence that had settled in. "Don't say I didn't warn you."

CHAPTER 7

"Step right on up to the fence, come on, come on. For your own protection, don't dare think about reaching over. You never know what will come at you next at the magnificent Major James Out West Show," screamed the show's namesake into a bullhorn before a thousand or more attendees. "Welcome to the only traveling show on rails today that will leave you longing for the trails of yesterday."

Major James basked in the spotlight and stood tall before the audience in front of him. His prized Union Pacific FEF steam locomotive served as the most pristine backdrop for the show they were about to put on. An arena designed by Major James and a team of professionals separated the train from the eager crowd who all drove out of Texarkana to where the show had set up for the evening past Loop 151.

He'd seen turnouts grow with each show as they

traveled from state to state, but this was undoubtedly the most impressive one yet. When he overlooked what he had made happen, he smiled.

The show sat next to a grassy pasture bordered by a wall of oaks and pines that looked untouched since the last train show came through town more than a century ago. A blazing sun was settling in to rest on a skyline made up of swaths of orange and purple stretching out in every direction. The threats of daylight leaving them all behind grew more intense by the minute. It would eventually fizzle out for darkness to take its place, but at least for now, Major James was the only star in sight.

"Tonight, you will see the arts of riding and roping once thought lost with the coming of the power lines and invisible transmissions. You will be amazed at the death-defying stunts in re-enactments of a history born on the heels of the old West itself. You will be serenaded by frontier voices previously known only by the livestock they kept in line. And for those who aren't afraid to stand in harm's presence, you will be shocked to see shooting prowess that only the state of Texas could bear witness to," Major James continued his speech.

The crowd showed their approval for his words with their applause. Kids raised up on their daddies' shoulders and a sea of cell phone lights recording his every move stretched out in front of the arena. The people had paid forty-five dollars per adult and thirty dollars per child to come watch the Major James Out West Show, where they would eat twenty-dollar cheeseburgers, drink eleven-dollar sodas, purchase thirty-five-dollar t-shirts and then go home believing they just had the night of their lives.

"If you need to find a chamber pot, I suggest you do it now, because you won't want to miss a single second of the show soon to start." Major James raised his voice as he spoke. A soft drumroll started at the end of his sentence, queuing up the performance to begin its two-hour and fifty-two-minute showtime. "The old West was indeed quite wild, but few know the tales of how it was tamed with gunpowder and lassos, and even fewer have seen it in action for themselves. Tonight, you will become among those lucky few."

A lone fiddle cried out at these words, and the audience seemed moved by its sudden appearance before any of the performances had started. The spotlight which bathed Major James in all the attention he could've ever wanted began to share its adoration, moving toward the crowd first, then back to the arena, before settling on one of the train cars that was fenced off. It hovered on the side of the car, shaking ever so slightly by the hand of a manual operator for the show who'd never shown their face before.

The drums picked up against the wailing of the fiddle as the side door to the train car fell to the ground with a jarring slam of steel meeting dirt. The spotlight showcased what was waiting for the crowd inside and they all gasped in unison—man, woman, and child alike. A white horse, standing on its rear legs, straddled by a lone rider with a white ten-gallon cowboy hat and a bandanna over their face, caught the attention of damn near all of Texarkana in a dramatic entrance.

Although the warmth of the spotlight was no longer focused on Major James, his voice still carried out into the dusk for every ear in attendance to hear.

"Behold, the one and only, descendant of the bull-dogger himself, brilliant with any bullet, and a new star shining over Texas—J.R. Pickett!"

As it always does, the crowd exploded with applause at a real-life cowboy riding into the arena before their very eyes. Not the ones you see kicking up dirt at rodeos, or those with glinting smiles on the television. A real one, with a gun strapped to his hip and a horse that stole the show. The crowd fell for the newest headlining act making his first entry lap to kick off the show, but the spectacle didn't start until his six-shooter came out of the holster and aimed up at the sky.

Major James watched his eager attendees as they hung on every movement with bated breath. He'd had riders take to the arena first before, but never to such an effect. J.R. could sell a show as good as the best of them. He watched as the man completed his opening lap with a single gunshot in the air that drew audible gasps from hundreds. The smoke billowed from the end of the barrel and although everyone assumed it had been a blank, they were even more shocked to find out that J.R. Pickett had just shot a very real bullet at a very real target which had been launched above their heads. An explosion as loud as TNT and as colorful as fireworks burst overhead before cascading down. The lights danced across the faces of the spectators as the horse J.R. rode reared up one more time and galloped back up the ramp into its train car.

The doors slammed shut behind them, and applause broke out once more. They were hooked almost immediately and Major James knew he'd done his job one more time. He faded away from the stage he took to at the beginning of every show and let the performers take over. From behind the train, he listened to the roars of the crowd and the sporadic gunshots that rang out, punctuating each showcase of grit, talent, and tenacity that he'd assembled so delicately.

As was usually the case when he wrapped his introductions, Major James was enjoying a few puffs out of his intricately carved corncob pipe. The smoke escaped his nostrils and mouth as he smoked the earthy tobacco with hints of clove and cinnamon. Somehow, it always made him think of home. The routine had become impossible to avoid these days. It had become his celebration of a life well spent, a chance to enjoy the fruits of his labor. Success had found him at last, and the hollers of the crowd at his back were all the proof he needed. The only thing that remained was to ensure history would remember what he made.

"Shut the hell up already." A voice broke his serene routine.

When Major James turned his head and exhaled a plume of smoke into the night air, he watched as two stupid young men stumbled their way from beneath the train. They were failing hilariously at remaining hidden from sight, so Major James humored himself and watched them continue about their shady business. He shook off any notion of hiding from the trespassers and puffed again on his corncob pipe.

"I heard he carries the dead bodies with him," the next one said. Plump as he was, he still moved like an athlete.

"No way," the first one exclaimed. He was lanky and awkward in every movement. "He couldn't carry the bodies with him across state lines and not get caught. They have checkpoints and shit like that. Haven't you ever watched *Law and Order*?"

They had both pulled silly Halloween masks over their faces in a half-assed attempt at disguising their identities. One was an expressionless face with barely a discernible shape, with a small elastic black band that wrapped around the back of the lanky one's head. The other, strapped haphazardly to the fat one, had an uncanny resemblance to the former President Nixon. It was an unusual pairing that Major James could only shake his head at.

They strolled nearer to him before coming to a stop in front of a train car that had been fenced outside of the arena. Major James watched with his pipe still in hand and allowed himself to sink back into his overly priced lawn chair that had become a second home. A trail of smoke lifted into the air in front of his face as he watched.

"From what I heard, bodies or not, there is money stashed all over the train. The old man hordes it all to himself and stays on the run," the lanky one said.

"Why does he have to run?"

"Taxes or some shit, how would I know?"

"Yeah, no, that makes sense," fake former President Nixon said with a sincerity that made Major James sigh quietly to himself.

The two had a plan and went right to work, no more than fifty feet from where Major James was sitting and smoking on his pipe. The crowd burst out in applause again as the band struck up their music. A fiddle took the lead and created a piercing soundtrack for whatever thievery the two men had in mind. The people's cheers and excitement at the Major James Out West Show made the man behind it all gleam with pride, but the young men who were forcing their way onto his train made him feel something else entirely, something much more sinister. He often lied to himself, saying he didn't want to be that man anymore, but this wasn't one of those times. His show needed him, the performers depended on him, and a chance at earning his own chapter in the history books was right at his fingertips.

"This whole dadgum thing is made out of solid steel," Nixon continued. "We ain't ever getting in that place unless someone lets us in."

"We researched this, remember?"

"Not like this, Jesse. No research is going to get us through solid damn steel."

"Don't use my real name, asshole, what if someone is listening?"

"Like who?" The fat one held his arms out but forgot to look around to make his point.

Had he remembered to just glance to his left, he

would've seen Major James sitting in the distance, puffing on his pipe as if nothing was happening.

"Like anyone, dipshit. This is the kind of thing that could put us away."

"Give it a rest already, there's no one around here. Ain't nothing going to happen, just like we ain't getting into that hunk of shit." The would-be thief slapped his hand against the train car and a hollow sound resonated from within for a brief second, only to be drowned out by the cheering of the crowd on the other side.

"Give the bar."

Crowbar in hand, the lanky expressionless one started to pry at the sliding steel door that sat unmoving above his head. His grunts and tugs betrayed his efforts as nothing happened. His accomplice, former President Nixon, just stood there with his hands on his hips like a construction manager in a hard hat during his annual visit to a job site. There was nothing he could do to help and they both knew it.

"It ain't trying to move at all." The lanky one finally gave in.

"You know, I don't like saying I told you so."

"Then don't you son of a bitch."

"What are we supposed to do next?"

Major James finally decided to stand up from his most comfortable chair in the dumbfounded silence that settled in between the two. He exhaled one more plume of smoke and smashed his thumb into the corncob pipe to stop it from smoldering. By the time he had set it down and allowed himself a casual stretch to loosen up his sore muscles and crackling old bones, the two idiots had started in again with the crowbar.

"Just get something and help me pull this damned door open."

"We only brought one crowbar, man. I ain't got nothing else."

It didn't take long for Major James to walk up behind the two, concealed completely by his own Wild West show unfolding for all of Texarkana not too far from them. As if right on cue, a revolver fired off a shot into the air to silence the crowd and before the smoke that poured out could clear the air, Major James decided to finally speak up.

"Howdy there, boys," he said nonchalantly.

"What the—"

"Shit!"

Before his friend could finish shouting the latest expletive of choice, former President Nixon was at a dead sprint. He yanked at his pants falling down his ass as he tried to put one foot in front of the other without ever looking back. He wasn't just a thief, but a coward as well, and his buddy had been left behind to learn what happens when you put all your faith in a yellow belly like that.

"The mask suits him, you know." Major James couldn't help himself as they both watched the young man run as fast as his short legs and hanging belly would let him.

"Look, mister, we didn't mean any harm." The thief tried to explain himself, knowing damn well it would all be in vain.

"I'm sure you didn't, folks like you never do."

The blank stare that met Major James told him everything he needed to know about the man he was confronting. Instead of threatening him with law enforcement or showing him the back of his own hand like he rightfully deserved for doing what he was doing, Major James the showman took a different approach—a tour.

"Rather than breaking and entering to pocket whatever you could get your slimy, thieving fuckin' hands on." Major James leaned up against his cane as he spoke in a monotonous tone. "How about I just show you what makes this place special enough to attract swarming flies like yourself?"

"What do you—"

"A tour, my boy. Let's take a stroll inside," the showman said with a sinister smile. "The show going on over there is for the children and the parents who envy them, but you're different, aren't you?"

Major James lifted the cane and stuck it up against the man's chest with enough force that shoved him back into the train car with a sudden *thud*. The swell of the crowd rose in response, becoming a soundtrack to the conflict breaking out behind the train in a pasture bathed in moonlight. There was something about crossing the border into Texas that changed them. The performers, staff, and stars of the Major James Out West Show—and even the showman himself—had all felt it. There was something freeing about being beneath the timeless night sky of the lone star state that shone bright in spectacularly dotted constellations that were anything but lonely.

"I don't wanna do nothing to make this any worse,

I just wanna be able to get on home now. Please, mister."

"No, no, my boy, it's a little too late for all that now."

With a swat of his cane, Major James pushed aside the thief and walked up to the train car door that was just under the duress of a coward's crowbar. He glanced back to ensure the young man was still standing where he'd placed him, reached up with his free hand, and grasped the handle above his head. He tugged it gently. The sliding steel door made a jarring sound before clicking open and rolling backward with a push of a single finger.

"Come along," the showman said, then stepped up with uncanny agility for a man his age.

As Major James made his way into the darkness of the train car just beyond the door, the thief stood motionless with his cheap plastic mask still covering his face. For just a split second, he contemplated sprinting in the opposite direction and never looking back, maybe even meeting up with the asshole who'd abandoned him to deal with this on his own, but something else beckoned him. The void inside the train called to him. He couldn't resist its pull, and he didn't care to try. The young man relaxed his grip on the crowbar that had failed to gain him entry and stepped up inside the train to follow the showman further into the train car.

What he saw was unlike anything that had been made real to his eyes ever before. He was far from a history nerd, but the museum-like room that unfolded in front of him made his knees tremble just a little and his eyes widen more than he'd ever admit. It was a sight to behold. A collection of antiquities right out of the pages of history books surrounded him in every direction. They were treasures torn from time. Ancient-looking firearms, finely carved busts and stat-ues, priceless artwork to even the untrained eye, falling piles of books, and barely legible documents yellow with age were only half organized throughout the inside of the train car. The most noticeable of all was the banner that read BUFFALO BILL'S WILD WEST AND CONGRESS OF ROUGH RIDERS OF THE WORLD hanging above their heads.

"What is this place?"

"A refuge from the inconveniences of the world outside, a vault of sorts, to hold within it the greatest secrets of our most daring days." Major James's familiar voice came from behind a stack of books so tall he couldn't be seen. "And I already know how much you like vaults."

The young man tried to pull his plastic mask up on top of his head but was met with a firm slap on the hand by the showman's cane out of nowhere. He yelped in response and jerked away.

"No more than the next guy, I guess." He tried to downplay his fears through the mask still covering his face.

"The world changed when civilization came for America at the turn of the century. Before justice was handled in the court of law, it was settled in front of the town. Did you know they used to hang people for the simple crime of stealing someone's horse?"

"Uhhh…"

"Don't worry, I'm not accusing you of stealing my horse or anything like that. I do indeed see why you might be getting nervous, however."

Major James stepped in front of the thief to come face to face with him. He'd seen more intimidating men in his day. A costume mask, soft hands, and a weak-spined demeanor made him wreak of irresponsibility. There was nothing to be afraid of when Major James looked into his eyes, but that would not spare him the wrath he'd brought down on himself.

"I have something I want to show you," the showman said to change the subject with a more upbeat tone. "I know a man of similar tastes when I see one, a man who can find enjoyment in the things no man has ever laid eyes on before. That is what brought you here, is it not?"

The thief refused to answer this time, unsure of where exactly it would land him. Instead, he joined Major James on a slow crawl through the inside of the museum on rails that he'd found himself in. They strolled by countless artifacts and objects in the dim yellow lighting from hanging bulbs above their heads as Major James explained the story of each piece down to the smallest of details. It was more than he could've ever imagined, certainly more than the anonymous tip he'd received had described.

It took only a few minutes to wind their way through the train car, weaving between stacks of books tipping over and ducking beneath banners of old West shows long gone from the public eye. The showman always did enjoy a chance to showcase his collection, and he'd be lying if he said that he wasn't finding some fun to be had during their tour, despite the circumstances it had arisen in.

"What's this one?" The thief finally decided to test his luck on the one thing that Major James had not thoroughly gone into detail to explain, lifting his finger to point at a small worn leather bag stowed in the corner. As his fate would have it, the bad luck he'd encountered outside trying to break into the place would only continue with him inside.

"I just knew you had an eye for the spectacular!"

"I don't know about all that," the young man tried to say through his expressionless plastic mask. "Curious is all."

"It's more than that, boy. This is one of the most inspirational pieces I've ever owned. You might even say this is the one piece of my collection that has allowed me to do everything you've seen firsthand tonight."

"It is?"

"Indeed it is."

Major James snagged a leather strap that looked as though it was barely hanging on by a thread. He slung it over his shoulder before walking back to his desk in the middle of the long and narrow train car. It landed on the hard oak tabletop with a hard *THUNK* that caught even Major James off guard. Before either could say anything, the showman glanced out of the corner of his eyes at the young thief and let a smirk cross his lips.

"You want to see what it is?"

"I don't really think I do, sir," the young man told him, trying to take a step backward as he did.

"Nonsense, boy, this one can't be explained. You just have to see it for yourself to believe it."

"I really just want to go now, if that's okay, sir."

"You take a goddamned look inside this bag right now and don't you fuckin' make me tell you again."

The harshness of the showman's voice fell over the young thief in an instant, terrifying him all the way down to his bones. He started to come closer to the leather bag on the old wooden desk, and fear washed over him in waves with every step. His fingertips began to tremble. In a matter of seconds, he was close enough to the showman to smell his musky cologne mixed with the scent of pipe tobacco. It was a smell that did nothing to ease his nerves. The showman stared at him with violent eyes as he anxiously waited to show him whatever was so important inside the leather bag that looked as if it was two hundred years old.

Before he could realize it, his hands were running along the worn-out stitching of the creased leather. The showman watched over his every move with a twisted smile stretched across his face. A metal clasp keeping the bag closed was rusted and difficult to undo. He fidgeted with it beneath the watchful eye of the showman only inches away from him before finally releasing its hold.

"Go on," Major James coaxed him.

He flipped the leather flap of the bag over at last and allowed his curiosity to take over. His wandering eyes finally peered inside and in a fraction of a second, the young thief was frozen in place at what he saw.

The showman exhaled a sigh of relief as if every

care in the world that plagued him was rinsed away by the young man who'd tried to steal from him only moments ago.

What took hold of the thief as he gazed down into the bag wasn't something that could be put into words. It was beyond comprehension of anyone who would become unfortunate enough to be caught in its view, and it did to the thief exactly what it had done to so many others. Behind the mask, the young man's eyes widened further than they ever had before, and his lips began to quiver. He released his hold on the bag and stood motionless, unable to look away or move at all. The quiver from his mouth soon took hold of his entire face before extending to the rest of his body. He was shaking violently and starting to mumble incoherently.

Blood began to drip from one nostril, running streaks of red down his chin, then the next nostril did the same. The bottom of his plastic mask soon turned deep red as it flooded down his neck. His eyes remained locked on the contents of the bag as blood poured down from his nose. The blood never stopped. It came next from each of his tear ducts, spilling from the holes cut into the mask for his eyes, but even then, the man stared without so much as blinking. He stood there, shaking and mumbling, blood rushing down his face.

The young man's unnatural response continued for only a few seconds longer before his chest began to swell and heave uncontrollably. The blood rushing from his body poured onto the floor in front of him as the heaving turned to shocking spasms that coursed throughout his limbs all the way into his fingertips and toes.

With a quiet exhale of the last bit of air that would ever leave his lungs, the thief collapsed to the floor, landing in a puddle of his own blood—becoming nothing more than food for the worms.

CHAPTER 8

There were plenty of old Western singers and poets who'd spun the lonesome yarn of being all by yourself in the world. Words of brokenhearted rejection and feeling so damn blue you could just die have been passed down from generation to generation like a beloved heirloom. Even the best wordsmiths couldn't quite capture the toll it took when you found yourself in such a place though.

That place was exactly where Cannon had found himself, spiraling, unable to stop the walls from closing in.

He was flipping through a leather notebook, spreading torn and wrinkled pages that were far older than he was, and sighing as he read the same lines he'd read a million times before. The pages of the notebook were made up of dozens of documents and journals through the years, musty from age, and fading into obscurity. He would have been more worried about losing what each page contained if he didn't have every bit of it memorized.

It was his ancestor's album. A collection of stories and records passed down from his family and locked away until his mom dug it up to hand it down to him. There was so much that went into finding the documents, so much sacrificed through the years. He knew firsthand what had gone into unlocking the secrets of his family. As he poured through the information in the hopes of finding what he'd never seen before, his heart twisted and turned at every dead end he found.

The hotel desk he sat at was lit only by a yellow lamp with a crusty white shade that had seen better days in its time. It barely provided the light he needed to read, and it was only serving to frustrate him further at this point.

"Son of a bitch," he whispered beneath his breath.

There were traces of his lineage all throughout his mom's family that stretched back hundreds of years. It was an unimaginable trove of information with names, birthdates, stories, and even some pictures, but it was only on his mom's side. There was nothing of who his father could be. No matter how hard he searched through every single line written on every page, there was never so much as a hint at where he should be looking to find out who the man was.

His father was a ghost, proven only by the fact that Cannon simply existed.

Cannon had stayed with his mom as long as he possibly could, helping her put back the pieces of her life that had been stolen and carry on with the park ranger she'd married. There was a life for him there. It was a life that most could only dream of after their family had taken back thousands of acres of land and enough money for their grandchildren's grandchildren which had been taken from them all, but his own dreams still carried him into the unknown. Despite everything that they had found, he could only seem to focus on what he'd never had before.

He'd given up speaking to his family for over a year now and refused to go back until he knew who his father was. The NHCP was his home away from home. They were backed by the family business and that gave him everything he needed. None of that ever mattered though. It all took him to the same place—nowhere.

What he couldn't tell anyone—including his family and arguably more importantly, the NHCP—was that his futile search had fallen into his lap out of the unknown. It had arrived in the middle of the media storm that raged on when the return of his family's fortune became public news. Amid the lines of reporters, constant phone calls, meetings with lawyers, and strangers showing up on their doorstep, it was a rather mundane letter addressed to Cannon Hunter that turned his storybook life upside down.

He reached into the back of his ancestor's album and slid an envelope out. It was the letter he'd read as much as any of the pages of his family's history, addressed only to him with a return label from a company named The Out West Outfits. Although he'd never heard of them before, what they had to say sparked something inside him. It led him speeding right onto the dead-end road he'd been traveling until Etta called him in.

Cannon let his eyes scroll through the letter once again and just like it always did, his stomach dropped when he was halfway through. He stared at the words in the hopes that he could look through the letter, and somehow find the answers it had promised yet never delivered.

"The last secret of the Hunters lies not in some buried crypt, but with me instead. I know who your dad is," the letter claimed.

The mysterious letter of The Out West Outfits company had proven to be the catalyst for his undoing. There was nothing in the letter that gave him any hint as to where his father could be, or if he was even still alive. Even then, Cannon could never forget what he felt when he read the final sentence.

He fought the urge to crumple the letter up in his hand and forget it ever existed. As much as he wanted to, there was too much inside him that couldn't let it happen. The letter took him from his family, from a life he fought and killed for, and he was ashamed of what it had turned him into. He couldn't give up the search though, not yet.

The hotel room had become nothing more than a place for him to stew in his misery for the night. Feelings of hopelessness always settled in during nights like this. His longing over the promise of the letter began to crawl over him, so he shoved the envelope back into the ancestor's album and returned to obsessively pouring over the same old documents he returned to every night.

It hadn't been more than a few minutes when he heard a hard knock at the motel door. The hollow echo forced his head out of his hands as he turned to look at the alarm clock glowing frightening red numbers that read 1:31 a.m. He sighed in response. The knocks came again and he finally decided to push his chair back to stand up.

"Open the hell up."

"Yeah, yeah," Cannon said to himself as he shuffled across the hotel room, rubbing his eyes.

After a wide swing of the door, he was staring right at Cathay. It was impossible to tell the mood she was in by her facial expressions, so he resorted to asking just to clear the air between them.

"You okay?"

"The fuck kind of question is that? You're the one who still has all the lights on in the room way past your bedtime." Cathay pushed her way through Cannon and into his room as she spoke.

"You can't just—"

"Your room's nicer than mine, did you know that? I'm going to have to keep an eye on you."

"I'm pretty sure they're all the same damn rooms, Cathay," Cannon told her as he gave up the fight and closed the door behind her. "Why are you here?"

"Couldn't sleep. Looked like you couldn't either, so I figured I'd just show my happy ass up."

"I *don't* sleep, it's different."

"Sure," she answered with a quick roll of her eyes back at him. "So, what exactly did Etta see in you anyway? She don't dick around with just anyone like that. I couldn't believe my eyes when she showed up at my trailer with you."

"We've worked together for more than a year now. She told me she didn't want me to get killed trying to bring you in, but now I know she just wanted to catch up with an old buddy. So, there's that, I guess."

"That don't explain as much as you think it does," she told him.

"You're probably right."

"So, there's a train, and a guy who's killing all these people just to get his hands on a bunch of shit that museums don't even want?"

"You really came over here to listen to my speech again?"

"Nope. I sure didn't. I just want to know why the hell he's so important that we gotta do all this." Cathay gestured broadly around her as she spoke.

"It's not enough that he's killing people and stealing millions while doing it?"

"Not really. That's pretty much just a normal day for the NHCP, and I ain't never seen them bring you in before. So, I'm thinking there is something else happening here."

Cannon fell back down in his chair when he heard her response. As he fought the urge to second guess why he said she'd be the best choice for their ragtag little team, he watched her shift uncomfortably. Her body language betrayed the attitude she gave to just about everyone around her. There was something else lurking beneath her intense gaze.

"He has something," Cannon tried to say. "Or at

least we think he might. It's going to be up to us to find that part out to be honest with you."

"Has what, exactly? Seems like y'all just forgot to tell me about all that."

"I wish I could tell you. All we know is that whatever he is collecting in that damn train of his seems to be leaving a trail of dead bodies. If you ask me, I think he's just killing anyone who has something he wants, then moves on to the next. Makes it look like there is more to it than there really is."

"Well ain't that just real damn convenient."

"I know it's not the answer any of us want right now, but we're going to find out what that asshole is up to regardless," Cannon assured her.

"You can bet your ass that I feel all warm and fuckin' cuddly about it now."

"Good, then it's my turn to ask a question."

Cannon and Cathay spoke for what felt like the next few hours—well into the morning—almost exclusively about the next member to join their team. Cathay had worked with some rodeo clowns years back and out of all of them, there was only one who was still getting up to the same old trouble. The man was a bullfighter, through and through. That wasn't the worst part though. The particular bullfighter they were going after was one who had a penchant for getting into more trouble than he was worth. The man Cathay described was one of unabashed devilry, simply put.

Cannon watched her closely as she divulged one terrible story after the next about the bullfighter. Just one of them was more than enough to make him reconsider what he was doing, but all of them together, was becoming more than he bargained for. He sighed more times than he would have liked at her firsthand accounts of what the bullfighter would get into, but eventually grew numb to the shock.

The hotel room they had found themselves in was musty and unwelcome, but for Cannon, it had somehow become a sanctuary of sorts. For the first night in as long as Cannon could remember, he wasn't furiously pouring over the ancestor's album until he passed out where he sat. The ritual had become ingrained into him. It put him at odds against his own failures and served as a constant reminder of what he became more and more desperate to find each night. As he listened to Cathay, he felt like he was finally able to belong somewhere other than with his nose in the same old pages.

This was about the furthest thing that he had signed up for when he told Etta he'd take this whole thing on for the NHCP. Despite this fact, along with being locked inside the smelly old motel room— Cannon had found purpose.

"I can see you're nodding and all, but I'm not so sure you follow what I'm telling you," Cathay said, snapping him out of his moment of reflection.

"I'm following."

"I'm trying to tell you the man is a cold-blooded killer. You get that? Always has been too. I had to get away from him, and when I did, I told myself I'd never be caught in his eyesight again."

Cannon considered whether or not to tell her that recruiting the man was his idea. He knew Cathay was telling him all these things to scare him away, to make him reconsider who to bring into the fold next, but every reason she gave was just proof that the bull-fighter was exactly who he needed on his side. A cutthroat with a gun, who knew how to be mean in a pinch would go a long way when it came time to face down whatever was waiting for them inside of Major James's train. Rather than waiting too long to let Cathay down, he figured he better go ahead and rip that Band-Aid off.

"We're going to need a little crazy on our side, you know," he told her, standing up and beginning to pace from one side of the hotel room to the next. "I told Etta when I agreed to all this mess that I needed one level-headed hand and one hand who didn't even know what that meant. Your name came up first, and his name came up second. I'm honestly just glad to hear you can back up what she told me."

"You're shittin' me?"

"I shit you not."

"Well in that case, you're damn sure gonna get what you wanted outta him. That man ain't had a level head since his parents dropped him on it when he was a kid," Cathay said with a smile forming on the end of her lips as she spoke.

Cannon allowed himself a few scoffs in exchange for laughter. As he did, Cathay reached behind her back and miraculously pulled out a bottle that made Cannon question where she'd hidden it this whole time. With a slight nod toward Cannon, she offered him a swig of whatever the brown bottle contained. He wasn't one to turn down a drink after a night like he'd just had, so he reached out and nodded right back to her as he did.

It took just a whiff to know that it was whiskey in the bottle. His heart fluttered at the first drop that hit his tongue when he turned the bottle upside down. Cathay's expression of dismay almost took him by surprise, but he let it pass as he chugged down more of the liquor than any man should in one pass. He smeared what remained from his lips onto his forearm when he was done and handed it back to Cathay. Before she turned the bottle up herself, she couldn't help but come clean herself with a confession all her own.

"You better believe we're gonna find out who your old man was."

Cannon stopped himself from saying anything brash in response. He let the words settle into his head. As hard as they had been to hear, they might've been the first time he'd heard any words of support for what he was going through. Although it took every bit of willpower he could find—and a pretty big swig of whiskey to top it off—he allowed himself to believe them, even if it was just for the night.

CHAPTER 9

I f you want to get around East Texas, there is a lesson which everybody learns whether they want to or not—you gotta drive everywhere. The roads are a second home. It's where you'll hold the hand of your spouse, or yell at the asshole on the other end of the phone. It's where you'll discover the love of a new song or stare endlessly into nowhere when you should be paying attention to where you're going. The piney woods roads will carry you to unimaginable beauty, or into the depths of abandonment, from one small town to the next with rolling pastures connecting each, all beneath a bright sun casting down humid heat what felt like all year round.

Cannon and Cathay were on their way to Gladewater from the other side of Carthage. Luckily for them, this drive was only about an hour long. Heading northeast on 1-49 up through Tatum and past Longview was their best route and it made for a simple drive, one that was no different than going to the store for those who lived here.

Etta had taken an emergency phone call back at the motel not too long after their thrills at the Panola County pro rodeo came to an end. That phone call led her out of the room and into the hallway where she wouldn't be seen again. The NHCP had a way of doing that to her, but Cannon had grown accustomed to it. He woke up the next morning after just a couple of hours of sleep to a text message from her which stated the obvious fact that she wasn't there anymore.

With nothing else left to do but push on, Cannon packed up the Ram 1500 pickup that had been left behind so they could hit the road. It was a minor upgrade from his old 1980s model Chevy that had gotten him through the years, but new didn't always mean better in his book.

Their ride quickly turned into a picturesque view once they went through Lake Cherokee. The water glistened in the sunlight with only a few clouds dotting the sky throughout the horizon. Homes lined the shore far in the distance with docks reaching out into the lake. There were only a few boaters enjoying Lake Cherokee when they passed by, but Cannon couldn't help but imagine himself as one of them, dropping a line and sitting back with a bottle of whiskey that he didn't need. The lake was the kind of gem hidden in the woods that made you want to call the place home.

"Would ya look at that." Cathay finally spoke up.

Cannon thought about answering, but their drive would only send them through the lake for only a few minutes longer. He glanced to his left to see the piers stretching out into the cove, trying their best to create an interconnected network of lakefront homeowners. With oaks and pines hanging their limbs overhead, Water Shield covered the tops of the water throughout the entire cove until the water took further out into the middle of the lake. The green pads reached deep down as they swarmed everything near the shoreline.

Soon, the scenic lake faded into his rearview mirror and Cannon was forced to come to terms with what was ahead. He looked over at Cathay. She had been staring at him this whole time with a squint in her eyes and a turned-up lip, like she was peering into his soul that had been splayed open by the view of Lake Cherokee.

Instead of acknowledging the awkward moment that Cathay had forced in between them with her behavior, Cannon turned his attention back to the business at hand.

"You know, I never did get the name of this crazed bullfighter we're going after today."

"Jim Bob Hicks," said Cathay, clearly trying not to laugh as she did.

"Jim…Bob…"

"Hicks," she confirmed. "That's his name. There's a whole thing to it, and I'm sure he'll be the first to tell ya all about it."

"Well, I'm looking forward to meeting our Jim Bob."

Silence once again fell over the two as they listened to the hum of the road. The quiet vibrations would take them right to the rodeo grounds at Gladewater, where they had a bitch of a time finding parking. It was a round-up like no other across the state, and more than eighty years old in the making. The facilities had more money in them than the rodeo out in Panola County, but that didn't matter to those competing. The dirt in the arena held the same opportunity for glory and pain.

Despite having most of the day to get there, the sheer amount of people who'd shown up to the small-town rodeo turned big time put them behind schedule. By the time they had found a couple of open spots on the hard metal bleachers, it was only minutes before eight fifteen p.m. when the event was set to kick off.

There was a towering wall of storied oaks that lined one side of the arena, just barely peeking their limbs over the stands that rose into the air as if they too wanted a view of the rodeo soon to unfold. The sun was already setting on the day. Orange hues reflected off the metal that made up the seating, siding, and fencing of the facilities. They'd found themselves in the middle of a green pasture, one that had been overfilled with pickups and trailers, turning it into a muddy mess despite not seeing an inch of rain in over a week.

"Feel like I was just doing this," Cannon quipped as they sat down.

"Just weird being on this side, honestly." Cathay didn't even make eye contact.

The rodeo began as customary, with the stars and stripes first and foremost waving alongside the voice of a singer just a bit more experienced than the last one they'd listened to. Dirt kicked up into the air as the horse made its lap through the arena. The woman holding old glory into the air refused to move even a muscle as they strode by.

Ropes and spurs were soon filling the arena as the rodeo powered on. The crowd was deafening here, and it put a stop to any conversation Cannon and Cathay might've had. Spare a few times where they just resorted to screaming in each other's ear trying to figure out when the bullfighter would make himself known, they just watched the age-old spectacle play out in front of them. Rodeos like this had become one of the last vestiges of entertainment born of the frontier. They found themselves in the position of carrying the torch for the Old West itself.

When the breakaway ropers lined up at the chute, Cannon couldn't help but notice Cathay leaning forward to put both elbows on her knees. She was locked in and not at all focused on what they were there for, but that was okay. Her intensity somehow got Cannon more interested and he followed suit. They fell into the emotions of the crowd, eagerly awaiting each ride and hollering through them all no different than anyone else in the stands.

The Gladewater Rodeo went by in a blur. Before they knew it, the announcer was calling on the bulls lined up in the cutes. With names like Hellfire Damnation, Devil in Disguise, Burning Rage, and Gunpowder, the crowd knew damn good and well they were in for a good time. Their excitement was palpable and it told Cannon everything he needed to know. The man he was after was surely coming up soon.

"Let's get ready to ride!" the announcer screamed over the sea of people encircling the arena.

The sudden clanking of the gate swinging open to the chute sent out the first bull rider hanging on for dear life. Slobber from the bull strung out in every direction as he kicked violently and spun with bewildering speed. The rider clung to the bull's back as if his life depended on it, and in some ways, it did. A trio of clowns circled the rider as the bull wore himself out to chants from the crowd. When a loud buzzer went off throughout the arena, the rider flew into the air all too ready to celebrate.

This went on several more times to varying degrees of success. Some lasted no more than two seconds while just three riders were able to feast their eyes on the coveted eight seconds lit up the clock for all to see. Just when it looked like they were out of bulls in the chutes, the announcer over the megaphone got everyone riled up all over again.

"We have a special surprise for you tonight! These tough ol' bull riders may be done for now, but it's time to buckle up, because the bullfighters are just getting started!"

Cannon shot a look over to Cathay. "Here we go."

"Ain't that right," she said. "That damn Jim Bob has these people fooled though. I know better."

"Remind me what it is again that's about to happen here."

"Think of it as running for your life, but you get scored on how close death gets on your heels in the process."

"Sounds like a good time."

"Get *your* ass down there then."

The lights clicked off around the arena before Cannon could dig his hole any deeper and the crowd went silent in response. The moths danced in the light of the stars that were making themselves known with the sun gone. For a few fleeting seconds, it was a moment of serenity that made Cannon forget about the weight of what he had just told Cathay about— and what he'd kept from her. When the lights powered back on, the serene feeling that had washed over Cannon melted away with the roar of the crowd who had just seen the appearance of a lone bullfighter standing in the middle of the arena.

"Here we go," Cannon heard Cathay complain to no one in particular.

The man responsible for the sudden explosion of cheers lifted his arms up in recognition and spun to bask in it. He wore denim overalls that were twice too big for him, held up with leather suspenders topped with a tall straw hat that looked like it had been trampled more than a time or two. His shoulders were wider than the bulls that chased after him, but he was light on his feet and seemed to truly thrive in the adoration of everyone crammed shoulder to shoulder in the bleachers.

"Let's give it up for Jimmy Robert Hicks, the bull battling bastard from Beaumont, Texas!"

The crowd was already giving it everything they had so they just kept it going when the announcer spoke up. This time Cannon and Cathay opted not to join in on the fun. They had to get their heads in the game. Cannon wanted to know for sure if this was the guy he needed, but Cathay was just hoping he might get gored by the bull's horns so they could find someone else.

Jim Bob Hicks bounced up and down in place as he stared ahead at the chutes and waited on a lane to open. There wasn't much else he could do but wait. This gave the announcer enough time to bask in the few seconds it took to send the bull up.

"He might be the baddest bullfighter this side of the lone star state, but he'll have to give it all he's got against tonight's matchup—Dead Man's Hand!"

The final words blared from the announcer's box filled with cowboy hat-wearing talking heads looking down at the arena. A black and white spotted Brahman cross bull with wide-set pointed horns came trotting down the lane. The bull held a deadly gaze on the man in the center of the arena and came to a sudden stop when he hit the dirt. A metal gate slammed shut behind Dead Man's Hand, who wasted no time in getting to work.

The first move was an easy sidestep at the last possible moment from Jim Bob who stayed light on his feet. A big white smile lit up the arena when he dodged and before too long, he suckered the crowd back into thinking he was in life-threatening danger once again.

"He's good," Cannon acknowledged.

"Never said he wasn't."

"Let's just hope he makes it out of this one so we can get to him."

No answer came from Cathay.

Meanwhile, the bullfighter was hard at work

putting on a show for everyone at the Gladewater Rodeo. He moved too quickly for the muscles packed on him and it seemed the bull was as caught off guard as the audience was. Jim Bob ran in a tight circle with the bovine athlete right on his heels and waved to the crowd with a smile as he did. The bull got angrier and angrier with each circle until Jim Bob broke the routine and set him up for a stunt.

The crowd was hanging onto every move with bated

breath. Dirt flew as loose as the snot of the bull. The announcer hollered something but no one was paying attention to his voice in the background. As Dead Man's Hand lifted a front hoof in preparation, Jim Bob squatted down low and waited for just the right moment. Each of the two found themselves squared off in the middle of the arena.

The bull moved first. Almost like they were playing chicken, they both ran directly at each other headfirst. Right before it was too late, the bull pushed its head to the ground and got ready to hurl its horns at the bullfighter with all eighteen hundred pounds of might it could muster. Jim Bob read every move the bull had, and with his palm placed right in the middle of its head, he leaped up to get launched another six feet into the air. The crowd gasped in response as he went flying.

The bullfighter was unfazed, though. He landed upright on his boots and never missed a step. The bull looked around to find its target once again and wasted no time in coming right after him. As the announcer spurred everyone on and the clock ticked down, Jim Bob set himself up for a spectacular finale.

"Here he goes." Cathay leaned over to tell Cannon. "He always does this shit; thinks we never see it coming."

Cannon nodded, unwilling to admit just how anxious he was at the bullfighters performance. It wasn't like roping and riding. Somehow, this was even more dangerous. Watching the man stare down a pissed off bull twisted his stomach, and he knew most of everyone else sitting in the bleachers felt the same way. That much could be felt even in the air. The crowd's roar motivated the bullfighter to continue on. As the clock ticked down to the final thirty seconds, the people began to count down louder and louder.

With just fifteen seconds left, the game of chicken started all over again. Jim Bob charged first this time. His boots stomped the dirt as if he was every bit as pissed off as the bull that was running right toward him. Jim Bob went to push off the bull's head with the palm of his hand, but things didn't go as planned this time. His boot slipped just as he tried to jump, and the bullfighter went down at the same time as the bull's horns. When he hit the ground, the bull was right on top of him.

All Jim Bob could see from the dirt were horns gashing left and right with wild ferocity. There was no more snot flying or applause ringing out, there was only a fight for his life—and he was on the losing side. The first bit of pain that coursed through his body flared from his rib cage. He did his best to ignore the cracking sound that filled his ears. There was no time to be concerned with his ribs, because the bull immediately landed on his thigh sending a burning sensation throughout the left side of his body. It was a crippling kind of pain and he screamed in response, though no one could hear.

There were only a few seconds of Jim Bob getting mauled by Dead Man's Hand in the middle of the arena before a trio of bullfighters came to his rescue, but it felt like an eternity to both the one on the ground getting attacked, and those in the bleachers watching it happen in real time.

"We might have to go back to the drawing board on this one," Cannon admitted as they watched the bull finally leave Jim Bob motionless in the dirt.

"Stupid son of a bitch," Cathay answered with a shake of her head.

"You think he's okay?"

"Definitely not, look at him."

Jim Bob was lying motionless face down in the dirt. His limbs were twisted unnaturally and his body was left mangled. The bull had left him a mess of a man. The crowd was waiting anxiously to hear the announcer say everyone was safe, but the affirmation never came. They watched as one of the rescuing bull-fighters grabbed Jim Bob by the safety vest beneath his shirt and overalls and dragged his limp body across the arena.

Every head in the crowd was bowed as the mega-phones came back on, but the regular announcer's voice didn't come through. It was the man who had led the invocation to kick off the rodeo instead. He'd stepped back into the booth to lead a prayer for the bullfighter who'd been beaten into the dirt by Dead Man's Hand. Every cowboy hat was in hand and not a sound was being made outside of the words of grace echoing out over the crowd.

It was a solemn moment. It was the kind of experience that would force any man's priorities into perspective without a second thought—except for the man named Jim Bob Hicks.

CHAPTER 10

The hiss and knocking of the Union Pacific FEF hugging the rails at speeds it shouldn't know firsthand was nothing more than music to the ears of Major James. The feeling of Big Betty racing toward the next small town in search of a larger audience was his second favorite part of the Major James Out West Show tour through the southernmost United States—behind only the collection that was hidden away in the middle train car.

He was standing front and center in the engine as the wind rushed by. They were on their way south through Marshall where they would host just a handful of stops throughout East Texas as they made their way west. The tour was set to come to a close on the other side of the state in El Paso, but that was still a long way off. For now, his view was filled with nothing but green on either side of the train. Pines and oaks mixed into the yaupon brush that lined the railway, separated only just wide enough to allow the tracks to run through them. The woods parted before him like the Red Sea itself and Major James couldn't help but feel a sense of power and control from where he stood.

"Sir, sir." Ned burst into the engine car just in time to ruin a good moment like only he knew how to do.

Major James did his best to ignore his loyal hand and savor the moment of reflection offered to him through the tree limbs stretching out over their head. It was a losing game though, as Ned was a persistent one.

"Sir? Can you hear me?" He was now standing no more than two feet away from the showman.

"Yes, Burwell, I can indeed."

"I thought you were at the armory. I was looking all around, calling your name. Then, I remembered you were here, so that's why I'm late," Ned explained for no reason. "But the reason I come down here to find you is to tell you something real important," Ned continued without missing a beat. Getting ignored by his boss wasn't something that was exactly new for him.

"Go on already.".

"I hear people talking, sir. All of them talk a lot on this train and most of it's good, it really is."

"But?"

"But I heard something not too long ago you'd probably want to know about from a couple of those riding actors."

"Walk with me, Ned." Major James put his hand on the small man's shoulder and nudged him forward.

They both felt the rumble of the train rushing

forward as they turned to walk back through the cars behind them. The vibrations were fierce and constant, all the while encouraging you to become numb to its effect. Their steps were no different than if they were walking on Mother Earth herself instead of the steel deathtrap hurling itself down the rails fueled by a fiery breath. Just as they exited the engine and started to make their way into the bunks through the brief gap of open air, Major James spoke again.

"What are the rumors of today, my old pal?" His tone was softer now that they were alone, and it coaxed exactly what he was looking for out of Ned.

"They are scheming to steal from you. One of the men got a glimpse inside car four and word has spread—quick. Some of them have gone and planned a distraction while the others are gonna try to break in from the back."

"At our next stop, I assume?"

"Yes sir, they said sometime tonight."

Major James ran his calloused hands through what little hair remained on top of his head. This type of thing was to be assumed, especially given what he was building just beneath all of their noses. "Understood," he finally said. "I thank you for your undying loyalty, Ned. They just don't make 'em like you anymore, that's for sure."

"Thank you, sir, thank you."

As they walked through the bunks surrounded by the real artists of the show—the ones who have perfected the craft of setting up a show and breaking it down in a single night—and the stench they brought with them, Major James spoke low and close to Ned so there could be no confusion.

"Now I am going to need you to do one more favor for me, and you gotta do it now, before they figure out what's best for them."

"Anything, sir. But the only problem is, I don't know everyone is going to be in on all of this. I only caught the one guy's name, Brad Dahlman. He plays Teddy Roosevelt and also…robber number three, I think."

"I don't rightly care about who it is, or how many it is," said Major James. "You see, there is a matter of principle at hand here that we must nip in the bud before it's too late. These kinds of ideas can spread, permeate through the very fabric of our great show here. Does that make sense?"

"I think so, sir. You mean that they are going to inspire others to go snooping around where they shouldn't?"

"Precisely so, Ned. It won't do just to go track down—what did you say his name was, Brad? No, no, we will have to do something else entirely. As soon as word gets out about what we have here at the Major James Out West Show, when they find out how special everything we've put together here truly is, the world will want it for themselves. It always does."

"Don't we want the world to see, though?" Ned was surprisingly forward about his question, having been taken off guard by the monologue of his boss.

"We want the world to see the show, Ned," Major James explained. "And that is not the same as them seeing what it takes to put it on. History will only remember the spectacle."

Ned decided to remain silent himself this time, not because of frustration or annoyance, but because he was made painfully aware that their conversation had fallen into intellectual capacities of which he was simply not privy to. Silence was the only reasonable response that he could make sense of.

"If we're going to put a stop to this the right way, to make sure we carry onward just as before, I'm going to need you to run along right now."

"Yes sir," Ned said without thinking. "Um, excuse me, but where am I running?"

"To go find our new gun hand, Mr. J.R. Pickett, of course."

CHAPTER 11

For most people, hearing a bull bell ringing like it's dinner time at the pits of hell while getting trampled half to death by a nearly two-ton bovine athlete would be more than enough to deal with in a single night. Jim Bob Hicks just wasn't like most, though.

Cannon and Cathay wound up finding the beat-to-shit bullfighter staving off every doctor in Gladewater from taking him to the nearest hospital for a full evaluation. His leg had already turned all different colors, most of all a horrifying purple, and his lungs felt like a thousand pocketknives rattling around in his chest with every breath. His eyes weren't quite able to focus enough to read worth a damn, but he could still spot a cop or a nurse from a hundred yards out if he had to. He knew just what to say to them, too.

"I swear to the Almighty himself, I told you to go get me a damned drink," Jim Bob hollered. "You get close to me without a whiskey or a beer in your hand, I'm just going to have to slap the shit out of all y'all."

Cathay rolled her eyes over to Cannon. "He's fine, by the way."

"Looks like we're in luck," he gave the one answer she didn't want to hear.

"I told you; I got places to be tonight," Jim Bob kept it up despite being surrounded by a swarm of cowboy hats and gloved hands. "Keep this up and I'm just gonna start swinging. We'll see how many of you are left when I get done."

They were standing behind the announcer's booth back behind the arena as nighttime in East Texas had found them all once again. The cicadas did their best to drown out Jim Bob's screaming and the humidity forced sweat to run down the backs of their necks. Towering lights that once basked the rodeo grounds in brilliant light were now turned off to let darkness mixed with vague shadows from the moonlight take hold. There was no more backdrop of trees, or city horizon in the distance anymore. A local spectacle had come and gone for another year, leaving behind what it always did—an empty arena, a closed off pasture, and a lot of empty hope for an even better time next year. Standing where they were, each one could feel the impending weight of a stark return to reality after the performance of the historic rodeo.

Cannon broke away from Cathay's side at last and made his way over to where Jim Bob was surrounded by people doing their best to help the man despite himself. His boots pushed down into the mud that had formed in the chaos of animals and people that had used it only minutes before.

"Get outta here," Cannon demanded as he shoved his way into the crowd. "Don't you hear the man? Go on and find something else to waste your time with, you useless pricks."

He reached down and put his hand on Jim Bob's shoulder. "You finally wake up from your nap, you lazy asshole? We gotta get to work."

Somehow, Jim Bob instinctively knew what was happening and played along like a charm, almost like they had rehearsed the moment long before the rodeo ever happened.

"About damn time you showed up," he told Cannon, ignoring everyone standing around him. "I been telling these dickheads to leave me alone. I feel fit as a fuckin' fiddle."

"Then we better get," said Cannon, grabbing the bullfighter by the arm and yanking him up to his feet.

The two pushed their way past the men who'd been taken off guard by the interruption. Most gave up the fight and wished the worst for Jim Bob, either throwing their hands up in defeat or actually taking the effort to cuss his name. That didn't stop either of them from seeing their way to the line of trailers leaving the rodeo grounds.

Cannon nudged Cathay to follow them as they passed her by. She took the hint with ease. They formed a gangly trio of misfits that had no reason to stick together other than a handful of half-truths and too much hope for something that would never be there. Yet somehow, they'd all found a way to cross paths.

"I appreciate what y'all did back there," Jim Bob said as he stumbled keeping up.

"Don't mention it."

"Your number's been called, asshole." Cathay wasted no time interjecting.

"The hell is she going on about?"

"Let's just get you outta here first." Cannon darted his eyes over to Cathay.

They kept walking as best they could, trying to get back to the pickup that had brought them out to Gladewater. Jim Bob's limp slowed them down, but all things considered, Cannon was still feeling lucky. Aside from his first recruit almost dying in a fight and the second one almost dying by a bull, his team had been assembled with relative ease. He would never tell either of the two walking with him, but it certainly put a pep in his step.

"I should tell y'all," the bullfighter started to say, this time with a tone most would have in the middle of an apology. "All that stuff I said back there about having to meet some people here in a bit…"

Silence came from both Cannon and Cathay. It was the kind of silence that falls over a family hanging on every word of a doctor after an emergency. Some news could only be bad, that much is just a fact of life. The only thing that's ever left to do in such a situation is to find out just how bad.

"Well, I wasn't lying about all that."

"What does that mean?" Cannon had choice but to ask.

"Means people are gonna be here looking for me. In fact, they're probably already here."

"Who are *they*, exactly?" Cathay cut in.

A bullet whizzed by their heads before Cathay could finish her sentence and slammed into the ground only a few feet away from them. It was as if gravity had increased a hundredfold and crumpled their bodies down with unrelenting force. Cannon, Cathay, and an injured Jim Bob fell onto their backs, unaware of what was happening. Before any of them could react, it was Cannon who had brandished a snub nosed .38 special revolver and fired off a round in the first direction he'd seen people moving in.

"Get the hell outta here!" he hollered to Cathay and Jim Bob before a barrage of bullets started raining down on them, sending them scrambling to their feet to sprint out of the line of sight.

"Holy shit!" Cathay let out as she left them all behind.

Jim Bob was doing his best to hobble out of the rodeo grounds to a fine tune of his own expletives, but there wasn't much cover to be found nearby. The closest thing to safety any of them could hope for was an old metal building that was almost falling down back behind the arena. None of them could see hide nor hair of who was taking pot shots at them from back in the stands, but there was definitely more than one judging by the amount of bullets coming for their head.

Cannon fired one more round from his black N-frame revolver that blended into the night until the blast of hellfire pouring from the end of the barrel gave it away. It was only a five-shot backup pistol concealed for crowded events, not good for much in the fight he'd suddenly found himself in. Even then, he was damned and determined to make the most out of the three rounds he had left.

He was standing in a field, all by himself, separating the gunmen from the team he'd only just met. The chance to run was now, but he couldn't bring himself to do it. Images of watching his own family succumb to the hands of unknown goons who mean only to harm had cracked his cold heart. With a quick glance back at the rusted tin pole barn that had long outlived its heyday, he watched Cathay and Jim Bob dive out of sight. The urge to join them hit, and he gave it a few seconds of serious consideration. Instead of giving in, he turned to face the arena that was no stranger to welcoming the potential for death and started his senseless charge into the firefight.

Three bullets left.

He knew there were at least two gunmen, and that gave him just one extra shot to spare if he needed it. Worst case, there were more than two and if that happened, he'd be just about screwed anyway, so none of that actually mattered. He stomped as he sprinted, forcing one boot down harder than the next as he waited on the piercing scream of bullets to tear by his path. They never came.

His sprint got him across the field and close to the arena sooner than he'd expected. He couldn't put into words the appreciation for the shadows cast by the light of the moon. It had granted him just enough visibility to spot movement in the distance. That was his first target.

They were running from the bleachers to a nearby building that looked to be a bathroom or office, and if Cannon had his way, the man making a run for it would never see the inside of it for himself. He bolted to his right to cut the man's path off and did his best to get as close with the snub nose as he possibly could. *Bam!*

Two bullets left.

The man who'd caught the.38 special bullet in his belly clutched at the gunshot wound and fell to the ground with terrible screams of pain and fear. Cannon knew it would get whoever was with them riled up and unfocused, maybe even scared for their own lives, so he let the man continue to wail.

"I ain't done with you yet!" Cannon hollered over their partner's screams. "I'm coming for every goddamn one of you."

Bam!

This time he fired needlessly into the air for the threat alone and stared wide-eyed in every direction around him. Carelessness could always rear its ugly head, even in a shootout.

One bullet left.

There was no response, nor shadow slipping away in the distance. He felt alone at that moment in time, more alone than maybe he ever had in his life. Hollering at ghosts who'd opened fire at him and the two people who were the closest thing to friends he'd had in a long time—even though they barely knew him—had a way of isolating his thoughts. It wasn't tunnel vision from the gunfight. It was something else, something that followed him around every corner he ever turned. He considered the one bullet remaining in the revolver clutched in his grip.

Another bullet suddenly screeched by his right ear until it ricocheted off the bleachers with a blinding spark. It was just what he needed to get his head back in the game, only this time, it came from behind him. What he saw when he looked back was enough to change damn near his entire outlook in life.

"Don't stop shooting, you asshole!" Cathay let loose as Jim Bob hobbled alongside her holding a 1911 pistol that looked like it was pulled from his grandfather's nightstand.

"What the…" Cannon couldn't help himself.

"We gotta get the hell outta Dodge!" Jim Bob said as he stumbled right on by him.

Cathay looked over her shoulder at Cannon to catch his attention. She nodded blatantly and wasted no time in barking the same order at him again.

"You coming or what? Those red and blue lights coming this way ain't gonna like this one bit."

She was right. Cannon looked out across the arena and saw the reflection of what happened when you in a gunfight in the middle of town. Flashing lights were growing closer by the second.

Instead of saying anything, Cannon followed suit and caught up to both of them. The arrival of law enforcement was the worst kind of backdrop for what they were doing and it only turned their escape into a blur of wild emotion. Somewhere far behind them, the screams of the man who'd been shot faded into nothing and Cannon wondered what his fate would be, but quickly abandoned his concern for anything that wasn't dealing with his own getaway.

The Ram pickup that had become their sanctuary would've blended right into the swarms of trucks that had filled the rodeo grounds during the big event, but as empty as it was now, they had no choice but to hope not to draw attention to themselves. Crammed inside the pickup all sweaty and out of breath, Cannon pulled out of the pasture they were parked in and turned left to meet the coming law enforcement head in.

They drove right on by. The flashing lights went from a threat coming their way to a near miss in their rearview mirror. Cannon turned down another street to put some distance between them and the rodeo grounds before they found a back road to slip out of town on. As he slowed down and listened to the clicking of the blinker, no one in the truck said a word.

Nerves were still coursing through his body, and from the look of Cathay and Jim Bob, a similar feeling had set in for them too. Everyone was just staring ahead, grateful to be in the peace and quiet of the dull hum of the 5.7 HEMI that had raced them away from all the action. Jim Bob was lying on his back, face up in the back seat, groaning at every ache in his body and for some reason, complaining about how hungry he was.

"I sure could go for a chopped beef sandwich about now," said Jim Bob with noticeable pain in his voice. "There's a place outside of town, mostly does pork, but they have a damn good, chopped beef with all the fresh peppers you can stomach. Don't that sound good right about now?"

"Are you really talking about food?" Cathay couldn't believe her ears.

Just as they turned onto the back road, Cannon glanced in his rearview mirror and saw a striking silhouette he didn't recognize.

"Who the—" he let out before Cathay cut him off with a loud shout.

"Shoot! Shoot his ass!"

"Wait! Wait!" Jim Bob yelped while curling into a ball in the back seat.

Before he knew what was happening, the silhouette held a pistol from the bed of the truck and was pushing it to the back glass. He was a split second from opening fire into the cab and ending their getaway right then and there, but Cannon beat the gunman to the punch with one last bullet fired directly behind him without even looking.

Bam!

Glass shattered in the cab all over Jim Bob hollering in the back seat, and both Cathay and Cannon reactively yelled their own curses in response. The once-deadly silhouette stumbled back in the bed of the truck, and Cannon reacted quick, slamming down on the gas pedal just as whoever was in the back grabbed at their neck. The last thing any of them saw was the person flying out of the back of the truck and crashing into the gravel of the back road, tumbling head over feet until he slid face down to a stop. He didn't move again.

"All out of ammo," Cannon said without reading the room or taking his boot off the gas pedal.

The three of them just raced off down the back road leading south, far away from anyone who'd know anything of what just happened.

CHAPTER 12

"What in the Sam Hill just happened back there?"

"We almost died."

"Well, no shit!"

Cannon heard the questions, he heard the shock in their voices, but he did nothing to acknowledge them. He stared ahead with a blank look on his face. The thoughts that raced through his mind were only on a single question—who were the men he'd just gunned down?

They'd stopped near Liberty City, a small town south of Gladewater that would barely pass as a town for most, but considering it had a Whataburger, it had everything they needed for the night. There was a place to park their vehicle and crash for the night just beside Rocky Creek running through town. Cannon had found their way to a quiet spot tucked away out of sight and killed the pickup that brought them there.

It wasn't the shootout that had thrown Cannon off. It was the fact that both of the people he'd picked from the NHCP reserves were in the middle of fights with people he didn't know. Sure, the rodeo types might have always been in some type of scuffle here and there, but not like this. There was something happening that he didn't understand, but he was damn sure about to figure it out.

He could feel the cool breeze making its way into the cab through the shattered back glass of the Ram. Humidity had given way to a familiar nighttime chill. The Texas sun had a way of fooling you into thinking it was hotter than it really was, but humidity was often the real culprit in the piney woods. When darkness fell and swaths of stars lit up the horizon, it often allowed a briskness to settle in whether it was welcome or not. This time it was. Cannon knew they had to get some sleep, but before he would even allow the other two to step out of the truck, he had to know what was happening.

"You're both about to tell me something worth hearing," he started in on them. "Cathay, you were staring down men twice your size when I found you, and Jim Bob here was about to get filled full of lead if we would've been one day late. I ain't gonna sit here and hear any more bullshit about what you've all been up to."

"What are you talking about, Cannon?" asked Cathay. "We're lucky to even be alive."

"I'm starting to think that a lot more of this is connected than any of us realize. I want to know what we're getting into. Both of you are hiding shit from me about what you've been doing and that ends tonight, right here."

He was staring straight ahead as his voice rose higher with each new sentence. It wasn't anger that was swelling in his belly, it was more like a hankering for what he knew was right in front of him that he just couldn't shake.

"Cathay, you start," he said, wasting no time.

"I already told you everything, dumbass."

"Then why were you about to get your ass kicked behind the trailers?"

"I think we both know I was never going to get my ass kick."

Cannon glared at her out of the corner of his eyes and didn't say anything. He knew she fully understood what he was talking about. It didn't take long for her to get the hint and continue talking.

"Look, some company found me a while back with more promises than money," Cathay started explaining. "First, it was just one guy who showed up at one of my worst rodeos yet, but he still found me afterward. There were offers floating around for me to perform exclusively for them, basically live with them like some damn carney folk."

Cathay finally broke eye contact with everyone in the pickup, but she didn't stop telling them about what happened to her.

"I started doing better on my own, hitting the right times at the rodeos, and people even started recognizing me. I stopped entertaining their promises of stardom and mounds of money, but then they started showing up more and more."

"They?"

"The guys you saw." Cathay turned again with a different look in her eye. "The guys who were threatening me. By the time you showed up, they had already followed me to three different towns. They told me that if I didn't come with them—"

"That they'd kill you with just a single look," Jim Bob cut in.

Cannon fought to turn around in the pickup as quickly as his body would possibly allow to see Jim Bob's face. He knew something, and it was finally starting to come out.

"A single look?" Cannon asked both of them.

Cathay was the first to speak up. "That's exactly what they told me too."

"These guys pulled the same shit on me," Jim Bob agreed with her from the back seat. "They followed me around from one fight to the next, always telling me this or that about how good I am, how much money I could make, or whatever else they could come up with."

"So, you both got offered to join some new kind of rodeo," Cannon was trying to put the pieces together. "And it was actively recruiting the likes of y'all? I wonder how many more are out there that they've approached."

"There's no telling, really," said Cathay.

"You said it was a company," Cannon asked her. "Do you remember the name of the company who was going after you?"

"Something Outfitters, I think," said Jim Bob, interjecting with less than helpful input this time.

"I don't really remember, honestly," answered Cathay finally. "I tried to block it out after one of the guys showed up at my hotel room one night and damn near broke my door down trying to get me to answer it."

"They might be our only lead at this point," Cannon urged them both, talking with his hands. "Major James isn't exactly hard to find since he's putting on a new show every two days, but we don't know anything about what's really happening inside that train. I think what was happening to y'all is connected to the dead bodies that the NHCP keeps finding everywhere that train goes. The Major James Out West Show isn't just some damn rodeo."

"Out West?" Cathay realized. "That was the fuckin' name of the company. The Out West Outfitters."

"Hot damn!" Jim Bob cried from behind them. "You're right. Out West Outfitters entertainment exhibitions to revitalize lost souls and win wandering minds."

Both Cathay and Cannon had turned confusion to look at him as he prattled on.

"Or something like that…"

Cannon was screaming inside his head. It was impossible. He hadn't heard anything from the strange company that adorned the letterhead of the piece of mail that had sent him down the rabbit hole to find his father in the first place. The Out West Outfitters was a shell of a company with no presence and no connections, yet the only two people he wanted on his side had both been in touch with the same people. It had to be connected to Major James somehow, and it would be their job to find out exactly how.

They were finally getting somewhere, but it wasn't prudent to let Cathay and Jim Bob know everything about why he was doing what he was doing. So, he turned the conversation back on what else they might know.

"Did they ever tell you to go anywhere, or meet anyone?"

"They always came to me," said Cathay.

"Same here," Jim Bob answered.

"Surely they had some way to contact you, though. If they were following you around like that, if they wanted you for anything, then they had to keep tabs on you with something."

"I did get invited to one of the shows one time. Never did find out where the show was supposed to be other than somewhere in Memphis, Tennessee, but I got the invitation by mail. I remember thinking it was weird because when you rodeo for a living, don't no one know where you're gonna be one night to the next, so letters ain't exactly something that comes your way often."

"I'm guessing you don't still have that letter, do you?"

"Damn right I do," Cathay exclaimed.

"Jim Bob, what about you? You have anything they gave you? Anything at all we can use?"

"I ain't got shit," he admitted. "First guy who showed up caught me after a horn to the rib cage, so I wasn't in the friendliest mood. I actually thought he was someone else at the time and being completely honest, I took a swing at him."

Cannon buried his eyebrows as Jim Bob spoke and once again fought the urge to let himself question why he considered approaching the bullfighter to begin with.

"Next thing I know, I'm up shit creek and surrounded by like five of the bastards. Made it through a few bouts with them, but I wasn't sure I was gonna this time though."

"Wait. So, that wasn't the first time they tried to kill you?" Cathay couldn't help but ask.

"Nope. Been a few times now."

"And you've just been dealing with it?"

Jim Bob shrugged his shoulders without saying anything.

Cathay looked over at Cannon who had already matched her concern with his own. They'd all stumbled into something much more dangerous than they imagined, that much was clear now. The realization of this washed over their faces at the same time. It wasn't just some overeager businessman or violent criminal hell-bent on a murderous rampage. There was something brewing beneath the surface.

The night dragged on as the three found themselves in an RV which looked like it hadn't been lived in for close to a decade. The inside was smaller than any of them had hoped for and there was a musty smell that could only come from too many years of too much moisture. With no room to spread out, Cannon, Cathay, and Jim Bob each found a corner they could call their own.

It should've been a time for Cannon to pull his trusty black felt cowboy hat down over his face and close his eyes, but he could do no such thing after what they'd just discussed. He returned to his familiar routine of digging through the same old family history book instead. The documents shuffling back and forth were the only sounds being made inside the cramped space, aside from an occasional sigh from Jim Bob, who never really did well sitting still for too long anyway.

It didn't take long for Cannon to get right to the letter he was looking for. It was an empty promise that had led him into an abandoned RV in a city he's never been to. The letterhead was burned into his memories —Out West Outfitters. The six horse stagecoach art that ran across the top of the letter made it look more respectable than anyone would care to admit. It looked like a letter from a lost world, one where people took pride in stationery and the craft it took to compose a message worth taking the time to send. For Cannon, it was as if he was able to hold the singular point in time that he had never been able to escape.

Without thinking twice about it, he did something he hadn't even considered since his mom passed down the ancestor's album that guided his every decision. He lifted the letter from the Out West Outfitters into the air to turn it over and show both Cathay and Jim Bob undeniable proof they were all connected in this fight. As much of a wild bunch as they were, the gun hand, the rider, and the fighter all crossed paths for a reason.

"I'll be a son of a bitch," Cathay let out as she sank

down in her makeshift seat made up of a pillow they'd found tossed on the floor.

Jim Bob shook his head, either in disbelief or because he didn't really know what the letter meant for them. Cannon caught the look in his eye and thought it might be best to go ahead and catch him up to speed.

"I got a letter from the same company who was going after y'all," he explained. "This was more than a year ago. It came at a time when I should've had everything I needed, but I couldn't leave well enough alone. I chased after those same lies they told you like I didn't know any damn better."

He stopped talking for just a second as he tucked the letter back inside the oversized book he lugged around everywhere he went. Cathay and Jim Bob watched him closely, not knowing what to say that didn't include asking what exactly the letter had promised him.

"This isn't where I thought I was going to end up when I took off on my own either, for what it's worth," Cannon admitted. "Now that I'm here, I'm starting to think it was always going to end up here, with us three sitting in this stinkin' ass RV together."

"I don't truthfully know about all that, Cannon. Hell, I don't even really know *you* all that well," Jim Bob finally spoke up. He was propped against the far corner by the front door of the RV. The beat-up bull-fighter didn't give the impression that he was in much pain, but then again, he had gotten pretty good at masking his workplace injuries. "But I know for a fact that you're supposed to be here."

An uncomfortable silence fell between the three after Jim Bob offered his best shot at making Cannon feel better. It seemed as though they were fated to wind up together. They had to be the ones to find what Major James was hiding in his rail cars, there was no other choice. That didn't mean that they had any idea of what they were supposed to be doing, though.

"Whatever we do, we have to make sure we find out what Major James is really up to," said Cannon without making eye contact just yet. "If there was anyone else who might be able to help us do that, they'd be sitting their ass right here with us. It's just us though."

"The NHCP really broke the bank on this team, didn't they," Cathay smarted off.

Just as she gave them a hard time, Cannon's phone started to vibrate from the bottom of his right-hand pocket. It broke the solemn mood that had overcome them with a distraction that was both welcome and warranted. The name written across the glowing screen made Cannon consider just how much in the world really did happen at random.

"Speak of the devil," he said as he swiped his thumb to the side and pushed the phone up to his ear.

Cathay and Jim Bob were back to watching. They listened to half of a conversation that didn't really go anywhere.

Cathay had already spoken to Etta back at the hotel in order to find out what the deal with Cannon really was. She made sure they'd already had their heart to heart before coming forward to let him know she was on his side.

Jim Bob, however, was in a room of proverbial strangers. He wasn't the type to make himself at home just anywhere, and the people that he was now surrounded with may have saved his life, but he knew his life wouldn't be easier now that they'd all gotten tangled up. Being indebted to another man wasn't something he took lightly, however. Even strangers couldn't stay that way too long after everything they'd already gone through. As someone who prided himself on shooting straight in life, it didn't take long for him to come to the understanding that he'd have to go ahead and throw his lot in with the people inside the RV.

As they listened to a roll of the dice answer from Cannon between yes and no—with an occasional acknowledging grunt—Cathay and Jim Bob didn't move or say a word. They knew whatever he was talking about concerned them a great deal. They also knew that they'd be the last ones to find out as well. Luckily, neither of them had to wait very long to hear for themselves.

"Okay, you're on speakerphone," Cannon said a little louder to get everyone's attention.

"Listen, I'm glad y'all are one big happy family enjoying a camping adventure in the wilderness, but you need to get moving," Etta wasted no time in explaining herself. "And you gotta do it now."

"Well hello to you too, Etta," Cathay shot back to her. "Don't think I'm over you just up and leaving us all behind you know."

"I'm serious. We don't have a lot of time," Etta ignored Cathay's antics.

"We got word that local authorities picked up another dead body up in Texarkana. This one looks like the rest, but an autopsy is being done now. The only thing that's going to do is confirm what y'all are going to put a stop to, though."

Cannon glanced over at both Cathay and Jim Bob, letting them know with an affirming nod that they were about to do whatever Etta told them. It was a mutual assurance, something that went a long way with the type of people inside the RV.

"Where you want us, boss?" Jim Bob hollered from the other side of the RV.

"It's not just where. The whole damn world knows where Major James is going to set up through his tour. It's like he has a full-time marketing team working constantly to bring in larger crowds at every new show. It's not just about where you need to be. It's about what I need you to do when you get there."

"No sense in beating around the bush," said Cannon.

"The Major James Out West Show left Texarkana headed for Marshall. He's got stops set up there, and on the other side of Longview. We don't have time to get there tonight, but the good news is you can be ready and waiting tomorrow when they stop north of Kilgore just over Bighead Creek."

"Kilgore, got it," said Cannon.

"And the bad news?" Cathay interjected.

"We think he's planning a mass casualty event somewhere in the state, and he's using the stops at small towns as practice. You'll have to find a way to break into the train to find out what Major James is hiding, and why he's leaving a trail of bodies behind him to protect it," said Etta.

"And then we need you to kill him."

CHAPTER 13

"Mr. J.R. Pickett, why don't you go ahead and tell us the full story—from the beginning now—just so I can be sure I understand what was done before making any rash decisions some of us might regret."

Standing in front of the showman in a damn near perfect line were half a dozen of his own staff of the Major James Out West Show. At the front of the line to his far left was his always dedicated assistant, Ned Burwell. Standing shoulder to shoulder next to him with a foreign-made six-shooter strapped to his hip and a black felt cowboy hat pulled down low was the gun hand J.R. Pickett. Continuing the line were four nervous workers who had no idea what was in store for them.

He knew their faces well considering he'd seen each one at work through the nights. They were Huxley Donnovan the trick rider, Juan Santiago the roper, Daisy Dickens the singer, and the man she was sleeping with—as well as the brains behind the whole stunt being pulled—Brad Dahlman the actor.

Not a single one of them would make eye contact with Major James, and for damn good reason. Every employee of the outfit knew what happened when they crossed their boss the wrong way. It was a chance few ever took, and even less survived.

The first one to step forward was J.R. Pickett, who was simply doing as he was told. His spurs rattled with each step and his boots knocked against the wooden floors of the train car. They were standing in the middle of Major James's pride and joy—his old West collection. Every aged book, piece of art, statue, and shelf full of antiquities looked like it hadn't been touched in years. It was just as he liked it. The place was doused in a yellow light that moved slightly to the swaying of the train rushing southbound toward Longview.

"It was like I told you earlier," said J.R. "Brad here wrangled himself up a crew of his own. Looks like they had a few meets before tonight judging from some of their messages."

"We didn't—"

"Don't you do it, Juan," Major James cut him off. "Please, continue Mr. J.R."

"Brad got with these others over the course of a few weeks from what I could tell. Started with a harmless curiosity about what you got going on with all this," J.R. gestured to everything stashed away in the train car they were standing in. "But after a couple weeks of spending all their pay on drinks and gambling away whatever was left, the ringleader got himself an idea."

"An idea to take what was mine, isn't that right?"

"Yes sir," J.R. said. "That's what I took out of it at least."

"How original. And how did that particular idea get to these others standing here?"

"Almost didn't figure out how that happened, actually. Turns out, ol' Huxley wasn't quite as on top of deleting text messages in a timely manner like his cohorts here. Once I found a group chat named *Stickup*, well, everything else fell right into place."

"They just make it too easy sometimes," said Major James. "Ned, remind me again how you found out about all this mess."

"The show has a life all its own, as you know," Ned started the explanation he'd rehearsed about a dozen times in front of the mirror before being called on by his boss. "It breathes and talks, if you know how to listen, you won't miss a single thing. I swear it."

"Please, get to it."

"Sorry, sir." Ned shifted uncomfortably and cut to the chase. "I was trying to find Daisy to give her a delivery that got here in the batch from Texarkana. I don't know what it was that I was delivering, but when I found her in the wrong bunks, I decided it wasn't so important that I had to get it to her right away. So, I sat back and listened for just a few minutes. It's a handy habit to get into, you know? That's when I heard her talking to Juan. She was complaining about something at the show and it caught my attention."

"Ned," Major James started in on him again.

"I know, sir, I know." Ned shook his head as he forced himself to catch up to speed. "I heard Daisy tell Juan that whatever they were planning had to be tonight because they were getting off in Longview as soon as we made it to the station. Juan didn't want to do it, though. He wanted to wait."

"Now that ain't—"

"Juan, goddammit," Major James cut him off again.

Ned wasted no time in continuing. "Juan got a phone call and right after, he agreed. I didn't know what they were doing and didn't think much of it. But just before I went ahead to deliver Daisy whatever she'd ordered, he made a comment."

"A comment?"

"Yes sir, a comment. He said he hoped you weren't smart enough to put it all in a vault, or if you were, that there was a stick of dynamite laying around somewhere."

"Seems pretty clear to me." Major James looked as though he was ready to wrap things up.

"Once Ned here told me what was going on," J.R. intervened. "I went looking for Daisy to see what I could find, and well, I found a whole lot more than her. She was with Brad and they were both—let's just say indecent."

Major James couldn't help himself but let out a laugh. He was the only one who found the remark funny. Luckily, he was the kind of man who didn't mind laughing alone in a room where everyone was staring right at him. This went on for an awkward few seconds before Major James waved his hand to urge him to keep going.

"I whipped my pistol out and they got to yammerin'." J.R. got the hint. "Daisy was the first one to break, and the first thing she did was throw Brad right under the bus. Said he was scheming to break into the boss's collection and rob him blind, and that he had a getaway driver lined up at the next stop. Even said he had it all worked out where Huxley and Juan here would end up taking the fall for it so she and Brad could ride off into the sunset together. Pretty dreamy, if you ask me."

"Well I didn't," said Major James. "I think that's enough. Anything I'm missing here, boys and girls?"

The showman turned his attention to the four being charged for their intent to become no good, thieving bastards. They responded all at once. Every one of them started talking over the person standing next to them. They dished out falsehoods and cast blame on everyone but themselves. Major James let them get all worked up for just a bit before he nodded at Ned who took to screaming at them immediately after. Once everyone had fallen quiet again, Major James spoke.

"I'm going to just go ahead and say no, I'm not missing anything. You four had a half-baked idea to come steal my shit, you got caught, and now you're standing here about to piss yourselves as you try to blame everything but your own damn actions."

The showman pushed his cane to the hardwood floor with a sudden click and took a step toward the accused. The yellow light seemed to darken as he walked, casting black shadows across his face that shifted and morphed his features. An ominous mood had come over them inside the train car. No longer did it feel like a museum dedicated to the history of Wild West showmanship. Instead, it felt only like a place removed from time where Major James would be allowed to enact any revenge he saw fit, free from any consequences.

The fear that started to weigh heavily on each of the four employees was enough to make anyone crack. Not knowing what was about to happen was the worst part. It was the kind of thing that could make people act against their own best interests. If Major James hired only the best of the best, he might've expected each of them to take what was coming their way without flinching, but that wasn't who he brought onto his show. The first among them to try their luck also just so happened to be the most lack-luster of the bunch.

Huxley moved quickly and acted alone, breaking the line with a hard sprint forward, directly toward Major James. Unbridled anger fueled his attack. Shock washed over the faces of everyone else in the train car, except for J.R. Pickett.

J.R. knew why he'd been brought into the show, and it wasn't just to play the role of the trick shooter during the performance, that much was made all too clear before he received his first paycheck. From a certain point of view, he was a man who was paid based on his reflexes alone. As long as he could move faster than people could see, he'd always be able to earn a living.

Unfortunately for Huxley, the hired gun hand would earn his paycheck once again. J.R. had retrieved the six-shooter strapped to his hip and aimed it right at Huxley's kneecap before anyone else knew what was happening. With a sudden cracking explosion of gunpowder and lead blasting throughout the inside of the train car, the revolver in J.R.'s hand spewed fire and smoke with furious intent. Huxley's knee turned to a red mess that splattered all over the hardwood floors and sprayed the pile of books to his side.

The ringing in everyone else's ears was nothing compared to the pain Huxley was experiencing with his knee blown to pieces. He crumpled to the floor and grabbed at the bullet wound all while screaming his lungs out in pain.

"You shot me, you son of a bitch!"

"Damn right I did," J.R. told the man crying on the ground beneath him.

"Damn right he did!" Major James backed his new gun hand up with renewed enthusiasm. The showman bent down to get on the level of the man who would've strangled the very air out of his chest had a bullet not interrupted his path. He looked at the pain surging behind the eyes of Huxley and he felt nothing. "You deserve worse, you know that?"

The remaining three being accused did everything they could not to react. Any reaction meant the target would be on their back next and they all knew it. As they all listened to Huxley continue to scream on the floor and roll in pain holding what remained of his knee, no one even bothered to offer so much as a word of concern.

Major James stood back up with a disapproving shake of his head. The tapping of his cane as he paced back and forth was drowned out by the pained moans from Huxley, before both were overcome by the coughing fit that found its way into Major James's chest. Ned and J.R. stared ahead without flinching as their boss hacked up a lung, but the accused couldn't stop from sharing a worried glance. Every cough was violent and caused the Major's back to hunch with each heave, but it wasn't enough to stop what was about to happen. There was still a price to pay for what was being conspired.

"You know, when I started this collection, if you can call it that," Major James finally held enough air to begin to speak, keeping his back turned to those still in line. "I wanted only to uncover truths lost to history that could change the future. I am still a man who believes that our best days are still to come, but we can only see them for ourselves if we look back to the days we've already spent. That's where the answers always are."

Ned and J.R. hadn't heard this speech yet. Their interest piqued a heck of a lot more than the employees who could only dread what was going to happen to them when he stopped talking. Their faces were nothing like the faces of the other employees. The difference was stark, but also symbolic of what it meant to be on the good side of Major James—as opposed to the bad side.

"I knew what my own family had hidden away from the world in their closets and I soon became obsessed with what I might find hidden by everyone else's family. I've spent most of my life collecting everything I could from the days before the automobile and telephones changed how we interact with the world. What I've found could change the lives of hundreds of thousands of people who don't know anything about where they came from, or what they've lost. What you see here isn't just knick-knacks or fodder for storage, it is the very history of our nation at a turning point for civilization."

Major James abandoned pacing back and forth in front of those lined up in his train car and allowed himself to explore the confines of the collection as he spoke. He picked up a small silver shooting trophy from the late 1800s and admired it, before turning to look at Brad with haunting eye contact.

"At first, I wasn't sure what to do with it all. I was using whatever money I could find to buy just about anything that came my way. There was no real goal other than to discover. But I soon learned that kind of thinking wasn't going to get me anywhere. The only thing that would do is land me in the crosshairs of people who think just like you all."

Major James hesitated for a moment before sighing for a little longer than he should have, then continued speaking.

"So, I got to thinking, how could I use all of this history at my fingertips? And more importantly, what could I use it for? Questions like that sure can get you down and out, let me tell you."

The next item from his collection that Major James held was a rope. It looked like an old lasso used on the Chisholm Trail. Though the showman held it with a delicate sensibility, the rope stayed perfectly curled just as it had learned from its working days so long ago. It twisted without fail and curled every way Major James hoped it would. The rope undoubtedly held many stories, but it would never share a single one. Maybe that was why Major James had taken such a fancy to it.

"As fate would have it, I was forced to reckon with the fact that the answer I was looking for wasn't in the artifacts. It was in what they could give me, and there was one piece in particular that could give it all. Everything else you see here was just a distraction, all of it leading me to just a single opportunity."

He tossed the rope back down onto the shelf with a sudden *thump* and watched as the dust billowed up into the air against a backdrop of faded yellow lighting.

"Strangely enough, the very opportunity that thrust me into the spotlight of our own little circus family here is the same one that will define everything your own lives have led you to."

Each one of the employees standing in front of him showed signs of confusion in their own way. They could barely follow along with the things Major James was telling him, much less determine what he was insinuating when it came to their own involvement. They just stood there, looking as dumbfounded as they had when they first arrived.

Somewhere along all the several-syllable words that Major James had thrown about, everyone had given up their concern for Huxley. The poor man had resigned to heavy breathing and staring endlessly into the metal joists of the train car while his knee bled out. His labored breaths were an unwelcome annoyance more than a sign of urgent care in need. When he finally summoned enough bravery to return to his cries for help, he was met only with a hard smack to the face with Major James's cane as he strolled by.

"I am going to tell you all a story, so settle in," said Major James, encouraging everyone to stay right where they were despite his insistence on doing the exact opposite. "It is a story of a man who inspired me to stand right where I am today. Despite your wretched thieving ways, I think that you might actually end up getting a real good kick out of it."

Leaving no time for anyone to interject or say otherwise, the showman fell right into the theatrics of telling a story he'd longed to share with more than the simpleton Mr. Burwell. This group would be much better than the mirror he'd grown accustomed to. He stopped walking and leaned on the cane wedged into the floorboards below as he spoke.

"You might be thinking of William Cody because of the sign," Major James said with a gesture to the Wild West banner that stretched out across the train car above their head. "Buffalo Bill was a trailblazer for men like me. He was a legend among men in his day, but now? A god damned myth."

He was still propped up against his cane and it didn't look like he'd be moving anytime soon. Ned and J.R. stood motionless, either out of interest in what was playing out or gratefulness that none of it was aimed at them.

"But if you were thinking of that man, you'd be dead wrong."

Major James let out a shit-eating grin for the first

time. Not even his right-hand man Ned had seen him make such a face. Its glint made everyone who caught notice of it shudder at what it might mean.

"The man that you all should care much more about was Lakota. He was a Chief, said to be from the Dakota territories. He was a warrior before all else, but he was also a performer. His name was Tȟatȟáŋka Íyotake. His story is known well enough to be recognized around the world. He traveled the United States to showcase the Wild West, and some believe he basked in the stardom this brought him, but others say it gave him an opportunity to do something else entirely."

"The days of the Wild West may be long behind us, but what was created then by the hands of men just like him has turned each one of us standing here tonight into who we are," Major James continued. "Did you ever consider that?"

Before anyone had the chance to say anything, the showman answered for them. "I bet not. But that's ok, because I am willing to bet that Tȟatȟáŋka Íyotake never did such a thing either. His contributions to the world were too many to list, but what he gave to me was something more special than any of you could ever imagine."

Major James finally stood up from his cane. He shoved one hand down into the inside pocket of his vest. The group assumed he was digging around for whatever he was talking about, even Ned and J.R. seemed to think so. They watched their boss swap pockets before scrunching his face and finding yet another pocket.

Ned allowed his eyes to dart over to the people standing next to him. He hoped he wasn't alone in wondering what was happening. His eyes soon met J.R.'s eyes doing the very same thing he was doing and they couldn't help but offer each other a slight shrug at the awkwardness. There wasn't much else for them to do but wait, so they sat there and waited while the showman shoved his hand into one pocket after another before finally yelping with joy.

Major James held up his hand to reveal an old, rusted key pinched firmly between his thumb and index finger. It wasn't a key you'd find on any ring today. It was a single bar with two prongs on the end that looked like it was made by hand. This wasn't what anyone was expecting the showman to pull out of his pocket, but he wasted no time before speaking up.

"To some, this is a lost key that leads to nowhere, and maybe never did," he finally said, letting his eyes drift to the key in his hand. "But for you all, you might as well see this as the key to your future, the key to unlocking something more valuable than you could've ever hoped to steal from this little old train car."

"Can I ask you a question?" Brad finally spoke up from in line, still ignoring his partner in crime bleeding out at his feet.

"Don't you dare," Major James told him. "What you can do, if you must know, is stand right there, shut your treacherous mouth, and listen to what I have to say. If you knew any better, you would use this time to think about what you are putting this family through with your schemes."

"Where was I?" Major James trailed off for a second as he struggled to find his thoughts again. It was the kind of moment he never wanted people to see him in, much less the employees of his Out West Show. A brief glimpse of weakness that he would never choose to allow anyone to see. When his train of thought returned, he played it off like nothing had ever happened.

"Tȟatȟáŋka Íyotake was a performer in the great Buffalo Bill's Wild West showcase of the American frontier. He brought authenticity to entertainment, and he was among the most treasured appearances in the entire exhibition," explained Major James. "He was also killed before he ever should've been."

Major James made another lap through his coveted collection. When he came back around, he was holding the key in one hand still and a creased leather bag in the other. It was the mysterious leather bag that had been stowed away during their tour so far, the one that remained locked shut. The lock stole all of their attention, but there was a new kind of twisted glare in the showman's eyes. He scanned each of the three accused left standing. Huxley was still alive but was coming to terms with the finality that was beginning to approach due to blood loss. Major James did all but step over the dying man on his way to come face to face with the would-be thieves.

"Law enforcement came for Tȟatȟáŋka Íyotake because they were scared of a movement. They were scared at what someone like this man could inspire. Because of that fear, they gunned him and his horse down. There's a lesson to be learned there. A lesson about the scales of justice, about the laws of nature and how men will kill anything that scares them to break those laws."

Major James was doing nothing at this point to hide what he was talking about. He leaned into the accused a little closer and before he spoke, he waved off both Ned and J.R. with a swat of his hand, still holding the key as he did.

"When you are poised to change the world, the forces that be will come for you every single time," said Major James. "My father always told me that we were doomed to repeat history no matter what we did in life, so it was best to just roll with the punches. I aim to do more than that, though."

Ned and J.R. graciously made their exit without the notice of any of the accused employees that had found themselves in such a dire situation. They were staring at the showman, frozen in fear. The screech of the monstrous steel door slamming shut urged the showman to continue. Every eye in the train car followed the key in Major James's hand as it was pushed into the lock and twisted.

"I'm gonna throw the goddamn punches," he said.

What was revealed inside when the bag gave way was beyond the recognition of human intellect, incomprehensible to those who gazed inside the leather bag and soon, their own bodies rejected what was right in front of them.

Three of the four accused stared wide-eyed without blinking for longer than anyone naturally should. Their blank stare soon turned bloodshot until the situation took a turn for the worst. Major James refused its effect for himself, but he knew their fate had been sealed.

The employees would never take another breath in this life. Their eyes ran with deep red blood that soaked their faces until they each succumbed to violent shaking, one by one. A hard thump of their bodies smacking the hardwood floors of the train car signaled the end of each of the employees. Daisy was the first to collapse, her face covered in blood. She gave her last breath to look over at Huxley who had long since died from blood loss. Juan followed soon after.

Brad was stubborn, though. He stood shaking in place with wild fervor, spitting and choking on the blood that poured out of him. His eyes were locked on Major James. He collapsed to the floor, eyes still following the showman with dying fury, and fought with everything he had to stay alive just a few more seconds.

The last thing Brad heard in his life was the off-kilter *click, click, click* sound of a cane tapping the floor, followed by the return of yet another violent series of sickening, guttural coughs as Major James left them all behind.

CHAPTER 14

No one ever talks about the pressure of finding something worth listening to on the radio during a road trip with people who are—for all intents and purposes—nothing short of strangers.

Cannon was right at home letting his mind drift from one thought to the next accompanied by nothing other than the dull hum of the road noise that made its way into their pickup. The truck now held a unique odor inside. It was the kind of musty aroma that even the tree hanging from the mirror had no chance of cutting through. His newest teammates had the etiquette and hygiene of true rodeo competitors. Even then, for some reason, Cannon didn't mind.

A life on the road wasn't anything new to any of the people inside the pickup. Despite Cannon's life being so radically different from what Cathay and Jim Bob had grown to know, the road had become home for all of them in their own way. It was among the first things they had in common, outside of their shared love of a good shot of whiskey, of course. As luck would have it, it was this love of whiskey that sparked just about the only conversation to be found.

"Only one place around we can kill some time if you ask me," said Jim Bob from the back seat.

"Don't recall anyone doing that," said Cathay.

"No, he's right," Cannon chimed in. "We're coming into Kilgore a bit too early. I doubt the train has even rolled into town yet. We should find somewhere to hunker down out of sight and figure out what the heck we're about to get ourselves into."

"We already know what we're getting into," Cathay shot back. "It's a damn circus and we're gonna blow the doors off it, take what we need, kill whoever needs to be killed, and get the fuck out of Dodge."

"We don't always agree, you know," Jim Bob said with a smile he couldn't hide. "But that sounds like a damn good time."

"It's not gonna be that easy, y'all."

"I don't see why not."

Cannon looked over at Cathay who was sitting next to him in the passenger seat and allowed his stare to do all the talking. The air conditioning was blowing loud enough to cover any music that was playing, and it made the long curly hair that draped down Cathay's face swirl around her.

"I'm being serious," she told him. "Etta was pretty clear about what we needed to do. I don't know what you heard, but I sure as shit didn't have any questions."

"I'm not arguing what's being asked of us, I'm only asking how we're going to pull it off."

The inside of the pickup fell silent at Cannon's question. Etta had asked them to pull the trigger on this Major James guy, take his private collection and help her put it in the public eye, but it wasn't any of that giving them pause. It was how they were going to get through the people he had working for him. There were sharpshooters, ropers, riders, fanatics, and carney hands all waiting to make sure they kept their job. On top of it all, men like Major James didn't get to their position without a few sycophants hanging on every word and every demand he ever gave. Those people would be the real threats.

Their conversation never did return to the talk of liquor that started the disagreement between them. Cannon drove in silence as they made their way closer to the World's Richest Acre out in Kilgore. The closest thing to a drink they could find wasn't too far from the city limits in a metal building buried alone in the piney woods. Pines blotted the hazy sky as they pulled onto the dirt driveway made of gravel from over a decade ago.

"Finally, this asshole has a good idea," said Jim Bob as he slapped the back of the headrest on the driver's seat. "No sense in being sober while we wait it out. I wouldn't mind having one for the road when we leave either, being totally honest with you."

"Please tell me road drinks aren't actually a thing." Cathay couldn't help herself.

"They can be, if you try hard enough."

Cannon didn't say anything as he pulled up to the

bar and threw the truck in park. The doors tried to unlock when it came to a stop, but he was quick to slap the button on the door panel to lock everyone inside. It was a universal sign that there were words to be had before anyone would be leaving the pickup.

They all knew what it meant and no one did anything to stop it. With the push of a button, the engine died, and the air conditioning came to a dreadful stop. Sweat formed on their brows in seconds from the uncomfortable humid heat that welcomed itself back. It made each of them long for the sweet breeze that swished the branches back and forth up in the trees. It would flood into the cabin as soon as they opened the door, but that would have to wait.

"I'm going to tell y'all this one time, then we never go back to it again," Cannon started, still looking ahead into the dense woods that surrounded the bar. "Cathay knows more than you Jim Bob, but you all deserve to know why I'm here, because it ain't justice, and it ain't contractually obligated demands of the NHCP."

Cathay allowed the beginnings of a smile to form on her lips as she listened to him. Jim Bob was lost and had no problem scrunching his face to show his confusion. The mixed responses were enough to urge Cannon on, but not enough to make him look in their direction.

"I've been looking for my dad for a long time now. I've gotten a lot of people killed doing it, almost even myself a couple of times, and it's gotten me absolutely nowhere. Etta is a friend of mine, and my family has been real good to the NHCP, so she pointed the way to

Major James because he might have something for me to find."

Cannon waited for a moment longer, refusing to break his concentration on the birds dancing in the brush of the woods ahead.

"Now, y'all heard her, same as I did, Major James has gotta die," he continued. "But if you could help me out and just not kill him until I can find something worth knowing. it'd sure mean a lot."

"Why the hell would Major James have anything on your dad? Y'all related or something?" Jim Bob was the one who couldn't help himself this time.

"I hope not. I'm sure you know you weren't the only ones that man tried to reach out to. What you don't know is that asshole reached out to me too. Might've even been the whole reason I got started in all this mess."

Cannon shifted his weight to reach his back pocket from behind the steering wheel. He fidgeted for just a second before pulling a piece of folded paper out and holding it up for Cathay and Jim Bob to see. Their reaction caught him off guard.

"I figured as much," said Cathay.

"Yeah, makes sense," Jim Bob agreed. "Ain't nothing new to us, right, Cathay?"

She ignored the man in the back seat and put her hand on Cannon's shoulder to offer even the smallest bit of reassurance. When she looked over at him, he couldn't bring himself to make eye contact. Instead, he watched the dance of the birds rustling in the brush.

"As much as I hate to admit it, dipshit back there is right," she told him. "We aren't just here because the

NHCP says we have to be. We've got our own reasons, no different than you."

"And mine ain't nearly as noble," Jim Bob cut in.

"So, we're all on the same page with what we need to do here?" Cannon was finally warming up to what was happening. They weren't pissed off at him like he would've expected. In fact, they didn't seem to be bothered at all.

"I really only got one question," said Jim Bob. "When the hell are we goin' in for a damn drink?"

Cannon had to let out a laugh in response. It was the only thing that seemed to come to mind after everything he'd been through. Life hadn't been reduced down to a glass of whiskey in far too long for him. Sitting in the truck—sweating his ass off since the air conditioner had turned off when he killed the engine—he realized he couldn't remember the last time he shared a drink with people who he could consider friends.

He slapped the steering wheel a couple of times to get himself worked up and turned to face Cathay and Cannon for the first time since getting everything off his chest. With a smile finally finding its way onto his face, he told them both exactly what they wanted to hear.

"Let's go get a drink."

The inside of the bar at the city limits of Kilgore looked like it was right out of a movie set. Exposed rafters of the metal building stretched overhead as humming neon drenched everything in an intoxicating blue haze. The light mixed with more cigarette smoke than any establishment should ever let linger inside. There wasn't an empty seat in the place, considering there wasn't much else to do in the area. Everyone inside looked like they had been there just about their whole life, only making it that much more awkward when three strangers walked inside like they owned the place.

"Don't stop on our account now," Cathay told everyone who'd turned to scowl at them.

"Remind me to not get whatever they're having," Jim said out of the side of his mouth.

The three moved to the end of the bar made of chipped wood and dented tin. It looked like it'd caught every spilled beer over the last decade. There wasn't much to look at inside the hole in the wall aside from liquor promotions and the occasional side eye from local patrons. Cowboy hats and mesh back caps dotted the building everywhere you looked. Buckets of bottled beer cluttered the few tables that were inside, leaving everyone else to stand around nursing a drink in one hand.

There was no dancing or blaring music from a live band tucked away in the corner. This was the kind of watering hole that had one shitty speaker with a long wire stapled to the wall. The speaker was playing a country radio station interrupted by static every so often. No one was paying attention to the music playing anyway, so they didn't catch the fiddle wailing in the background to create a soundtrack worthy of a classic Western film.

"A round of whiskeys," Cannon hollered to the other end of the bar, finding a man twice his size pouring drinks with both hands. "Doubles. Three of 'em."

"And don't go too far!" Jim Bob followed. "We'll be needing your most valuable services, good sir."

"If we're supposed to be working tonight, we damn sure don't need him to hover for too long. Might not be able to walk out of here, much less go introduce ourselves to the Major."

Few words as wise as those would be said for the rest of their time at the bar. Once the first glass of whiskey hit each of their dry mouths, the second and third were soon to follow. Cannon would've never done such a thing when he was working by himself. He let his guard down more than he should with these people, but it felt warranted for reasons he didn't understand. Before long, all three of them were working in unison to put away more of the bartender's stock than he would've liked.

While they did their best to drink away any nerves that had settled in, they ignored the reaction from everyone else in the bar. If one of them had taken the time to look around, they would've seen there were some who didn't take too kindly to some strangers getting hammered drunk on the only good whiskey in the joint. They'd already made a bad impression without talking to anyone there. It was only a matter of time before someone else had enough drinks to find the courage to tell them so.

The confrontation no one asked for started with a simple tap on Cannon's shoulder. When he turned around to see who was trying to take him away from his drink, he was knocked violently backward over the bar by a wide, hairy fist he never saw coming. The one who'd thrown the punch was a burly, bearded, man over fifty wearing a cutoff camouflage button down shirt. There were no reasons given for his attack and no heads up that it was coming. Worse than that, the old man also had just enough buddies to keep Cathay and Jim Bob busy. They'd all stumbled into an old-fashioned brawl.

Shattered glasses rained shards down around Cannon as his head crashed into the floor. He went head first over the bar but was lucky enough to still be conscious after the blow. His hands and knuckles were already bleeding from crawling on the glass, leaving red stains on the floor as he moved. In a quick scramble to get to his feet, he dragged his knees through what felt like tiny daggers and winced at the stinging pain. When he was up and ready to fight back at last, he couldn't help but notice Cathay and Jim Bob both with bloodied faces, swinging wildly at anyone in sight.

Without a second thought, he joined the fun.

Cannon leaped back over the bar with blinding speed and went furiously into the unknown man who'd picked the fight. They went tumbling backward into a hard wooden table. People scattering out of the way and hollers from others egging them on drowned out the pleading bartender trying to save his business from any more damage. Cannon didn't pay attention to any of it.

He pulled himself up onto his knees and let loose a devastating cascade of punches right into the old man's scruffy face. He was determined not to stop until he was sure the fight was over. A burst of blood popped out of his nose after a strike, but he didn't stop throwing his fists. The old man was trying to push him off, or at the very least protect himself from one rage-fueled blow after another. Nothing was working though. Cannon broke through every attempt at defense, and it seemed like every strike only brought out more blood.

When he watched a cut on the old man's lip bust open and turn the rest of his face bloody red, he finally snapped out of his tunnel vision. Cannon flicked the blood off his knuckles and stole a look around the bar. Cathay and Jim Bob had long finished their fight. They were standing on either side with scrunched faces from watching the unknown assailant get beaten damn near senseless.

"I think you got him," said Jim Bob.

"No," Cathay interjected. "You definitely got him."

"Why the hell did they start this? We didn't even do anything to the assholes."

Cathay pointed over to a shady corner of the bar. Cannon's eyes followed her hand to find one man left from the group who hadn't joined the fight. He was surrounded by a table full of empty beers, and he was looking right at them with his mouth still just barely open. Plastered right across his chest on a baggy, wrinkled T-shirt was the face of the same man they were about to go find, alongside the name of his touring performance—the Major James Out West Show.

"I guess we were being a little too loud."

Cathay nodded and glanced over to the man left watching them. The bar had almost emptied out by now. The blue haze of neon and static from the old radio were all that remained. Everyone else had abandoned the place, including the bartender.

"What exactly did you hear?" Cannon was already walking toward the last one left.

The surviving man was shorter than the rest and had an awkward cropped haircut that sat crooked against black-framed glasses. His shirt looked like it had been worn a hundred times over. When he spoke, his high-pitched voice betrayed how old he actually was.

"Nothing worth gettin' my ass beat like that over."

"What's your name?" Cannon tried to be cordial despite being covered in blood.

"I ain't gotta tell you that."

"You're right, you don't. Big fan of the Major?"

"Been following the tour for months. The guys you just pummeled unconscious were my ride. Didn't know 'em all that much, though. They just joined up back in Texarkana."

"You going to the show tonight then?" Cathay joined in from behind Cannon.

"I was—"

"Good." Jim Bob stepped forward. "Because we're gonna be your new ride."

Cannon played along and nodded to urge him to agree. It only took one more look at the bloodied and broken faces of his former buddies to convince him to try his luck with the strangers.

"Yeah, sure, why not?" he told them with more worry in his voice than he'd shown so far.

It was almost as if Cannon, Cathay, and Jim Bob

had the same idea at the same time. They'd convinced one of Major James's biggest fans to become a personal guide for the show in Kilgore. It was just the kind of inside knowledge they'd need to have an advantage when they came in ready to shoot the place up if they had to. They all decided unanimously, without a word spoken, that they'd found their way in.

Cannon grabbed the man by the arm and led him out, leaving blood stains smeared onto his clothes as he did. Before they started walking, he asked the man's name for a second time.

"What do we call you?"

"Newton is what the government calls me," he answered as he was halfway dragged through the destroyed remains of the tables and chairs inside the bar. "Newton Thomas, actually. If you don't leave my ass dead in a ditch somewhere, you can call me Newt."

"All right, Newt," said Cannon, still holding on to him. "We ain't going to leave you dead nowhere, I can promise you that. Even those dipshits you were running around with back there will be fine."

"Eventually," Cathay cut in.

All four of them exited the bar into the dimming light of dusk to find an empty parking lot. It was finally time to make their way to the Major James show undoubtedly hard at work setting up for their performance in Kilgore. Cannon and Cathay tossed Newt into the back seat as Jim Bob climbed in from the other side to make sure he wouldn't make a break for it. When the doors slammed shut, Cannon realized he'd been in yet another bar fight, but this time he was the one who walked away.

Once they were all packed inside the truck and ready to head out, Cannon took a second to admit one last thing to Cathay and Jim Bob, almost forgetting that Newt was crammed inside as well.

"Thanks for y'all's help back there," he told them, the scent of whiskey lingering in the pickup from his breath. "Last time I got into a scrap like that, I didn't even remember getting carried out."

"You ain't fighting by yourself anymore."

"That's right," Jim Bob hollered a little too loudly from the back seat.

"Well, it means a lot," Cannon answered. "Now we just gotta do the same damn thing to Major James. We'll make sure he pays for what he's done, whether he ends up dead or not."

Newt had been staring out the side window contemplating his choices in life until he heard what Cannon had just said. He finally perked up, turned to look at the three who'd just kidnapped him and cleared his throat.

"Wait—what?"

CHAPTER 15

The stars had once again found their familiar home over Texas, this time shining their light down through dozens of oil derricks that lined the famous Kilgore train platform. It was once the greatest concentration of oil wells in the world. Now, each derrick stood tall as a monument to their own historic legacy. The structures reached upward into the night and turned the nearby skyline into an iconic, picturesque view that immortalized the small town's beloved heyday. Their steel framing towered above, adorned with brightly lit multicolored stars that set the stage for a once-in-a-lifetime performance from the Major James Out West Show about to kick off.

"I'll be a son of a bitch," Jim Bob was the first to speak, as always, when they pulled into a crowded parking lot downtown. "This place is gorgeous."

"It sure is," Cathay agreed without realizing who had spoken.

"We get in and we get out—tonight," reiterated

Cannon for the hundredth time. "You heard Etta, we might be saving countless lives tonight. There ain't any room for error."

"I don't want any part of—" Newt tried to talk.

"Well that's just too damn bad," Jim Bob cut him off with a slap on the shoulder. "You didn't have any problem letting your buddies get one over on us, so you just sit over there and shut the hell up."

"Actually, you're going to be the most important part of all this, Newt," said Cannon. "You've been to the show more than once, you know how it works, and I'm willing to bet you know how to get inside that train of the Major's without being spotted."

"You're screwing with me, right?" Newt couldn't believe what he was hearing. "You *can't* get onto the train. That's the whole point."

"I ain't one to play around. If you don't get us in, I guarantee what you saw us do to those guys back at the bar will be the least of your worries."

"You don't get it," said Newt. "You think we don't know what happens to people who try to sneak one over on Major James? You guys are nothing, that man there is ruthless. Real fans of the Out West Show keep up with the news, ya know, we all see the headlines that follow the tour around. It's one of the reasons why it's so popular. It's like he's bringing the actual Wild West into town for a night. Anything can happen."

"Then you know all it takes to get out alive is to be quicker on the draw," Cannon quipped while pulling his shirt up just enough to reveal a revolver tucked inside his waistband.

"Ever heard of being outgunned? Major James doesn't just employ performers."

"We'll take our chances," Cathay warned him.

"Look, I'll help you out, but you can't make me go with you in there. I don't have the death wish you three have."

"We'll make that deal."

All four climbed out of the truck and began the mile-long walk from the parking lot in downtown Kilgore. They soon joined a crowd on the train platform already swarming with people hoping to catch a glimpse of the show torn from time. The original purpose of the oil derricks had been restored after so many years, becoming their guiding light and taking them right to the main attraction. The stars lined up in the night sky called them closer as the noise from the gathering crowd began to swell louder and louder.

The train wasn't nearly as long as Cannon would have imagined, coming out to less than ten cars long. It rested like a behemoth behind the small blue and red building of the platform. The steam engine that carried the show into town was still smoldering inside, sending plumes of white smoke out as if it was exhaling the very fires of hell from its depths. The train's presence served as an unusually menacing backdrop to the whimsical Western show soon to play out.

As they approached the platform, Cannon was surprised to find a fenced-off arena filled with dirt, no different than a local rodeo. It wasn't empty though; it was staged with set pieces like an old, covered wagon and a twenty-foot-tall water tank which seemed to be begging to have a few bullet holes shot through it for dramatic effect. A full orchestra was tucked away in the corner, hard at work providing a soundtrack to transport the crowd back to the days of the frontier. Fiddles battled back and forth against the plucking of an acoustic guitar as the tempo rose and fell.

The crowd was dressed for the occasion, too. Straw cowboy hats and enough denim to blanket the whole town filled the area in front of the train platform. They were loud enough to force Cannon into yelling at Cathay and Jim Bob.

"We aren't going to get anything done standing out here with all these people."

"Gotta get around all this shit," Cathay told him, pointing over to the oil derricks that stretched down either side of the road. "That way."

"Newt, time to earn your keep," said Cannon, grabbing at Newt's shoulder and dragging him closer. "Not too many train cars here. I imagine some are used for horses and cargo, others for lodging. You point out the one that belongs to the Major. Got it?"

"I do that and you let me go?"

"No. You point it out and get us inside. Then, maybe, we'll talk about how you walk away."

With a heavy, noticeable sigh, Newt lifted a finger and pointed to the right-hand side of the crowd, behind the orchestra that carried on without end. Hidden behind the oil derricks and locked into place right after the flatcar loaded with crates strapped in place was a nondescript steel-clad car. "Over there, fifth car in, that's where you wanna be."

"Why that one?"

"I don't know." Newt shrugged. "Rumor is that's where he keeps the bodies of the people he's killed so far. But if you want to pull this off without catching a bullet to the face, you'll need to wait until the intermission. Trust me, it's the only time to actually get inside. Y'all can blend right in during the set changes."

Cannon turned to look at Cathay and Jim Bob for their acknowledgment but was interrupted by the voice of an announcer whose voice blared out over the speakerphones placed strategically throughout the crowd. He was louder than the orchestra, but even then, they each seemed unfazed by his intrusion into their perfectly rehearsed songs.

"Welcome to the Major James Out West Show," the announcer's deep voice began. "The show is set to begin shortly where you will be transported to a time lost long ago. Remember, there is no flash photography or recording of any kind…"

The announcer's voice continued listing off rules and regulations for those attending the performance while Cannon did his best to scan the crowd. If the plan was to wait until intermission, he could at least make sure he was familiar with his surroundings. There didn't seem to be anything out of place from what he could find, but he knew there were secrets nearby that Major James would kill to keep hidden away. If they were still on that train, they would have to find them before taking down the show's leader. Anything less would be a disaster.

"Prepare yourselves to witness a spectacle on horseback…" the announcer continued.

Cannon knew he wouldn't find any bodies left

behind by Major James. Etta had made it clear that she'd already discovered the death that followed that steam locomotive's path. But he also knew that rumors weren't always baseless. If there weren't bodies hidden away inside the train, what was?

"Behold an artistry of gunpowder and lead…" the announcer's voice carried on.

There were so many questions surrounding what they were about to break their way into. Whatever Major James was keeping away from the world—and whatever he was planning to do with it—had to be the priority. He'd be lying to himself if he ever thought this was about anything other than the answer to who his father could be. He knew what he wanted could be lying no more than a few hundred feet from him. The thought alone made him giddy enough to charge right in.

"And experience the harrowing tales of history that shaped the way of life of an early nation."

Just as the group started to push their way through the crowd that had formed in front of the arena, a series of gunshots blasted into the air. It felt like every single person in the town of Kilgore burst into applause. Cannon turned to look at Cathay with worry in his eyes, but all she could do was lift her finger to point ahead.

At first, his voice didn't come through the speakers as clearly as the announcer's. The words were broken and whatever did come through was lost in the deafening roar of the crowd. Cannon darted his eyes around the front of the arena before finding the spotlight that had settled on an older, gentlemanly figure perched on top of the train car. He could just barely make out a thick white mustache and pot belly pushing through a striped shirt. The man leaned against a cane with a grin stretched across his face. His voice finally cleared through the speakers and Cannon knew immediately who was speaking.

"Welcome to the only traveling show on rails today that will leave you longing for the trails of yesterday," exclaimed Major James.

"That's the—" Cannon tried to say.

"We should do it now," Jim Bob cut him off.

"No!" Cathay shoved Jim Bob while speaking through her teeth. "We have to get inside first."

Newt was quietly trying to push his way deeper into the crowd. It was clear he was only trying to watch the show. After the production value they'd seen so far, Cannon couldn't blame him. Instead of dragging him away by his arm yet again, he watched the Major James Out West Show begin its routine himself.

"If you need to find a chamber pot, I suggest you do it now, because you won't want to miss a second of the show soon to start," the Major continued his introductions.

The crowd clambered on throughout the speech and Cannon couldn't help but notice just how synchronized the performance played out. Everything was fine-tuned and precise. The orchestra hit every note to punctuate Major James's words at just the right time. As the showman brought his speech to conclude with the introduction of the first act, Newt raised his hands to join the crowd's antics.

"Behold, the one and only, descendant of the bull-dogger himself, brilliant with any bullet, and a new star shining over Texas—J.R. Pickett!"

A steel door of the train car fenced into the arena slammed open and a masked rider on horseback came riding out at an unnatural speed. He made a lap around the arena before whipping out a revolver and firing a round off into the air. Cannon watched as the bullet struck something in the sky and fireworks blasted out with a loud explosion. The crowd roared in response as the colorful burst of fire rained down around them in shades of a prideful red, white, and blue.

J.R. Pickett made another lap around the arena through the fireworks, this time chasing a calf that had suddenly been let loose. He leaped from the horse and tackled the horned steer. Man and steer went tumbling through the dirt as hooves and spurs kicked around. When J.R. Pickett stood up—covered in dust that billowed out with every movement—the steer remained tied up lying on its side, unable to move.

The bulldogger threw his arms into the air to garner more love from the crowd before he hopped on his horse and rode off back into the train car. Before anyone knew what was coming next, an entire outfit of riders came flying out from behind the building at the train platform.

Bandannas covered their faces as some fired revolvers into the air and others waved torches in fury. They screamed and hollered through a lap around the arena before encircling the covered wagon. One of the men climbed down from his horse and walked up to the wagon without saying a word, but he was met with the business end of a shotgun. The barrel popped out of the wagon first, to laughter from the crowd almost on cue, before it extended further out and pushed the vigilante back.

"The Jarbridge robbery marked the final one of its kind in the Wild West." The announcer's voice returned to narrate the performance unfolding. "It's a tragic tale of sacrifice, heroism, danger, and above all else—a gamble for riches."

Newt turned to find Cannon with a beaming smile on his face. He looked like he'd never been happier any other day in his life, despite being captured against his will. Cannon couldn't hear what he was saying at first, but the crowd soon died down enough to make out his words.

"This is new!" he was yelling over and over. "This spot in the show used to be a Teddy Roosevelt reen- actment."

Cannon scrunched his face in confusion. He didn't understand the significance of a lineup change for a show like this, but Newt had certainly keyed into something.

The Major James Show continued on with one performance after another, some including ropers and riders, and others showcasing a host of talented actors playing out famous historical moments of the old West. Cannon watched in disbelief at the pageantry and stunt work being pulled off without a single misfire. It was like a rodeo on steroids, like they were watching the filming of a Hollywood movie. He'd never seen anything like it.

They settled into their place in the crowd as the Major James Out West Show continued on. There was just about every type of performance imaginable in the first hour of the exhibition. Though, despite all the theatrics, Major James never did show his face again before intermission. His entrance set the stage for the event, but that was all the crowd would see of him.

When the last of three freestyle bullfighters had flipped headfirst over a charging bull to applause from the crowd, and the orchestra had reached a climax in the old West theme song they were playing, the announcer came back to the speakers.

"Ladies and gentlemen…" the voice began.

Newt turned to find the group who'd brought him into the show. When he saw the three standing next to each other not too far behind him, he waved them down. There wasn't much time to make their way through the crowd in the brief intermission, so they had to move quickly.

Cannon had spotted the Major himself in the frenzy of the swarm of people, though. He recognized the mustache and cane immediately. The only problem was the man disappeared as soon as he spotted him. He clenched his fists and gritted his teeth in response. Frustration was swirling in his belly with every second he couldn't locate the owner of the show.

Seconds ticked by as he frantically searched the crowd eagerly waiting for the show to continue on. He couldn't find him. Before he knew it, a hard jab hit him in the ribs.

"We gotta move." Cathay shoved Cannon forward.

"That was the—"

"We know, we know," Cathay cut him off. "Newt is leaving us behind; we have to catch up now if we're gonna do this tonight."

"We're not blending in just standin' around like this," Jim Bob urged them both. "We gotta go, now."

Cannon allowed himself to listen to them and shook his head to focus again on what they had to do. He turned and looked at Cathay and Jim Bob. With their help, he felt confidence begin to replace the frustration in his gut.

"Let's go get that son of a bitch," he told them.

CHAPTER 16

The real performance of the Major James Out West Show wasn't happening in the arena surrounded by hundreds of screaming fans. It was happening behind the train, performed by dozens of stagehands and staff members scurrying about like their lives depended on successfully completing more tasks than any one man could keep up with. It was nothing less than coordinated chaos behind the scenes of the show.

The smell of horse manure wafted all throughout the area behind the train. It had a way of permeating everything around like nothing else ever could. Dust swirled into the night sky, kicked up from muddy boots and rushed hooves. The sounds of men barking orders and others not-so-graciously accepting them filled the air. They were setting up the next performance, breaking down the last one, and loading everything needed to get back on the rails so they could do it all over again in the next town the following night.

"How the hell are we supposed to find anything in all this?" Cathay said in dismay out of the corner of her mouth.

"We already know where to go," Cannon told her. "All we gotta do is get through this crowd and onto the fifth train car." He reached his hand up to point before having it slapped down by Jim Bob.

"Let's just go," the bullfighter said. "Got a bad feeling here."

"Keep your heads down and don't draw attention."

The group continued through the crowd, each of their faces hidden from view with eyes locked forward only to ensure they didn't stumble. They shrugged their way through, blending in through sheer luck. Guys whose backs were loaded down with bags of feed shoved past them as another group lugging buckets of water came from the other direction. Cannon almost shoulder checked a horse being walked by, barely missing what could've been a devastating collision for the group judging by the evil glare from the man holding the reins.

Just when they were midway through the myriad of backstage business, a booming voice echoed from behind them. It wasn't hostile, but it wasn't the voice of a long-lost friend either. Cannon was the first to turn around. All he could see was a lanky man in glasses looking down his nose. He was pointing his finger right at them and his face was turning more red by the second.

"You three!" the man hollered at them. "I ain't

never seen your faces before, and I've seen *everyone's* faces!"

Every stagehand in a ten-foot radius around stopped what they were doing to look at the three trying their damndest to get by without being noticed. Cannon thought their half-baked plan had already been cast into ruin despite only just getting started. A lump formed in his throat. Blood rushed to his extremities and his mouth went dry.

"Get yer asses over here!" The man continued his shouting. "Every one of ya!"

The crowd seemed more accustomed to the stranger's yelling than Cannon had thought, though. They quickly returned to their scurrying about. A hushed silence that had fallen over them soon faded back into the familiar roar of fleeting conversations and the demands of too many bosses.

With a deep exhale, Cannon turned to face the music. He stared down the man who was shoving his way right toward them. His crooked nose barely held his glasses and the black vest draped across his back looked more like a costume than anything he would seriously wear. Against the shadows of night cast across his face, he looked like a man without a single thing to smile about in the world. That made him dangerous.

"Now look here—" Cannon started to formulate a lie out loud.

The man that had set them on edge moved right by them without so much as a word. Just as soon as he brushed past Cannon's shoulder, he continued yelling at three random men carrying a large trunk above their heads. All three of them dropped the trunk at the same time and returned their own senseless yelling at the manager. Together, they joined a chorus of incomprehensible howling.

Once again, Cannon felt a jab land into his ribs and he knew just what it meant. He glanced at Cathay who was already pushing him forward as discreetly as she could. Her eyes kept low and her lips stayed pursed.

The only thing that was left was to make it to the right train car and their night would get a whole lot better. The ceaseless chatter that surrounded them soon fell to their backs as they continued on. Sweat began to run down Cannon's brow as his breathing gave away the anxiety settling in the pit of his stomach.

He couldn't check on his partners in crime, but he knew they were still there regardless. The hunched-over silhouette of Newt shuffling ahead just in front of them slowly changed his path to circle back the way they came once the fifth train car was well in view. It was an expected tactic from a coward like that, but Cannon was one step ahead of him. He sidestepped Newt and casually shouldered him back on track with the rest of the group.

"Not yet, you little bastard," he whispered just loud enough for Newt to hear.

No answer came from the Major's biggest fan. Instead, they approached the flatcar leading to what Newt described as the place they needed to be. With every step, Cannon began to wonder more and more if the man should be trusted. Fear could only force someone to do so much in life. Adoration was a much more powerful motivator.

Before any of them could come to their senses, the trap was sprung.

The man who'd ridden out to kick off the show stepped out front behind one of the train cars with a six-shooter on his hip and a mares leg lever action tossed haphazardly onto his shoulder. It was J.R. Pickett, and he wasn't showing up to give them an exclusive backstage tour of the train.

"Here we go." Cathay was the first to speak.

"Maybe it isn't what it looks like," said Cannon.

"The hell it ain't," Jim Bob chimed in.

Newt turned around before they could say anything else and held up a cell phone in his hand. The screen was too small to make out any of the messages that were pulled up, but Cannon knew it wasn't anything good.

"Gotcha," he said with a sly smile forming on his lips.

J.R. took a step forward and waved Newt to come closer to him. His posture and demeanor changed effortlessly as he scrambled ahead to find safety behind the hired gun hand. He was dressed in his performance clothes, tight denim and black leather boots with a wide-brimmed cowboy hat built for riding. A holster was strapped to his thigh, holding what looked like a shiny new Colt revolver. His hand rested gently on the hammer of the pistol with a dip in his shoulder that made him look like nothing less than a good old-fashioned gunslinger.

Cannon knew this posture all too well. He'd used

it himself from time to time, and lucky for him, he also carried a firearm to the confrontation. Shortsightedness had put him in a regrettable situation, but he was backed up by the only people he could want in such a dangerous situation. Knowing those rowdy sons of bitches Cathay and Jim Bob were by his side gave him a confidence boost that helped spur on his next words.

"You sure looked fancy riding that expensive horse out there," he said to J.R. "Hate for you to get those fine linens all dirty."

"You sure you wanna—" Jim Bob leaned in for a word of caution.

"Shut up," Cannon cut him off.

He'd been in plenty of phony old West quickdraw fights in his time and never met a pull quicker than him. Cannon was focused intently on the man in front of him. There was something about J.R.'s quiet presence that pushed his buttons, but seeing the coward Newt standing behind him like the rat he was only made matters worse. Cannon nudged his cowboy hat up on his forehead just a bit to get a better field of vision. Then he allowed a smile of his own to stretch across his face.

Tunnel vision had set in for Cannon, but Cathay and Jim Bob still had enough of their wits about them to notice three other shooters who'd emerged from the crowd. These men didn't bother to holster their guns. Although J.R. had a penchant for the cowboy guns, the ones who were circling around their group seemed to be just fine with ARs.

"Cannon, you might—" Cathay tried to catch him

up to speed but was cut short no different than Jim Bob was.

"Not now, dammit."

Facing down a man with intentions every bit as lethal as his own, Cannon looked J.R. up and down. They were two sides of the same coin when it came down to it, but neither would admit any such truth. Each of their hands hung steadily over a revolver tucked into their hip.

Flies attracted to the manure starting to pile up from the horses in the show found their way over to the standoff in progress. Their relentless buzzing should've been a distraction, but it only served to drown out the ongoing circus behind them. Cannon focused on his opponent's hand, waiting for him to make a move and ready to ensure it was the last one he'd ever make.

"I know why you're here." J.R. finally spoke up.

"Then you should get outta my way," Cannon told him.

"Can't do that."

"Sure you can, just head on back to wherever you came from. Easy as that."

"That's good advice, you know," J.R. quipped with a smirk.

Cannon darted his eyes over to Cathay to see her shaking her head vigorously. He never expected to have her permission to do something as reckless as he was about to do. When he rolled his eyes over to Jim Bob, he saw only boiling anger. There was a fight to be had, and he'd be damned if he was going to back down from it now.

"We better get to it," said Cannon. "Wouldn't want you to miss your curtain call."

"Ain't gotta be this way," J.R. urged with a slight nod to either side of Cannon.

When he turned to look at what the gun hand was trying to bring to his attention, he saw the other guns aimed right at them and knew their situation was about to go from bad to worse.

Jim Bob turned to square up against one of the men with ARs. Cathay followed suit. The men they faced were covered in black gaiters and matching baseball caps. Their eyes were emotionless and locked on the three intruders. Whether the showman had hired a private security team or simply armed a few of his employees didn't really matter at this point. They were facing down the kind of firepower that only came with money, power, and fear.

Muggy humidity brought sweat down their faces and made it difficult to catch their breath. Both Cannon and J.R. refused to move a muscle until the time was right, not even to wipe the beads of sweat running into their eyes. Flies continued to swarm around both of their faces in a desperate search for one of the few harmless passes for blood to be found. There was every reason imaginable to swat at one, or wipe the sweat from their brow, but neither moved.

The stars above flickered as they always did, dotting the sky with brilliant displays offering a welcome distraction from the violence brewing behind the Kilgore train platform. It may have once been a sanctuary to weary travelers stumbling into a booming future, but tonight, it would only serve as the backdrop to a story as old as time—a shootout between two men too stubborn to back down.

Cannon gave no indication of what he was about to do. He gave no word of warning, and he damn sure didn't plan on giving any apologies after the fact. In a split second, his hand slammed down into the revolver on his hip, yanked it from the holster tucked into his waistband, and aimed it dead ahead to put an end to the gun hand in his way once and for all.

Bam!

Only one shot rang out behind the train, and much to his surprise, it wasn't Cannon's. When he looked down at his right hand still grasping the wood grips on his.45 revolver, he saw half of the otherwise blackened stainless steel painted bright red. It was his blood.

"Mother—" Jim Bob said from behind him.

Bam! Bam! Bam!

The gunshots started in rapid succession all around him at first, but Cannon could only hear the piercing ringing in his ears as he stared down at his hand—or rather what was left of it. He could feel the phantom presence of his trigger finger immediately. It felt exactly where it had always been, yet he could see plain as day that in its place was only a mangled stub. Thick, deep red blood gushed from the open wound and covered his pistol before falling to the ground.

Flashes of light from the muzzle blasts of every firearm behind the train lit up like the fireworks that kicked off the show. Men were dropping like flies around them as Jim Bob and Cathay went to work, but Cannon could only stare blankly.

"We gotta get the hell outta here!"

"Grab him! We're going now," Cathay said.

"Let's go, dipshit." Jim Bob grabbed Cannon's arm with one hand and fired off another round with a pistol in the other. "It's just a scratch."

Cannon watched the crowd of people swarming in front of him. There were men groaning in pain from taking bullets to the gut and more than one who'd fallen silent for good, but Jim Bob and Cathay didn't take any time to linger around. As he was dragged away, he watched J.R. still slouched to the side, holding his six-shooter hip level, aimed right at him. He was unharmed. It was a sight that was burned into his brain.

Bullets danced off the ground all around them as Cannon finally got enough clarity to run on his own. Dirt flew up in clouds at their feet and it took everything they had not to yelp at each one. Their retreat was unlikely, but it had to be done. There was no other option. They'd stumbled into something that was over their head and their only hope was the adrenaline forcing one foot in front of the other to a soundtrack of gunfire aimed right at them.

The stars that dotted the night sky were only a blur to Cannon now. Burning sensations began to flare up in his legs as he ran as he fought his eyes from watering to make it all worse. Nothing compared to the searing pain in his right hand, though.

"My damn trigger finger!" he finally shouted.

The trauma that was setting in for him was met only with laughs from Jim Bob. Cathay did her best to hold hers in, but even she couldn't help but shake her head. Chaos unfolded around them and Cannon was frantic about losing arguably his most treasured asset. His asshole partners could only find the humor in what had happened, though.

"This can't be real! Holy—"

"It's real, buddy. You just need to go ahead and wrap your head around it." Cathay tried her best to comfort him. "You finally found yourself a quicker draw."

"Ain't that the truth," said Jim Bob.

Cannon didn't pay much attention to either of them as they ran. While they were doing their best to make a clean escape with cover fire, ammo was running thin for both of them. The sprint was never ending down the rather short length to get to the other side of the train. If it hadn't been for the fleeing crowd —who were understandably scared shitless by the real-life shootout that had spilled over from just behind the train platform—the three of them might've not made it out.

"They were waiting on us," Cathay told Jim Bob.

"It was that damn kid," he said. "We never should've trusted that yellow son of a bitch."

"Well, we did. Now we gotta live with it."

Cannon was listening to them while they ran right into the crowd scattering in every direction, but he couldn't say much of anything. A flurry of people were screaming and clamoring to get out as quickly as possible, held up only by the few trying to catch it all on video. Cannon, Cathay, and Jim Bob blended right in with the panic-stricken crowd as they continued pounding the pavement to get back to the pickup that had brought them into town.

The oil derricks held a much more menacing presence now, towering over the nightmarish scene of people running for their lives. The stars on top that lit the way for everyone's scramble for safety were no longer beacons of inspiration—they were glaring signs of suffering, warning anyone near to stay far away.

CHAPTER 17

"We've been ruined by those assholes. We're never going to recover the good-will we've fought for."

Major James was as pissed as a bull left in a chute too long and was looking for something—or someone—to inflict pain on. The shootout at his show in Kilgore was already headline news everywhere he looked. There wasn't a single media channel, online armchair crusader, or otherwise who didn't have his name plastered on everything they could.

"Killers loose in local Kilgore showing of Major James Out West Show," read Ned out loud against his own best interest. "Kilgore train tour terror—"

"Enough!"

The two were standing alone in the collection car of the train as it rushed down the rails as far from Kilgore as they could get. Hissing interrupted their words as steam billowed out to mix into blurs of green foliage.

"Sorry, sir," Ned said. "It's just that everyone's talking about us."

"Don't you think I know that already, Ned? Can you not read a damn room every now and then?"

Ned took a moment to contemplate whether or not that question was rhetorical. After a few seconds, he decided not to answer. Instead, he chose to wield what little influence he had acquired with his boss.

"What was the old saying about press?" he asked in a casual tone so as not to inspire a harsh response if it turned sour.

Major James cocked his head to the side. Ned was a man of simplicity and that was always his strongest trait. It wasn't often he spoke with any sense of intellect about him. When he did manage to contribute something worthwhile, however, his timing was near impeccable.

"All press is good press," Ned continued without waiting for a response from Major James. "I've never seen so many people talking about us, sir. You gotta look at this."

Ned lifted a beat-up old phone that was barely legible through splintered cracks on the screen. He scrolled furiously through messages sent to them in just the last hour. There were thousands of them. Most were negative or rather downright rude, but every now and then, there were a few words of support.

"What are you showing me?"

"We might have done exactly what we set out to do," said Ned. "Just not at all how we thought we were going to do it."

Major James took a moment to think about their

situation. This wasn't supposed to happen at all. His blood pressure had skyrocketed after the first gunshot last night and it hadn't come back down since. It made his hands tremble and his throat dry. Renewed anger swelled and receded with almost every breath that quickly revealed itself to be another violent coughing fit. He felt the anger surge with every rough heave into his balled-up fist. Through watery eyes, he stared at his assistant.

All it took was an unexpected realization at what Ned had told him to change his outlook, and with it, ease the coughing that had turned into a metallic taste in his mouth. A lightbulb had just clicked on. Major James was a man capable of changing his opinion when it was warranted, after all, or at least he liked to think he was. This wouldn't be the first time it happened to him, either.

The Major James Out West Show may have started out as a tour to celebrate his passion for the myth of the West, but when he uncovered the cursed artifact of Thathánka Íyotake, it became something else entirely. A switch somewhere deep inside Major James flipped and he knew that he'd been chosen to do something far greater than placate the masses with mindless entertainment. He'd been charged personally, given an uncompleted mission that had been lost to history itself. There was no other way of seeing it in his eyes. The passages of history at long last had turned their focus to him. It was unexpected, and it changed his life forever.

With a quick glance, the showman turned his attention to the unsuspecting leather bag tossed in the corner of the train car out of the way. Inside it contained his very reason for existing. Knowing what still had to be done, he considered what Ned told him.

"We need to push everything up. West Texas isn't happening," he said with a renewed laser-sharp focus.

"Wait," Ned answered. "Shouldn't we be putting this place behind us? West Texas is a pretty dang good start."

"You were right, as much as I hate to admit it."

Ned thought once more about whether or not he should answer Major James after what he just heard. It wasn't often that he was told he was right about anything, by anyone, much less his boss. His risky gamble of saying something out of line was paying off.

"Everyone knows we exist now, Burwell. There is no one else left worth telling. If we wanted the spotlight, we sure got it now."

"Yes sir," Ned agreed instinctively with the same shit-eating grin across his face that he'd learned from watching Major James. "We sure do."

"That doesn't mean those damned instigators won't pay for what they did to us, though. They embarrassed us at our own show, on our own platform. The performance may never be looked at the same after what happened. The faces of people running for their lives are not easily forgotten in the public eye, you know."

"What are we gonna do now?"

"*You* are going to go ask J.R. Pickett to please bring us the ones I'm paying to fail us so miserably. That's the next step."

"I thought you might say something along those

lines," Ned began. "So, I went ahead and took the liberty of tracking them down with Mr. Pickett."

"Is that so?"

"Yes sir. They're waiting for us just outside that door," he said with a quick gesture to the steel door that led to the front of the train through the flatcar ahead.

"You know, sometimes I wonder why I pay anyone at all, especially when I'm the one having to pull all the weight day after day after godforsaken day," said Major James. "But you, Ned, have a unique way of showing me why signing all those paychecks can pay off every so often."

This time, Ned knew it was a compliment and it made him beam with pride. "Thank you, sir," was all he could get out.

"You go out there and tell them the boss wants to speak to them," said Major James. "But don't you dare come back in here yourself and be sure J.R. stays out there with you. We're gonna need to talk to him afterward."

"Sir?"

"It wasn't all bad news. If not for J.R.'s unwavering loyalty, I might've been killed back there, or worse. That man will play a vital role in what's to come, as long as we're the highest bidder. For now, he's gonna be our ticket to tracking down those who infiltrated our show, who brought chaos to our little family here. Every single one of those bastards are gonna die, I promise you that. In the meantime, I want you to round everyone up and bring all three of them to me."

"Everyone?"

Major James just glared at Ned in response. His eyes said everything that needed to be said. Ned wasted no time in following the exact orders that were given to him. He scurried off through the stacked-up collection inside the train car, doing his best to move delicately. Despite everything that had happened, the man felt like a million bucks after the praise he'd gotten from his boss. There was a pep in his step that couldn't be taken by anyone but the man that had given it to him in the first place.

Major James listened to Ned hurriedly make his way out of the inside of the train car to follow his exact orders. As far as assistants go, he was more content with his service than he was dissatisfied, and that was a heck of a lot more than he could say about some of the others that had filled the position in the past. He could never tell Ned just how replaceable he was. However, after the conversation they just had, even he had to admit the sniveling, brown-nosing man had earned his place.

A dull yellow light swayed gently against the rocking of the train powering its way down the tracks through the East Texas woods. The musty air surrounding his antiquities had become as familiar as home to him through the years. Every now and then, whenever he was by himself, he would breathe it all in to calm his nerves and bask in what he'd built. He was putting himself in the middle of history, one way or another.

His heavy boots echoed throughout the inside of the train car with each step as he walked over toward the old leather bag tucked away in the corner. There were few that even knew what was inside existed, and even fewer who had been in its vicinity. Major James wasn't like any of them, though.

He slammed the bag down onto his cluttered desk, sending more papers than he was proud of scattering into the air. When he had learned about the curse of Tȟatȟáŋka Íyotake that was spoken during a single lap to begin each performance of Buffalo Bill's Wild West Show, even he disregarded it as a myth. There was no proof any such thing ever existed. That was years ago though, an entirely different lifetime for him. As he reached to unzip the leather bag, memories of his first time grabbing that same zipper more than a year ago flooded back to him.

It was before he went out and found the Union Pacific FEF, before he surrounded himself with relics of the old West, and at the earliest days of planning what would become the greatest frontier spectacle on rails seen since William Cody walked the earth. A gray-haired and grouchy elderly man saying goodbye to the last of his possessions had tracked him down one day. They would cross paths for only a few minutes throughout their lives, just long enough to reach out and take the aged leather bag for himself. He remembered its weight when he tossed it on his shoulders, and the decay that burned his nostrils whenever he got near it. Little did he know, it was the weight of the entire world he'd just slung onto his back.

Major James patted the top of the cracked leather bag and allowed himself to settle into that same familiar fragrance of unfiltered death that came from inside. He was a showman without a show for most of his life, but not anymore. If there was one lesson he learned from the story of T̆hath̆áŋka Íyotake, it was that in the end, if you do not charge headfirst after those who stand in your way—they will only do it to you.

"They will remember the performance we give to the world together..." whispered Major James to the ghosts he knew followed his every footstep, "...my greatest attraction."

Everyone's days were numbered in this life, and Major James knew that he was no different. The only difference was that his name would be remembered apart from the sea of people lost in the back of the glossary of the history books. Major James was determined to have his own chapter. Not just as another deadbeat carney, but a herald of one of the most memorable spectacles to ever exist. His face beamed with delectable pride at just the thought of it.

Just as he became lost in the ideas of what he was going to leave behind, the steel door entrance to the train car he was waiting in slid open. Major James would have to leave the magnificence of his own dreams and deal with the same type of people who'd always held him back from what he was truly capable of.

There were five men in total who walked in with their heads hanging low, each one suffering from the same sinking feeling of their own failures. That much could be seen from a mile away. The men trudged slowly up to him and stopped in a single file line, likely just as they were directed by Ned.

Before the door could be shut, however, a sixth

man poked his head inside before shuffling into the train car. This one was a shrunken disgrace unable to even make eye contact. He wore a baggy T-shirt featuring the face of Major James himself and glasses that were too big for his face.

Major James couldn't believe what he was seeing. "If it isn't the one and only Newton Thomas!" The showman hollered when he finally made out who was dragging up the ass end of the ones who'd disappointed him.

"I only did what you—"

"Get in line with the rest of them," Major James directed without waiting to hear yet another rehearsed explanation. "Go on."

Newt did his best to drag out his walk of shame to the back of the line as long as he possibly could. He'd never been invited onboard the actual train, despite following it for so long from city to city. It was like a backstage pass pulled right from his own nightmares, one that he would never be able to escape. The Major James Out West Show was the only thing Newt had really found a passion for, and that fact was written all over his face as he stood before the Major.

"From what I hear, you all have Newt here to thank for what happened," said Major James. "My biggest fan, who turned out to be nothing more than a tool to be used for my own destruction. Isn't that ironic?"

"It wasn't—" Newt tried again.

"Not yet," Major James cut him off with a wag of his finger. "But I can promise you, your time is coming, boy. You can be sure of that."

Major James paced slowly through the line of men

that had failed him. The very men that had taken his money week after week, who had but one job to do when it mattered most. It took only a few paces to grow so disgusted enough with the lot of them that he wanted to just get it all over with.

He was distracted, though. Thoughts of what people were saying about him after the news of the gunfight had spread—and how he could capitalize on it by any means possible—filled his head. There was little he could do about what happened, but these men standing in front of him just might prove useful one last time.

"You all might think you're just here to take an ass chewing. Sit here for a few uncomfortable minutes, then simply go on about your lives," Major James started. "Maybe you even made plans for later tonight to help soothe the pain of your boss being an asshole just before the weekend?"

No response came to the Major's prying.

"Well, I've got nothing else to say about what you all allowed to happen. How's that? You know you fucked up. Newt over there especially knows he fucked up," Major James continued. "I'm not going to keep bitching at you, but what I can tell you, any plans you thought you had tonight are damn sure about to be canceled."

The men stood silent. Some were watching Major James with fear for their lives coming in waves, while others refused to meet his twisted gaze. Newt, however, had resigned to what fate had in store. He was the only one who'd be able to put the pieces together before it was too late.

Major James caught a glint in Newt's eye and savored the moment with everything in him. There were such few times in life that two people could be in such synchronicity, weaving through time to its finite end with unimaginable understanding. What the showman had in store for them all, and what Newt knew he was about to confront, was the very definition of a curtain closing experience.

He slammed his cane down with agitation in every step as he walked back to the leather bag sitting on top of his wooden table. The shadows that danced in the corners gave the place an unnerving presence, and Major James's soured mood only made things all the worse. Each of the men watched him perch himself on the tabletop, gripping the bag tightly just in front of him. While almost caressing the bag, the showman's eyes glazed over as he studied every detail of the bag. Then he spilled his heart to them.

"I'll be the first to admit," he started. "We haven't reached our true potential here at the Major James Out West Show. We've sure gotten some big crowds together, and even gained some rather dedicated fans. Just look at Newt over there, dumb as a sack of hammers, but as dedicated as you'll ever find."

He patted the bag with one hand and lifted up his finger with the other.

"This right here, though, this is going to take everything to new heights. A brand new stratosphere for Western entertainment. What's in this bag will change our lives, and the lives of everyone who bears witness to it, forever. So, even though I have to be stuck here dealing with the likes of you all, suffering through your willful incompetence—I know that I still have a purpose to fulfill."

Major James stayed right where he stood, still leaning on the tabletop and watching each of the men with a stern look painted on his face. His tone was that of a scolding father speaking over a room full of his own children.

"This train isn't the stage that so many believe it to be," he continued. "No, no, it's simply the ferry that Charon himself steers with an undeniably divine purpose. You might think that I stand here in front of you thinking I'm some sort of ferryman myself, and you are the lost souls in desperate need of transport, but you'd be wrong."

The showman's trademark twisted smile stretched once again across his face as he shifted his glare back to the men in front of him.

"We're all lost souls here, just along for the ride," he told them before settling into an extended pause that turned awkward in a hurry.

"The destination here isn't the afterlife, however," Major James finally picked his speech back up. "Your role in this divine purpose was a simple one. It was a charge given to you so that we may continue our journey to an inevitable end worthy of history's remembrance, and honestly, who wouldn't want that?"

The Major threw his hands up into the air with his last comment. With a scoff and a quick look around the room, he started to realize he was losing his audience. Even he could admit to himself that he'd always been a little too fond of tangents. He allowed himself a few seconds to collect his thoughts amid the gentle swaying and roaring commotion of the train barreling down the tracks.

The showman lifted his index finger again and pointed it right at his self-described biggest fan standing in the room with his head held down.

"Newt, I told you your time was gonna come," he told him. "Get your ass on up here."

Without hesitation, Newt did as he was told. He dragged one foot in front of the other to get himself up to his former hero, Major James. He knew better than to speak before he was asked, so he waited in silence, unable to make eye contact. Whether it was a bullet, or blunt trauma, he knew the ultimate price that was about to be asked of him.

"You might think my attention is the answer to your life," the Major told him. "But it isn't my attention that will change your life, it's the crowd's."

Major James began looking behind Newt at each of the men who faced him as he spoke. "What we need right now is the one who can headline our greatest performance yet. It's a big role, maybe the biggest we've ever had a need for. Instead of rightfully firing each of you and maybe worse, I'm going to give you one more chance to prove yourself."

The next few minutes were both horrendous and hopeful all at once. The prospect of salvation through such a menial task was promising, much less the idea that they might even walk out of the train car alive. Major James instructed each of them to approach the bag one by one. Their job would be to hold what was inside long enough to make a single lap around the arena. If they could pull this off, they would earn their place back in his good graces and lead the greatest performance Major James would ever unveil—or at least that's what he told them.

As Newt was last in line, he watched in terror as each of the men made their way up to the bag, unknowingly experiencing their last seconds to suck in air as they did. It was a cruel trick. Not only that, it felt aimed right at Newt, like an insult to his own existence. The first to look inside froze immediately before falling into violent spasms with blood pouring from his face. Newt shuddered at the clacking of his body thrashing on the hardwood floors. The second man to face the bag didn't fare any better.

At this point, it was safe to say Newt was pissing his pants. Fear made his knees wobbly and his breath labored. It surged through his extremities in waves that never seemed to ease. Major James had something at his disposal that was unnatural, and as the bodies piled up lifeless on the floor in front of the open bag, Newt realized that his life had amounted to nothing more than another of the showman's poor victims.

Three bodies were on the floor now. Blood leaked out from the pile in every direction, soaking into the wooden floors to leave deep red stains that would take years to fade. The fourth man stepped into place before reconsidering what was about to happen to him. His eyes darted to the side just for a second, then his body followed. He was making a break for it.

"He'll find out," Major James said. He motioned the next guy to step forward, leaving Newt next in line.

Just as the fifth man in line stepped over what was left of the bleeding corpses beneath him, a gunshot blasted out from the other side of the steel door. It echoed throughout the train for just a moment before Major James beckoned the trembling man forward again. When he did as he was told, he joined the ones still lying lifeless on the floor with blood dripping from his eyes and ears.

"My biggest fan," Major James said with a smirk. "I have faith in you boy. Tȟatȟáŋka Íyotake calls to you, he calls to continue the legacy. He is speaking right now. Can't you hear him?"

"No—"

"You can hear him," Major James told him. "Just listen and do what needs to be done."

Newt swallowed and took a step closer. Sweat was pouring from his face, his mouth was bone dry, and metallic air caused by blood loss tinged his nostrils. Tunnel vision was setting in behind his fogged-out glasses. With tears of desperation, panic, and defeat running down his cheeks, the fanboy of the Major James Out West Show stepped up to lock eyes with his hero.

When he summoned enough courage to finally look down into the leather bag that sat between them, his pupils blew out and the tears that streaked down his cheeks turned red.

CHAPTER 18

"**M**y fucking finger is gone!"

Cannon was still in shock at what had happened to him in the shootout. Where most would've passed out from the pain or even just the sight of how much of his own carnage had filled in the inside of the pickup, he only found burning fury.

"It's gonna be all right, you're gonna be fine." Cathay was trying to console him to little avail with her foot slammed into the gas pedal.

"She's right," Jim Bob said. "You don't even need that one, I've seen you shoot. Any of those fingers will do just fine. Trust me."

Cathay turned to look at the bumbling man sitting behind Cannon. Jim Bob shrugged in response and turned his attention back to Cannon. They were doing close to eighty miles an hour on the highway in an attempt to put some distance between themselves and the scene of the shootout. Half-ton pickups weren't made like the heavy clunkers from decades ago, this one handled those kinds of speeds with surprising ease. There wasn't even any intrusive road noise to break through Cannon's frantic hollering.

He was wrapping his hand with a spare T-shirt while listening to Cathay and Jim Bob bickering. They said everything they could except the most obvious thing of all—they just got their ass kicked. The gun hand protecting the train wasn't one to be messed with. He'd single-handedly gotten the best of all three of them.

Cannon groaned with his right hand held as high as his shoulders. Just thinking about making the call to Etta Daugherty to tell her what just happened was enough to make him wish the bullet that took his finger had just taken him out instead. As blood began to seep through the navy-blue T-shirt tied around his hand, Cannon let his frustration out.

"We had one damn job. We had one thing to do out there," he vented. "And we just stood there like a bunch of jackasses. If I ever find that coward Newt, I'm gonna—"

"The only thing you're gonna do is not bleed to death on us," Cathay cut him off.

"I'll kill that little shit," Cannon finished anyway. "I'll kill him, that gun hand, and the one who runs it all."

"That's all fine and dandy," said Jim Bob from the back seat. "But we barely got outta that place alive as it is. Before we start trying to hightail it back into that death trap, we might want to find a place to get off the road and get Cannon's nub there to stop bleeding into the upholstery."

This time, there weren't any vengeful comments or words of support to be had. The group sat in the speeding truck without any ideas as to what they were supposed to do next. The mission to take down Major James and put a stop to what Etta had described as a mass casualty attack still remained. They were no closer to accomplishing their mission than before any of the three had even met, though.

After all they'd fought for, Cannon could only see their glaring failure staring right back at him in the road that carried them on their escape. The searing pain in his hand was nothing compared to the sting of defeat that they were just forced to swallow.

Whether any of them welcomed a distraction from getting their ass handed to them or not, the rearview mirror of the pickup showed another one of Major James's hired hands coming up on them. Cathay noticed the sedan speeding up behind them first. She pushed her foot down on the gas a little harder without saying anything. They hit ninety miles an hour on the highway before Cannon finally took notice.

"What's going—"

"Company," Cathay cut him off. "Let's get back to it y'all."

Cannon looked down at the wrapped-up stub on his right hand again before turning his attention back to Cathay.

"Jim Bob," she said, still looking right at Cannon. "I think this one's gonna be on you."

"You got it, boss lady."

They were headed south on Highway 259 as fast as their truck would let them. The black sedan wasted no time in closing the distance and trying to rear-end them. Soft clicks of bullets dropping into a cylinder filled the inside of the pickup, becoming a sort of metronome to ensure the upcoming cacophony of gunfire would play out on cue.

Jim Bob slammed the cylinder to his revolver close and nodded his head at Cathay through the mirror to let her know he was ready for whatever she had planned. There were no cars out to stop the chase from hitting lethal speeds in a matter of minutes, and no matter how hard Cathay jammed the gas pedal to the floor, the sedan stayed right behind them.

"We gotta do *something* dammit!" Cannon finally yelled at them.

Without saying anything, Cathay reached down and rolled the backside passenger window down to let a rush of air come flooding inside. It was unsettling at first. The window crept down much slower than it should have as the pickup flew down the highway trying its damndest to reach a hundred miles an hour. The roar that followed when the window finally stopped set them all on edge.

"You know what to do?"

Jim Bob stared out the window for a second before a lightbulb finally went off over his head. "Oh hell yeah I do. You're a crazy son of a bitch!" He scooted over to position himself behind the passenger seat and watched Cathay for her nod.

"It's gonna be quick," she told both of them in the truck. "Just hold on."

"Wait!" Cannon tried to catch up as best he could. Just as he finished shouting, a gunshot cried out from behind them and a corner of the back glass window blew out into pieces inside the cab.

Cathay wasn't lying when she said it was going to happen quickly. One minute they were hauling ass down the highway and the next, the tires on the truck were screaming against the pavement. Cathay had stomped on the brakes and jerked the steering wheel to the right, almost rolling the truck in the process. They turned completely sideways to make their way onto a back road off the highway, bringing Jim Bob face to face with their chasers as he hung out of the passenger side rear window. One of his hands gripped an old revolver pointed at the sedan and the other hand carried the task of flipping off whoever was inside of it.

Cannon would probably never forget the way that man howled as they made such a violent maneuver. The bullfighter was a madman, through and through. His maniacal laughter continued as the revolver in his hand blasted out one bullet after another. The windshield of the sedan was the first thing to go, revealing two men with arms up over their faces to block the glass from slicing their faces.

Bam! Bam! Bam!

The shots from Jim Bob left them all with ringing ears. Between the high-pitched sounds that echoed in their heads, both Cannon and Cathay could still hear the crazed cackling from Jim Bob. He was enjoying the shootout a little too much.

Bam! Bam!

"Did you get 'em?"

Only more laughter came in response.

"Jim Bob!" Cathay cried out to him as she kept the truck speeding down the winding back road taking them westward.

Finally, the bullfighter threw himself from the window into the back seat again with a smile plastered across his face. He took the time to push the over six-inch barrel, still smoking hot from firing off so many rounds, into his holster before speaking. With a smack of his hands together, he composed himself and spoke.

"All good."

Cathay's eyes went right to the rearview mirror where she saw the black sedan coming to an abrupt stop in the road before veering off into the ditch with a hard slam. Her eyes widened.

She hid her reaction and adjusted the mirror to see Jim Bob's smiling face again. They settled into the drive down the country roads while the rest of their adrenaline got out of their system. When the truck turned back onto Highway 259 to continue moving south, it was Cannon who spoke up.

"Gotta get off the road. Whatever we started back there looks like it's following us," he said. "Blood loss has got me all woozy. I'll be no good in a fight."

"Well too bad," Cathay told him. "Because if you haven't noticed, we're already in one."

Jim Bob looked around at each of the windows around him.

"No, dipshit, not literally right now," she said without looking back at the bullfighter.

Silence fell over the group as they kept a steady pace on the highway. Cannon's hand was pushed up to his chest. The T-shirt tied around his wound was soaked red, but it had done its job. His eyes rolled around in his head before they could focus on the road ahead. He was in and out of clarity and fighting to keep conscious. When the soft glow of a neon sign filled his vision, relief settled over him.

Cathay and Jim Bob carried a groaning Cannon into a room of a hotel that didn't even look to be open when driving by. It was just the kind of spot they needed to hide the car, and themselves, away for enough time to think about what came next. Unfortunately for them, there wasn't much talking done inside the room.

Cannon passed out almost immediately after hitting the creaky mattress. The musty carpet and broken air conditioning didn't seem to bother him a bit. He drifted on a wave of endorphins that took his mind away from his missing trigger finger. Sleep found him like an old friend eager to enter a warm embrace for hours on end.

BANG. BANG.

"Wake the hell up!" Cathay's scream rang out through the hotel room.

BANG. BANG.

It took everything Cannon had to peel his eyes open. He saw Cathay firing off rounds and Jim Bob crouched down below the window loading his revolver again. He saw people scrambling just outside like shadows scattering from the encroaching sunlight in the distance.

"They're back! They're back!" Jim Bob was hollering while jamming brass down into the cylinder.

"No shit," Cathay told him. "Stop talking and start shooting. I don't wanna die in this nasty ass hotel room."

"Think he can make it?" Jim Bob said with a quick gesture to Cannon still trying to gather himself in bed.

A bullet blasted through the window of the hotel, sending glass raining down on Jim Bob before slamming into the wall just behind Cannon. Sheetrock dust billowed out from the strike before two more bullets whizzed by and slammed into the same wall.

Cannon instinctively rolled himself over the bed to hit the floor for cover. The men outside were relentless. They kept all three inside the room pinned down with no option to return fire. It went on like this for several agonizing seconds before the bullets flying just over their head finally came to a sudden stop.

"They're waiting for us," Cathay said.

"Give me the gun," Cannon told her, reaching out with his left hand.

"Are you puttin' me on?"

"There's no time, Cathay. Give me the damn gun," he said. "We gotta go, now."

She shoved the revolver into his hand without saying anything else. The weight of the firearm and the gunpowder residue that wafted into his face was more welcome than even he'd like to admit. Before he could think about what needed to happen next, he acted.

The first gunshot he fired from his left hand found its target, sending a red spray spewing up from behind a familiar-looking black sedan across the parking lot. The second shot resulted in another man screaming in the distance as he took a bullet to the stomach. Before he could fire again, bullets continued to rain down on all three of them stranded inside the hotel room.

"How many of the bastards are out there?"

Cathay's question might as well have been rhetorical. It didn't matter how many were bearing down on them. Cannon knew they only had two choices—move or die. Time was running out. Shells continued to pound the wall behind them, stopping only to give the gunman enough time to jam a new magazine into the rifle he was using to pin them down. Cannon counted the seconds between the shots and each break. Two seconds between the gunfire and more than five seconds to reload.

"One, two," he counted under his breath.

Another shot fired off over their heads, this time lodging itself into the lamp on the stand next to the mattress and sending it flying into the air. It crashed into the wall riddled with bullet holes behind them but was drowned out by the deafening blasts of constant gunfire. When another shot went right by their heads, Cannon started counting again.

"One, two," was as far as he got before another shot interrupted him.

"We're moving after the three more rounds," Cannon tried to say between the cover fire that continued above them.

"Are you crazy?" Jim Bob screamed.

The next two shots happened quicker than he'd guessed, and even Cannon started to second guess his timing. Once the third bullet flew by them to send another plume of drywall dust into the air, Cannon was on his feet and running before he could think about it any longer. He stole a quick glance behind him to make sure Cathay and Jim Bob were following. All he could hear between the gunshots trailing right behind him was the cussing from Jim Bob that came with every step he took.

"Shit, shit, shit, shit," he hollered the whole way to their pickup.

They made it inside in one piece, but the windshield took the first shot. It spiderwebbed out in every direction as Cannon tried his damndest to throw it in drive. His mess of a right hand didn't do him any favors. With no index finger, he struggled at first to grasp the shifter on the steering column but made do with what he had to get the heck out of Dodge. They were still taking gunfire as they spun out of the hotel parking lot.

"What is happening right now?" Cathay asked from the passenger seat.

"We're screwed, that's what," Jim Bob answered.

"It's Major James," said Cannon, ignoring Jim Bob's pessimism. "He's onto us. There's gotta be some kind of hit out that we are just now learning about."

"It hasn't even been twelve hours since we left. How does he already have so many people chasing us?"

"I'm surprised there aren't more. He's got the money and the connections," Cannon answered her.

"And he's probably pissed," Jim Bob cut in.

"He's definitely pissed."

"What are we supposed to do next?" Cathay couldn't help but ask.

"We split up," said Cannon. "We go our separate ways and turn everything over to authorities who are equipped to deal with this shit. None of us are going to survive this if we keep pushing."

Cathay couldn't believe what she was hearing. She turned her head to see if Cannon was laughing his own comments off, but what she saw was pain swelling in his eyes. It was inescapable and contagious. He was falling down the rabbit hole of despair, triggered by what he could only see as yet another devastating failure. Hope was no longer fleeting, it was gone.

"We're done," he said. "It's over."

CHAPTER 19

"So, you just give up?"

"It's not like that."

"Sure it is," Cathay blurted out. "If Major Asshole back there is so protective of whatever's inside that train, how do you know it won't lead back to your dad somehow? You probably still have his letter on you right now saying that he's got the answers you're looking for. Don't you?"

"This isn't about who my dad is anymore," he told her, still focusing only on driving.

"If you ain't gonna be honest with us, you should at least be honest with yourself," said Cathay.

"I am being honest. This is over."

"Horseshit it's over," said Jim Bob, finally catching up to what was happening.

"I'm serious, we've had three close calls in a matter of hours. We're gonna pull over, call Etta to send in the cavalry of whatever state agents she works with, and then we'll figure out the best way to split up from there."

The inside of the pickup fell silent after Cannon's demands. A dull drum of road noise lulled them into thinking their situation wasn't as deadly as it was. It seemed the only one who could hear the ticking clock getting louder and louder was the one who'd gotten them into the mess.

They were south of Kilgore, way out in the sticks with towering pines forming a green blur as they drove. The highway stretched on through the trees leaving them more time to think than they'd ever want. This dragged on for half an hour or so before the clicking of the truck's blinker snapped everyone back into reality.

Cannon steered the truck off the lane and into the shoulder of the highway. He found the closest exit leading them into a rest station. There were a few park benches scattered around a tiny building with grimy restrooms and the most unappetizing vending machine imaginable. It was mundane, but just what they needed to figure things out in the safety of the public eye.

The three of them sat at one of the picnic tables and listened to the cars rush by on the highway. They stared silently, waiting for someone other than themselves to start the inevitable process Cannon had just begun. Before any of that could happen, Jim Bob reached into his back pocket and pulled out a dinged-up metal oversized flask.

"Sure couldn't hurt," he said as he screwed the top loose.

No one answered him, but they also didn't refuse the flask when it was passed their way either. Cannon, Cathay, and Jim Bob each shared a large swig of lukewarm American-distilled whiskey, shaking aside any visible reaction as best they could. The sun crept over the horizon of trees all around them as the all-too-welcome burn settled into each of their throats.

"Jim Bob," Cannon finally said something while stealing another mouthful of whiskey. "You might be the only smart one here."

"Now, you know I don't buy that for one damn second," he answered, grabbing the flask with a quick jerk.

Cathay sat stoic and silent with her elbows propped up on the table. Her body language said that she was ready to give the middle finger to both of the men next to her, but she held her tongue. Instead, she was simply glaring right at Cannon.

"This is all my fault," Cannon admitted only after locking eyes with Cathay.

"Don't say all that—"

"No, it is," he cut Jim Bob off, still looking right at Cathay. "I've been willing to get all of you killed on some misguided hunt for a man who's never spoken to me. My mom did everything she could do to give me a life back on her own, but she needed me to play my part first. I spent too much time with people I shouldn't have been around. It made me careless."

Still no response from Cathay. She finally pulled her elbows from the table to show that she was at least listening. Cannon took that as a sign to continue.

"I couldn't accept failure. I couldn't take no for an

answer. But after this shit, I have to," he said while holding up his right hand wrapped up like a bloody club.

Cathay finally leaned forward, keeping her glare right on Cannon, and spoke with relentless anger dripping from her words. "You're lying."

Cannon's expression dropped. He was pouring his heart to them in an attempt to prove he was genuine when he said he was done. How could she say he was lying to them? Words escaped him.

"That's right," she doubled down. "You think I didn't notice you taking those dickheads down back there at the motel with one shot? You were screaming this and that about your trigger finger, but it was like you hadn't even missed a beat when it came time to shoot."

"What's she talking about?" Jim Bob asked.

"She's confused, that's all," said Cannon.

"Confused? You're bein' a real son of a bitch, you know that? You'd have better luck telling me to calm down. Go ahead, try."

"Cathay—"

"No," she pushed. "You forgot I ride horses for a living. I know a dominant hand when I see it. A gun ain't no different than a rope, and you are not about to sit here and tell me otherwise. You're a lefty."

Cannon fell silent and watched her expose him.

"Well I'll be damned," said Jim Bob, throwing his hands in the air but never relinquishing his grip on the over-halfway empty flask.

"That doesn't change what's happening," said Cannon. "It doesn't mean anything."

"Maybe not, but I think you lying about that means you'll lie about something else, like why you want to quit on us all of a sudden. Or did you forget you were the one who dragged us into all of this?"

"It doesn't matter what hand I shoot with. The only thing that matters is stopping the Major and whatever he's got planned. Our best bet of doing that is bringing in more guns than him. There's nothing we can do to change that. The three of us just ain't enough."

"From what I saw, we got all the guns we need," said Cathay.

"You're wrong," Cannon told her without hesitating. "You're just wrong, okay? I'm not getting you two killed for nothing."

"Look, if you haven't figured it out by now, I'll spell it out for you. We ain't going nowhere. Jim Bob and me are in this whole thing for the long haul," she told him.

"That's damn sure right,"

Just as Jim Bob spoke, the routine rush of wind from cars passing by died down to let the crunching of gravel beneath tires take its place. Someone was pulling into the same rest stop they'd found themselves hiding out in. It was another black sedan, no different than the one that had trailed them not too long ago.

The car put them all on edge. They didn't know if they were still being followed and didn't want to take the chance of getting caught off guard. All three slowly rested their hands on their firearms. A black sedan wasn't exactly an uncommon car, so there was nothing they could do but wait. It rolled ahead into the open spot next to Cannon's pickup before coming to an inconspicuous stop.

"You've gotta be—" Cathay tried to say before a door swung open from the car and cut her off.

A wide-brimmed straw cowboy hat popped out of the passenger side door, followed by a pair of blacked-out baseball sunglasses tucked right beneath it. The three at the picnic table saw the glint of the man's white smile before it was replaced by a steel-framed pistol eager to dump a magazine at every single one of them.

Jim Bob was the first to start cussing as he flung himself to the dirt. "Shit, shit!"

Cathay reached for her hip as the gunman's arm extended out from behind the passenger side door of the sedan. Before she could grip her revolver and get it aimed at the man trying to kill them, a shot rang out.

Bang.

The man who'd rolled up on them was flung backward by a bullet ripping right through his chest. He was hidden behind the car, but his dying groans gave away everything he was going through.

Bang.

Cannon fired one more time through the windshield of the sedan on the driver's side, causing a splatter of blood inside. The sedan's engine sat idling restlessly. Both of the men who'd found them soon passed on, leaving all three at the picnic table right back where they were before the sudden fight.

Cathay threw her hands into the air in frustration at the interruption. "Can't even sit here in peace!"

"I guess we just gotta stay on the move," said Jim Bob, opting to take another swig of whiskey.

"Might have to. It's gonna be the only way to keep from getting ran up on by these bastards," Cathay answered, holding her hand out to encourage Jim Bob to pass the flask again. "You know where we can go next?"

She'd turned her attention back to Cannon, but he wasn't listening. He'd pushed the revolver back into his holster and tipped his cowboy hat up to think better. It was pretty clear that the Major had too many hired hands for them to just shoot their way into the train. Cathay was right though, any leads on your dad would be hidden inside. Giving up wasn't something in his nature, but neither was getting other people killed over him. Especially not people he'd actually started to like.

"I could use some food," Jim Bob answered in the silence that followed Cathay's question. "Should be able to find a chopped beef sandwich somewhere around here, right?"

"What did you say again?" Cannon asked out of nowhere.

"Me?"

"Yes, Jim Bob," Cannon answered. "What did you just say?"

"I want a chopped beef sandwich?"

"He does this all the time, you just gotta ignore him," Cathay cut in while rolling her eyes.

"No, earlier. You said that we just had to stay on the move."

"Right..."

"Give me that," said Cannon as he reached for the flask.

After holding the flask up to his lips just a little longer than he should have, Cannon scrunched his face before exhaling to soothe the whiskey burn. He didn't explain himself immediately. Instead, his eyes wandered aimlessly as he became lost in thought.

Cathay could see it all over his face, but she wasn't nearly as patient as the others. Rather than waiting for him to speak up, she nudged his elbow to get his attention. When she saw that he'd snapped back into reality, she gave him a look that pressed him to start talking.

"We just gotta keep moving…" Cannon repeated before drifting off. "He'd never see that shit coming."

"I'm not following," said Cathay.

"I realize I just said there was no other way to pull this off, and maybe it's the liquor doing all the talking, but Jim Bob really does have a point."

"I do?"

"He does?"

Cannon finally let out a smirk and his entire demeanor shifted, like a weight was pulled from his shoulders. "We learned the Major makes his money setting up and breaking down that ungodly show of his. He's thought of everything when it comes to each and every stop on the Major James Out West Show. We were damned fools to think we could just waltz right in, no matter how many guns we had."

"Well, that part sure is true," said Cathay.

Cannon leaned forward. "I'm willing to bet he

doesn't give second thought to what happens while they're traveling between stops."

At this point, Cathay couldn't help herself but to laugh. Although Jim Bob didn't quite fully get what Cannon was insinuating, he went ahead and joined Cathay too. Before he knew it, or understood why, Cannon was laughing right alongside them. It was a silly idea, one that warranted such a response. As humorous as it sounded, it was also the only idea that could get them inside the Major's train to find out what he was hiding.

"I was serious when I said this was over, though," he spoke up again. "Etta knew Major James was leaving a trail of bodies behind him after every performance. She also seems to think he's just getting started, that he's on his way to pull off some kind of mass casualty event."

"Which means a lot of people are gonna die," Jim Bob said without thinking.

"That's right."

"Which is why we can't quit yet, you asshole," said Cathay.

"Well, there's no denying we got our asses kicked. I know I damn sure did," he said while letting his eyes drift over to his right hand. "Thinking we could just do the same thing and expect something different to happen just won't cut it with so many lives at stake. We don't know where he's going, what he's planning to do, or how he's even gonna do it."

"I thought you were done with all this woe-is-me nonsense." Cathay nudged him. "Didn't we just make it clear that we ain't going nowhere?"

"I just realized, none of that is actually important," he told her before looking at both of them at the table. "All we need to know is where he's at right now. He came through Kilgore headed southbound and those train tracks ain't gonna get up and move. That should tell us everything we need to know about how to catch up to him."

The vehicle that had rolled up onto the three of them still sat in the otherwise empty parking lot idling to no end. A hot Texas sun had continued its climb above their heads, doing its part to make each of them start wiping the sweat from their brows as they spoke. There was no breeze rolling in through the trees surrounding them and the highway traffic had died down in the distance. With a blue sky dotted with clouds stretching overhead, it almost seemed like too nice of a day to deal with the trouble at hand. A dead body still bleeding out into the concrete was a stark reminder of what they were facing down, however.

"You're serious about this?" Cathay asked him with a tone she'd never used before with either of them.

Jim Bob still hadn't quite caught up to what either of them were talking about, but he did his best to play along in the hopes that no one else would notice. "Don't be jerkin' my chain. If you're sayin' what I think you're saying, just go on ahead and get it out."

"We're gonna pull off a train robbery that would give Butch Cassidy a run for his money."

CHAPTER 20

"If we don't make it to Houston, everything we've worked for will be flushed down the damned drain! We've got every eyeball in the southern United States looking right at us. If I say now is the time, then right goddamn now is the fuckin' time!"

Major James was heated. It seemed as though things were spiraling out of control since the shooting in Kilgore. Staff members were dropping like flies. Reports of police turning their attention to him were starting to reach his ears. Even his right-hand man, Ned Burwell, had started to cast his own doubts. It was something to keep an eye on, as Ned was the only one who knew about what was going to happen during the final performance of the Major James Out West Show.

Although it had always been planned for Houston, the finale wasn't supposed to happen for several weeks. They were meant to travel to West Texas and back, thereby giving them enough time to find the right man for the most important job. All of that was going out the window in a hurry, though.

"None of those men were able to stand it?" Ned asked, knowing the answer before he spoke.

Major James cast a glare in his direction. It was the kind of stare down that would make a coyote tuck its tail and cry.

"Figures," said Ned, trying his best not to think twice about the look he'd just been given.

"We already know there isn't anyone alive today who could pull off such a feat. There's no sense in trying to find anyone. The only thing that matters is getting this train into downtown Houston and the curse of Thatȟáŋka Íyotake in front of as many people as possible."

"I've already called for a meeting tonight where we will put the word out that the rest of the tour is canceled," Ned began to explain.

"Canceled?"

"Well, yes sir. There are more than a couple dozen stops that we had planned to make between now and Houston. We'll have to cancel them, sir."

"You'll do no such thing."

"I don't—"

"Of course you don't understand Ned, I wouldn't expect you to," Major James assured his assistance. "If we tell the world we have put an end to the show, it would put too many on edge before we arrive in Houston. There's no telling what kind of story would be told about us, or where we'd be going next."

"What do we tell the crew then?"

"Exactly what is happening," Major James answered with a smile finally stretching across his face. "We tell them that we are going to make history together. We're not canceling the tour by any means, we're expanding it. We tell them we've added a new stop, one that simply can't wait."

Ned let his eyes wander through the dimly lit collection as his boss spoke. Stacks of books were falling over with every rough bump in the train. Spiderwebs scattered the corners of the ceiling and layers of dust had started to accumulate on every surface. It was the kind of place that history buffs and flippers alike would give anything to spend just an hour inside. At that moment, Ned felt like he'd spent a little too much time in the train car with Major James. Life was getting grim, and the shooting in Kilgore had only exasperated things.

"Sir, can I ask a question?"

No response came. It was something that Ned had grown accustomed to. More often than not, it meant he could continue on with whatever he was trying to do. Hoping that was still the case, he continued with his question.

"When you found that bag, you seemed sure that it would put you shoulder to shoulder with the greatest showrunners in history. You told me that if I stuck by your side when the history books told your story, I would be right there alongside you."

"Is there a question in there?"

"Yes sir," said Ned. "Why the hurry? I just don't see it."

"You've been the best assistant I could ever hope for, you know that, right?"

Major James's response caught Ned off guard, visibly so. He recoiled at the question that his boss had just asked him. Rarely was he ever given such a compliment, much less one such as praiseworthy as that. It was like he'd been handed a million-dollar check.

"I don't know what to say," was all he could get out.

"I'll be honest with you, Ned," Major James continued. "I'll be more honest with you than I've been with myself for the better part of a year now."

With a familiar clicking of his cane smacking the hardwood floors of the train car as he walked, Major James moved throughout his coveted collection of old West history until he was standing beneath the sign of the Buffalo Bill show. When he finally took his eyes away from the relics of a time lost to look at Ned, his eyes were frosty and reddened.

"I'm dying."

Ned gasped uncontrollably and pushed his hands to his mouth to stop it. He watched in horror as Major James struggled to lean his cane up against a nearby bookshelf overflowing with piles of books stacked every way imaginable. The old man fumbled at his pants leg stained with mud and dirt from days spent on the tour. He tugged it upward to reveal a plastic leg that went up halfway to his knee, almost covered by his custom cowboy boots.

"This isn't even my leg anymore, had it hacked off a few months back in some backwoods hospital south of Sixty Six, South Carolina. I got bit by a tick rummaging through this man's collection he had stashed away in a half-collapsed barn. Next thing I know, I'm getting treated for sepsis, listening to some doctor explain amputations, then having to hear about timelines, and quality of life this and that."

Ned wasn't listening to the explanation; he was focused on only one word that he'd heard come out of his boss's mouth. "What do you mean exactly by dying?"

"Same as it always means. You gotta keep up. My days are numbered here, and those numbers are just getting smaller and smaller," said Major James as he dropped his pants leg and gripped his cane once again. "There's no more time to waste."

"I don't understand, sir."

"Don't really have to."

Major James limped his way back toward his assistant, finally willing to stop hiding the pain behind every single step he takes. When he made it no more than a foot away from Ned, he stopped walking and his posture changed entirely. His back straightened and his gut sucked in just a little bit. There was a dire glare in his eye that was inescapable.

"Houston is my last chance. It's the only chance. Tȟatȟáŋka Íyotake has put this on me and I am the only one who can see it through," he said through his teeth. "I am meant to be known throughout the world."

Ned reached out and put his hand on his boss's shoulder. "You will see it through, sir. I'll lay my own life down to be sure of it."

"Hopefully that won't be necessary."

There wasn't much else that could be said between them. Major James and Ned stood beneath the banner stretched out from end to end of the train car. Yellow light swung above their head to cast moving shadows that danced between stacks of books and across the dozens of pieces of artwork strung up. With another pat on the shoulder, Ned broke the moment of reflection between the two to start pacing back and forth as he tried to find some clarity.

"You really think Tȟatȟáŋka Íyotake's curse will kill hundreds like you said before?"

Major James lowered his glare at last, before answering with just a single word. "Thousands."

"We draw the biggest crowd we can, and we roll out the main performance," Ned continued, almost talking to himself at this point. "Everything else will take care of itself?"

"We've gone through one headline performance after another trying to bring a crowd to the great Major James Out West Show," explained the Major with a new sense of grandiose rising in his voice. "We've made a name for ourselves. Drawn in hundreds over and over again. Texarkana had just over a thousand ready and waiting for us, and Kilgore sure tried to top it before…"

Major James turned and walked away as he spoke, showcasing the demeanor that he'd been known for. His stroll was that one that would convince anyone he was as healthy as a horse. He was making his way back to his desk in the middle of the train car when he stopped once again to turn and look at Ned.

"We need to be sure Houston puts those numbers to shame, or else my chapter in history will be lost into local newspapers and forgotten once the next breaking news story hits," he said. "I refuse to be forgotten due to the likes of some politician's infidelity or dime-a-dozen carjacking."

"I thought you might mention something like that," Ned told him before reaching his hand beneath a stack of dusty old documents. "You just need to see for yourself."

From the top of a bookshelf filled to the brim with anything but books—including statues and trophies of names no historian has ever seen before—came the clicking sound of an old television powering on. It was the kind of TV that was as deep as it was wide and took two able-bodied men just to move across the room. There was only static at first, but the face of a woman with shoulder-length hair and thick lipstick soon appeared. Ned stood close by with a plastic remote in his hand. As the volume got louder, Major James's jaw sank lower and lower.

"The Major James Out West Show garnered controversy during a recent outing in the small town of Kilgore, Texas, following a shooting that broke out leaving multiple dead and more injured," the woman on the television said. "We've received word that the owner now plans to reveal a brand new headlining act to capitalize on the attention at a newly booked show in downtown Houston."

"Ned, you have outdone yourself this time!" Major James was nothing short of ecstatic. "We're about to be shittin' in high cotton when we get to Houston."

"Wait, wait," whispered Ned with a smile. "Listen to this right here."

"Presales have topped over five thousand tickets sold so far for the highly anticipated showtime in Houston, putting it on pace to be the highest attended show in the short-lived history of the tour."

CHAPTER 21

"Can't believe we're actually going through with this."

"You better," said Cathay. "Shit's about to get real here in a few minutes."

"Stay focused y'all," Cannon told them.

They'd reached the train tracks headed southbound parallel to Highway 59 only an hour ago. All three were perched up on a hill tucked away behind a tree line of pines and yaupon bushes to hide their ambush lying in wait. The sun was beating down on them. Each one fidgeted with unease and wiped sweat away from their faces every few seconds.

"I get why we're gonna ride up on this train comin' through any minute. Trust me, I do." Jim Bob was working his way back through the plan they'd discussed a half dozen times already. "I do want to ask something, though."

"Here we go," Cathay chimed in.

"Why do we gotta be on horses again?"

Cannon reached down and ran his hand along the neck of the mare he was perched on top of. He gave the horse a quick pat and readjusted his grip on the leather reins clutched in his right hand. They were slick with sweat, and his horse had become sensitive to even the slightest nudge. He looked over at the horse next to his, a much softer chestnut with unique white markings across its head.

"We have to be able to get close to the train at just the right speed, then dismount without causing a pileup that will ruin everything we're trying to do here," explained Cathay.

"We've gotta use every advantage we've got." Cannon joined her. "If we want to get on board unnoticed, this is the best way. It's the only way."

"Yeah, okay. I guess that makes sense."

A few more seconds ticked by in uncomfortable silence as they continued to wait for the Major James train to rush by on the tracks no more than fifty feet in front of them. Cannon let his horse drift sideways a couple of steps before signaling it to come to a stop.

"One more thing," Jim Bob started up again.

"Come on," said Cathay.

"Why couldn't I have my own horse?"

Jim Bob pulled his arms from around Cathay's waist to gesture to Cannon as he asked his next question. He was pushed up against a saddle too small for the both of them and struggled to get adjusted every few seconds. Cathay gripped the reins and stared straight ahead, ignoring the complaints coming from just behind her.

"Cannon got one. You got one too, Cathay. Seems

like I would've been just fine on a horse of my own," Jim Bob said with an annoyed tone finding its way into his voice.

"It's because you gotta be the first one on the train, buddy." Cannon tried to ease the embarrassment he could see washing across Jim Bob's face.

Amid the sweltering humidity of the East Texas air bearing down on them and the occasional group of overly curious flies swarming around, they each sat patiently waiting to enact their plan. It was an improbable plan at best, but it was all they had. Chasing a train on horseback was something that could only come from those three being paired with a few too many swigs of liquid courage.

Cannon knew it was unlikely to work. He knew it was far-fetched from the start. Cathay had convinced him of the horses against his own best wishes simply due to the fact that their pickup would draw too much attention for any secrecy to be allowed. Somehow, even the most doubtful scheme proved to be enough to pull Cannon out of the pit of failure that he'd fallen into after losing his trigger finger. His eyes fell to the reins in his hand. He noticed again the missing finger resting right on top of the saddle, but this time, he didn't lose himself. For a reason he couldn't explain, having those two riding next to him did wonders for his mood.

The minutes ticking by soon turned into hours and what was once patience that kept the group waiting behind the tree line soon turned to anxiety. The horses drifted from side to side with an occasional toss of their head in boredom. There was too much time available to think about what they were about to pull off and it was making each of them nervous in their own way. Cathay was surprisingly the first to break the silence that had overtaken the group.

"Did we miss them?"

"Couldn't have," Cannon answered. "There's nowhere else that train could possibly go to. They've already been promoting the next show in Houston and this is the only track they could've taken from Kilgore down south."

"We didn't see anything on the way down here," she commented, not paying much attention to Cannon's certainty. "Can't hear anything either."

"The only thing we need to be doing is making sure every single gun we got is loaded," Jim Bob cut in, still clutching Cathay's waist from the backend of their horse. "We gotta be ready to make a beeline right to the train the second it comes around the corner."

"We will," said Cannon. "But before that happens, I want to tell both of y'all how much I appreciate you sticking around."

"Well tell us how you really feel," Cathay told him with a smirk.

"Just means a lot is all. I've been chasing these answers for who my dad is by myself for over a year and being completely honest, I'd forgotten what it feels like to not have to take everything on alone."

As he was talking, the familiar sound of a lid from Jim Bob's metal flask being unscrewed punctuated his words. He was struggling to get it open from his place on the horse, but he made do with what he could.

Before Cannon had finished his sentence, Jim Bob waved it toward him to encourage one last drink.

"And drinking by yourself is never a state of mind you want to be in for too long."

"You can say that again," Cathay said as she reached for the flask from Cannon's hand.

The flask that was being handed around was almost bone dry at this point. Luckily, there was just enough to get them to go through with their plan. When the last drop had fallen into Jim Bob's mouth, he gave out a hard swallow and pushed the metal container back into his pocket. A buzz had settled into each one of them. It was the kind that made every idea seem like it was worth chasing, and while all three had no problems summoning the courage to attempt reckless antics every now and then, the liquor kept them eager to get on with it.

Their last toast brought in exactly what the group was waiting for. A chugging echo came first through the trees they were hidden within, bouncing around them as it swelled with each passing second. First it was an easily missed clamor in the distance, but it would soon grow into a deafening roar that could have easily been mistaken for the opening of the gates of Hell.

"Y'all ready?"

Cathay and Jim Bob didn't say a word, or even acknowledge his question. Instead, they bolted out of the woods without looking back. It was an encouraging sign for Cannon, who took half of a second to find a sense of gratitude for those who would charge headfirst into such a fight at his side. If he did discover anything about who his father was, it would be because of those two wild asses riding off toward a speeding train rattling its way down the tracks. He couldn't help but smile.

Cannon slammed his heels into the horse and pushed his knees together to hold on as they picked up speed. The ride out of the woods was the very definition of organized chaos. Cannon squinted his eyes in focus as the wind rushed by. He held his breath until his lungs burned and squeezed the reins hard enough to make his knuckles go bone white.

Their plan was a simple one. It had to happen fast and without mercy if it had any chance of working at all. Everything hinged on how well they could surprise the outfit headed to Houston.

The first few seconds happened only as a blur. Hooves pounded into the dirt as the roaring engine of the train drowned everything else out. Thousands of pounds of steel thrashed down the tracks, engulfed in a relentless cloud of smoke. It soon became impossible to see more than a few feet ahead. The smoke swirled into Cannon's lungs as he rode and he fought the searing pain in his lungs that begged him to cough. Through the cloud, he could see the horse in front of him and a twirling rope above the heads of two silhouettes.

Cathay had found her mark and the rope in her hands spun above her head with the most welcome familiarity she'd felt in a long time. She was at home doing exactly what needed to be done. The bullfighter behind her could only focus on getting ready to become a one-man army. It was no different for him to face the horns of a pissed off bucking bull than to face down the end of a barrel. All he had to do was give Cannon the opening he needed to get on board.

All three made it within a few feet of the train as it barreled down the tracks. It was now or never and Cathay was ready to step up to the challenge. Against the screams of the engine just ahead of them, she could hear Cannon's voice booming behind her.

"Go, go, go!"

She glanced back at Jim Bob through the rough bouncing of the horse's gallop, only to see that he was focused with deadly intent on the train ahead of them. Her hand spun the lasso above her head with elegant grace despite the chaos unfolding around them. Out of the corner of her eye, she spotted a steel handle that made the perfect target to rope, and after only a couple more spins, she let loose.

Cannon watched as Cathay hurled the lasso toward the train. It yanked tight within a matter of seconds like it was always supposed to be there. Cathay tied the rope to her saddle within the blink of an eye.

"Jim Bob," she hollered as soon as she was done. "Now or never, you mother—"

"Just go!"

Jim Bob didn't pay either of them any attention. Holding on to the rope for dear life, he swung a leg over the horse and reached out with the other to step onto the train. It was supposed to be as easy as pulling himself onto the platform, but with the wind and smoke blasting him in the face, it was anything but simple. His boot slipped on the slick metal and he leaned back off balance. If not for the rope he was gripping so tightly, he would've gone face first into the dirt in a matter of seconds.

Cannon moved his horse closer to the train and listened to the squeak and ringing sounds of the steel rolling down the tracks as they moved. Jim Bob barely leveraged his weight to get steady on the platform before he was pounding against the door leading into the train car. As Cannon was reaching for the rope amid the blinding smoke billowing from the engine ahead, Jim Bob's shoulder landed into the door over and over again.

With his revolver in hand tucked at his chest, Jim Bob gave one last furious shove and the door gave way. The entrance of the door flashed several times in what Cannon could only assume were gunshots drowned out by the deafening banging and whistling of the train. Jim Bob was doing his part, going right into the fire first and Cannon wouldn't dare let him take it on by himself for too long. Before he could bail from the horse running at full speed to match the train however, one shaggy-haired frantic man somehow came flying through the door Jim Bob had just entered. The poor stagehand found his own most untimely fate on the other side. Cannon stared wildly as the man was shoved off the train car, screaming louder than the gunshots blasting from his pistol into the side of the train, before careening into gravel, dirt, and trees never to be seen again.

When his boots hit the platform and his horse suddenly trailed away from them to be lost in the distance behind them, Cannon drew his revolver with his left hand and stepped into the train car. He did his best to follow in the footsteps of Jim Bob who'd already cleared out half of whoever was inside.

There were bunks lining the walls and center aisle, each made with the same bedding. Some were all made to be tidy, and others were left in a typical mess of someone who just climbed out. The people who claimed those beds were not too happy at all to see both Jim Bob and Cannon barge right in. A few held their hands up to surrender without knowing what was happening. Those were the ones who had something to live for, something that was worth more than the train tour that employed them.

Not all of the people onboard were so willing to roll over, though. Jim Bob had fired two of his first six rounds in the cylinder of his .357 magnum, but Cannon couldn't even tell which of the men were targets. With one slow step in front of the other, he weaved through the bunks holding his own revolver at his chest. The only thing he could control now was his own anticipation of whatever may come.

Just when he thought he was ready to call out for his partner somewhere inside the train, he was caught off guard from just a few bunks down the row.

BANG!

The gunshot echoed from all around him and rattled off the metal walls to leave his ears ringing. It was a deafening sound that he hoped he didn't have to experience again anytime soon. He took off without hesitating. The pounding of his boots carried out as he ran, but he didn't pay any attention to it. When he saw Jim Bob, he had his revolver outstretched in one hand with a man pointing a snub nose of his own right back at him from the ground.

BANG!

The same ear-splitting reverberations from the gunshot stunned Cannon in a haze of smoke and burning gunpowder lingering in the air. All he could see was a splattering of red on the floor of the train car. It was then that Cannon realized what was happening —they'd brought fire and brimstone to Major James's front door. If he did have something capable of causing the death of thousands, there was little doubt it would show itself soon.

"We can't stick around here," said Cannon, trying to pull his eyes away from the mess in front of them.

"I put two rounds through the wall to scare 'em off. Not everyone ran, though."

"Yeah, I saw," Cannon acknowledged.

"This one had his hands up like he was surrendering. Before I knew it, he had a gun."

"You okay?"

"Never really done it so close before," said Jim Bob. "Nothin' like the TV makes it out to be."

Cannon reached up with his wounded hand and patted the man he could now consider a friend on the shoulder. He gave him a few seconds to admonish the death he wrought for the sake of preserving his humanity. There just wasn't enough time, though.

As they stood there motionless, the last ones remaining in the train car did their best to sneak by and flee for their lives. Cannon paid them only enough attention to ensure no one was trying to pull a fast one like what was left of the man on the floor in front of them. People scuttled by in a hurry until a voice called out from behind them.

"Y'all giving up already?"

Cathay had caught up to them and she was holding a wooden stock lever action rifle in the crook of her arm.

"What the—" Cannon tried to let out.

"Found it," she cut him off. "Figured a good ol' dirty-thirty sure couldn't hurt matters."

"I ain't mad at it."

"Me either. What's his problem?" Cathay gestured at Jim Bob with the end of the lever action rifle.

"There'll be time to talk about it after," said Cannon as he grabbed Jim Bob's arm to pull him back to Earth. "We gotta move right now."

All three had pulled off the impossible task they hadn't been able to do so far—get on the Major's train. The wind rushing by them created a constant dull roar throughout the inside of the train car that took some getting used to. It was disorientating at first, especially for Cannon, but now they could reload their firearms and get ready for the next impossible part of their plan.

"Major James is on this train," Cannon told them. "First we find him, then we kill him. Simple as that."

"Well, in that case." Jim Bob finally spoke up in a tone that was much more familiar for the bullfighter. "Let's go track this son of a bitch down."

The rest of the bunks looked much more rundown now that they had been cleared of anyone inside. The place hadn't been ransacked, but it dang sure looked like it. Cannon took the lead this time with Jim Bob falling behind and Cathay bringing up the rear, still shouldering the rifle she'd picked up. They moved in unison through the rest of the bunks to find the door leading into the next train car.

All three were forced to cross a rather tumultuous gap between the cars that was every bit as frightening as jumping from their horse onto the train. They soon found themselves inside the stable. Every horse, steer, cow, and dog used in the Major James Out West Show was penned up and the musty air hit them all like a ton of bricks.

Cannon ignored the bellering steers and pushy horses begging for feed and walked delicately with his revolver outstretched in front of him. With his team at his back, he made each step forward more confidently than the last. When one of Major James's paid goons stepped out from behind one of the horse pens with a 1911 pistol aimed right at them, Cannon was on target in a split second and firing. Two bullets slammed into the unknown threat's chest, and he fell to the ground without a word.

"Don't hesitate y'all," he said to Jim Bob and Cathay.

Just as he spoke, his voice was drowned out by Cathay's rifle from just a few feet behind him.

Bam!

Bam!

The lever action went to work quickly. Cathay was as accurate with the rifle as she was with a rope. It took only fifteen seconds to move from one end of the stable train car to the other before they found the next doorway leading out.

Bang!

Jim Bob blasted off another round from his revolver and a man hidden away behind a few square bales of hay was left screaming in pain. His panicked hollers for help were muted behind the hay, but they soon turned into desperate cries as he realized his life was coming to a violent end.

"No sense in stopping now!" Cannon called out to each of them amid the gunfire.

"Just go," Cathay responded. "We got your back."

"Right behind you," Jim Bob reaffirmed.

Without thinking twice, Cannon pushed his revolver back into the holster at his waistband then turned to shove the steel doorway open. On the other side was yet another awkward gap to get across. The blaring wind rushing by threw him off balance, but this time there was no doorway on the other side. It was an open flatcar piled high with crates.

Cannon jumped across with a careful step. With both of his boots planted firmly on the wooden plank floors of the flatcar, he reached up and held the top of his cowboy hat down against the wind blasting into his face. When he was able to get his bearings, he lifted his eyes to find a blur of trees and limbs as the train powered its way through the piney woods. Humidity mixing against the rushing wind made it difficult to breathe, and the rocking of the train as it barreled to its next, and possibly final destination, made it difficult to stand. He dragged one boot in front of the other until he was up on the train car and locking eyes with a man he knew all too well.

The most prominent gunfighter on Major James's

payroll was standing at the other side of the train car with his hand resting gently on the revolver strapped to his hip. His own cowboy hat was pulled down low over his eyes. A deep, gravelly voice came across the wind to reach Cannon's ears as soon as they made eye contact.

"How's that hand of yours?"

CHAPTER 22

The East Texas sun was burning overhead as two gunslingers with a history of crossing paths only once before stood facing one another. Wind rushed by giving only sparing relief from the sweltering heat. A blur of trees came and went as they passed through pastures and towns of a couple thousand people here and there. It wasn't high noon yet, but it was damn sure about to be.

Cannon felt a familiar shock that started at his shoulder before shooting down his elbow and into his hand. This time it manifested as only a phantom feeling in his missing trigger finger, a piece of himself taken by the man standing across from him.

J.R. Pickett stood motionless ahead of him. He was a menacing silhouette of a man. Cannon had unfortunately grown all-too familiar with what he was capable of. The standoff between the two carried on for several awkward minutes as gunfire popped off behind them, cracking into the air like firecrackers on the fourth. It was a racket that would send most running for cover, but not these two. Instead of fleeing, they stood in place matching stoicism and grit, sizing each other up without saying a single word.

Before Cannon could so much as flinch, the gun hand across from him took a step forward. Without thinking, Cannon did the same. This dance played out as both hesitantly brought themselves closer and closer to the end of a gun barrel once again. Halfway down the flatcar, Cannon finally made the decision to say something for himself. Not to plead for his life or to shy away from the fight, but instead, to antagonize. There was still time to get under his skin.

"You looking forward to dying for what you did to me?"

"Ain't no one gotta die today," J.R. called back to him.

"Except for you."

Cannon took a step closer.

"Nope. Not even me."

J.R. did the same.

"We might not have come here looking for the likes of you." Cannon was just barely loud enough to get his voice over the relentless gusts. "But I can't tell you how happy I am to see your ugly ass face again."

"You never answered me, you know," J.R. ignored his comments. "How's that hand holding up?"

"Come on over here and I'll show you."

A deep chuckle whispered through the wind as the rattling train did its best to stay on the tracks. While neither man would show it, their knees wobbled with every step and their posture leaned into the swaying of the train threatening to throw them off balance. A few more gunshots popped off behind Cannon and this time, he saw bright white teeth behind a forced smile on the man he was facing down.

"You think any of this is going to work out for you? Do you even know if your friends are still alive?"

Cannon lowered his brow and fought the urge to think about anything other than what was happening back there without him. "I'd be more worried about what's gonna happen to you."

Another chuckle came through the wind, setting off Cannon's nerves. They each took a step closer, this time in unison, bringing them no more than ten feet across from one another. They were close enough to see the whites in each other's eyes, as well as the deathly intent that was hidden inside.

"You're on the wrong side," Cannon told him. "You're not gonna win this."

"I don't know what you want, and I don't want to either. I do know you've got this all wrong, though."

"You're about to get real familiar with what I want."

Both Cannon and J.R. took one more step closer to each other, rolling their boots from heel to toe in an attempt to maintain their balance against the rocking of the train. Their voices were easier to hear now, though still muddied by the engine roaring ahead and the constant swell of wind.

Cannon squinted against the sunlight that passed through the trees into his face and fought the urge to wipe the bead of sweat that had started to run down his cheek. He stopped walking and squared up with the hired gun hand just a few feet in front of him. For a fleeting moment, he felt as though he was standing in front of a mirror. He saw his own deadly glare looking right back at him in the eyes of J.R. and in that moment, his stomach sank.

"I know you don't care. You probably don't get paid enough to care, but before we do something we can't take back here, you *should* know what we're doing here."

"You can't control Tȟatȟáŋka Íyotake's curse. No one can."

Cannon was caught off guard and made no attempt at hiding it. "The hell?" he finally let out.

Thunderous pounding of the train rattling onward punctuated the unsettling silence that had fallen between them. Inhaling the smoke without end caused Cannon's eyes to water. He let out a swear beneath his breath and began to find himself hoping that Cathay and Jim Bob would be catching up soon.

"I'm here to find out who my dad is," he said without thinking. "I'm here to find something in Major James's massive historical collection, anything that might even point me in the right direction. I'm sure you already know his reputation precedes him every-where he goes. He brought me here."

"Unless that old man has some bastards I don't know about running around, you're wasting your time then," J.R. told him with a cold tone. "Why do you need to find your dad so bad?"

Cannon hesitated before speaking. He gave himself just long enough to let anger wash over him at the question. "I'm gonna walk by you—or through you—

to the other side of this fancy ass train and I'm gonna find everything that man is hiding from the world. I don't give a damn if it's Sitting Bull's curse or the answer about my family that was promised to me over a year ago. I'm goin' in there."

The gunshots that had been popping off sporadically started to grow more frequent. It sounded like Cathay and Jim Bob were in the thick of it, but Cannon knew they couldn't possibly have the ammunition needed to hold out for much longer.

"It ain't getting any better for them," said J.R. as he moved his right hand closer to his waist. "Or you, for that matter."

"Let me ask you something. You the kind of man to sit back and let thousands die for a paycheck?"

"What are you—"

"Mr. Pickett!" A third voice pierced through the wind with shrewd intensity.

Boots too light to make a sound carried in a man of frail stature around a pile of crates. Slouchy posture, greasy hair that was slicked back to hide a bald spot, and eyes pushed too far together made for a man who wreaked of inadequacy. He strolled out with an unfounded confidence, eyes darting nervously, betraying what little ego he tried to project. This was a man who wasn't certain about his next meal, much less any threats he was trying to cook up in his head. When he finally did speak, his high-pitched, raspy voice confirmed what Cannon had already come to know about him. He wasn't cut out for the job at hand.

"I'd sure hate to tell Major James about how you were out here conspiring with this lowlife. I'd hate even more to have to be the one to tell him about how one of his star performers went and got himself killed."

"No need for all that, Ned," said J.R. without breaking his gaze from Cannon, or lifting his hand from his hip. "We were just gettin' to all that."

"I'm not so sure," Cannon answered. "He never told you what he'd been planning to do, has he? That show in Houston—the one that y'all are all of a sudden in such a rush to get to—that's a suicide mission. Did y'all know that?"

Ned increased his pace to catch up to where J.R. was standing. He may not have been as tall as the gun hand, or as dangerous, but he was every bit mean in his own way. Not many people had the misfortune of learning firsthand that he could spit fire with the best of them, especially when his boss wasn't around.

"The only suicide mission is the one you're on, you no good piece of—"

"Ned," J.R. cut him off. "I told you I got this. Go on back and wait for me. Tell the boss it's all handled."

"Yeah, run along," Cannon smarted off simply because he could.

"Not until I see it," Ned hollered. "Not until I see you pull your gun out and shoot that man down!"

"You think it's just me here? None of y'all are gonna get away with this. If I don't put a stop to this, my friends back there will. And if they don't, the people who sent us are only gonna send more in our place." Cannon was doing his best to either hold out until his help could finally fight through to him, or one of the men in front of him slipped up.

"That may be true," said J.R. "All those people who you keep talking about might show up. They might not, too. Either way, from where I'm standing, those people won't be able to help what's about to happen to you."

"You think so?"

"Kill him, J.R. Pickett!" Ned was spewing saliva as he screamed, but he quickly caught himself. "Once we get to Houston, the Major will explain it all, I can promise you that."

"Like I said before, ain't no one gotta die right here," J.R. said, this time turning his eyes back to Ned standing behind him. "My paycheck clears all the same regardless of how many bullets I shoot."

"You seem like a reasonable man," Cannon told him. "You want money? The people I work with will never stop coming up with new ways to get you paid. It's what they do. With your skillset, you'd be hard pressed not to be richer than your boss could ever dream of in a matter of months."

J.R. finally let his eyes fall before speaking. "How many did you say the Major was trying to kill?"

"Mr. Picket!" Ned was getting more and more furious. "If you do not kill that man standing in front of you, I'll be left with no choice but to fix this problem myself. Am I the only one left in the world with a sense of loyalty? With a sense of humility?"

Cannon moved his left hand over to his hip to match J.R.'s just in case things started to turn south in a hurry. His palm was damp with sweat, but his fingers were steady. The rattling train was far from an advantageous background to what was happening, but if he was being honest with himself, he'd certainly been in worse positions before. With a hard swallow, he spoke up again.

"It'll be the death of thousands if Major James isn't stopped," said Cannon. "That's what you'll die for, and what you'll always be remembered for. That what you want?"

"I will not tell you again!" Ned demanded, his voice cracking in and out with self-righteous fury that was unbecoming of his own position.

As if they were summoned by his very words, one gun-wielding paid mercenary after another came pouring out of the train car from behind the sniveling Ned. Their assault rifles were equipped with double mags, red dots, and suppressors that gave them the appearance of being more deadly with the firearms than they most likely were. They were silent as they spread out behind the piles of crates that filled the flat-car, until all at once, an all too familiar clanging of the rifles being racked to chamber a round.

Their synchronicity felt rehearsed. So much so that Cannon couldn't help but to let out a chuckle. He shifted his stance and kept his hand hovering over his trusted revolver. It had gotten him out of far worse situations than what was unfolding in front of him. Despite the numbers he was facing down, his eyes remained locked on only one. He'd been beaten to the draw before by the man standing across from him, and he damn sure wasn't about to let it happen again.

It was the calm before the storm, settling in like a death penalty verdict waiting to read aloud. No one expected to lose their life on a train rushing to Houston, much less over some old man's power trip. Cannon knew better, though. He knew his last good hand was about to be forced. Before the calm was interrupted in the soon-to-come drowning cacophony of gunfire aimed right at him, Cannon saw the gunman dart both of his eyes to Ned, still standing as pissed as ever at his side. Then, J.R. winked.

That was it. The line in the sand had been drawn and the sides were set. It was all Cannon needed to see to urge him forward. He took no qualms with being the first to let loose the fires of Hell. There was too much at stake to do anything otherwise. Like a bolt of lightning flashing into the sky, Cannon yanked out his .45 and spewed flame and smoke and even death itself before anyone else could think to react.

BANG.

Instead of setting off a crossfire of head-hunting lead, Cannon's draw was admired by every person on the train holding a gun. The smoke from his shot cleared in the rushing wind of the train speeding down the tracks, but no one collapsed.

J.R. remained still. His hand was locked onto his hip and his eyes stayed forward to not give anything away. He was the first to hear the gurgling sounds coming from his side. Strained breathing laced with shock was growing frantic by the second. The ragged gasps for air that haunted the rushing wind of the train would never be easily forgotten.

Cannon watched as Ned came to terms with what had just happened to him. The right-hand man felt blood streak down his forehead and sting his eyes first. Then, his knees began to wobble, and the blackness creeping into this vision sent his mind into a frenzy. Everyone hopes to see their life flash before their eyes when death begins to take hold, but in those few fleeting moments, Ned saw only a smoking gun pointed right at him.

The bullet fired from Cannon's revolver found its mark in the middle of Ned's forehead. A bloodied mist sprayed out from behind his head. An exit wound the size of a half-dollar coin revealed itself, matted with hair, flesh, and bone. Despite the wind and the clanging steel of the train hurling itself forward, each person standing on the flatcar could hear Ned fighting with everything he had to stay alive with jarring clarity. After those handful of excruciating seconds, the longtime right-hand man of Major James fell lifeless to the ground.

A hard thump of his body falling snapped the tension. J.R. spun around, pistol in hand, and slapped the hammer three times, blasting out shots that sent three men to the ground right along with Ned. He lunged behind the crates to his left just as Cannon scrambled for cover on his right.

Just as the bullets began to rain down on the two men who'd found themselves in the line of fire once again, the steel door behind Cannon was thrown open and his odds of living improved just a little bit. Jim Bob led the charge through the doorway, his revolver cycling through rounds faster than it should have. Cathay was right behind him, rocking the lever action on her rifle to send one shot after another down the flatcar. They moved in unison, step by step, matching each other as if they didn't actually bicker like an old married couple every chance they got. With gunpowder and smoke blasting in every direction, they carved their way into the fight.

"Hell yeah!" Cannon screamed with a four-fingered fist held into the air.

"Thought you was gonna have all the fun without us?" Jim Bob called out as he let loose the last two rounds in the cylinder. "She almost made us late."

"Wouldn't do us any good to get shot in the ass once we got here," said Cathay, who followed close behind, ducking her way out of incoming fire. "What happened here?"

"Killed one. The other one saved me."

"Glad to have you on the winning side," Jim Bob hollered ahead to the double-crosser. "Got a name?"

"Pickett," he hollered back. "J.R. Pickett."

Cannon watched as J.R. twisted out from behind the crate he was kneeled behind and shot three more rounds. This time only two men cried out and hit the ground. The third bullet slammed into a wooden crate only inches away from a hired hand's face. Shards splintered out from the crate and the man it protected swung himself behind for safety. It was the move that Cannon needed.

Determined to finally start taking control of the gunfight, Cannon stepped out from behind his cover and went to work.

His first shot went through the neck of a man doing his damndest to get out of the way, leaving him scrambling to the floor with his hand clutching his throat. The next bullets found a home buried in the chest of two men. Cannon walked forward without flinching, gripping his revolver in his left hand. He fought for every inch of the train car with relentless force. With every squeeze of the trigger, he advanced just a little further. He soon stepped over the deceased body of Ned Burwell, still bleeding out into the floors of the train car, and fired off the last of his remaining three rounds.

BANG. BANG. BANG.

He watched two of the hollow point bullets go to waste as they slammed into a crate. The third nestled itself into the shoulder of a man who'd gotten the jump on him with a rifle, failing to stop him from returning fire. The 5.56 rounds from the rifle luckily whizzed by without any accuracy, leaving Cannon with just enough time to step behind a new stack of crates for cover. He pushed the cowboy hat back down further on his head before he started the process of reloading his revolver. The clinking of six brass casings dumping to the floor joined a similar symphony as just about everyone else took the same opportunity to reload.

Sensing the break in the gunfight, Cannon took advantage of the timing by only shoving three rounds into his cylinder before slapping it back into place and pulling back the hammer with a familiar click. With his reload cut in half, he popped out from behind cover, fired off a round into a surprised gun hand who fell over clutching his gut, then turned to grab the man hiding while trying to push a new magazine into his rifle.

Cannon gripped the screaming hot barrel of the rifle and lifted it into the air, letting out a painful yelp as he put all his weight into it. With his revolver tucked closely to his hip, he aimed at the stomach of the man still trying to pull his rifle back down and fired off two more rounds into his torso. Blood began to flow freely from the freshly opened bullet holes. The man bellowed in response. His eyes widened, creating more wrinkles on his already aged face hidden behind an overgrown beard. It was a cry that was more fear than pain. A faint splatter of his blood streaked across Cannon's face before the man fell unconscious to the ground only seconds later.

As Cannon stood over the man reloading his revolver once again, Cathay and Jim Bob pushed forward in his absence, clearing out the rest of the flatcar with newfound aggression. Severe burns on his palm that were too raw to scab over made each shell he dropped into the cylinder hurt all over again. Between each click of the round finding its place, Cannon allowed a new feeling of regret to wash over him.

He'd gotten himself and two people he actually cared about mixed up in the most deadly stunt he could think of on the off chance of finding answers about someone who'd never been in his life before. Anyone could play hero and foil Major James's plans to kill thousands likely with the curse that J.R. had mentioned. It wasn't anyone onboard the train though, it was him.

It was too late for any of that to stop him now. Regardless of what got him onto the train, or even whatever it was inside him that needed to find out who your dad was so desperately, there were people who needed saving. Focusing on these simple truths was the only thing that could keep his mind on track. It didn't help that he was forced to use his already-mangled right hand to grab the barrel of that man's rifle. The burns stinging his hands were disorientating and distracting.

"We're clear for now." Cathay's voice came from behind him, pulling him back into reality. "You all right?"

"Yeah," he said without looking up. "Cathay, I gotta tell you—"

"Not yet," she cut him off. "We ain't done yet. Whatever it is you need to get off your chest can wait until after we're through with this mess."

He turned to face her. With a gentle nod, he patted her shoulder with what was left of his right hand, leaving a bloodstain on her shirt from his wrappings that had started leaking in the fight. It was the only moment they could have before it was time to get back to the job at hand.

"I don't know who you are, and I still don't forgive you for taking my damn trigger finger," Cannon finally spoke to the man still leaned up against a stack of crates. "But I owe you one."

"More than one," said J.R. "I'll be waiting to hear from you about that money you promised me."

"It was a job, actually."

"Either way, you remember what happened here when the authorities start showing up and asking about all the dead bodies. I don't want none of this coming back to me."

"Before you go, I'd like to ask, why did you turn on the Major?"

"I'll tell you the same thing I told him—I go where the money goes."

Before Cannon could respond, J.R. turned and pushed his way through a pile of crates that had fallen over in the fight. He made his way over to the same door Jim Bob had burst through when he and Cathay joined the fight. The once headlining act of the Major James Out West Show passed into the doorway and out of sight without so much as a glance back.

"I like him," said Jim Bob.

"I do too," Cathay agreed. "We should've told him to stick around a little longer."

Cannon let out a sigh as his only response. The trees that had lined their path down the tracks toward Houston had started to give way. Small towns and crossways backed up with traffic were sprouting up here and there. All three could hear the dinging of yet another blocked crossing approaching in the distance as they tried to figure out their next move.

"Being completely honest, I never thought we'd get this far," Jim Bob admitted.

"We ain't done." Cannon finally spoke up. "Not even by a long shot."

He walked to the front of the flatcar and gazed out at the seven dead bodies mixed into overturned crates splattered with blood. Overlooking the devastation that he and those who stood next to him had just brought with them, he came to the understanding that all three of them together could take on the world and maybe even see it through. An auspicious confidence arose in the pit of his belly. It swelled inside him until it manifested itself into a smile wrapped across his face.

"But thanks to the both of you," he continued without making eye contact with either Jim Bob or Cathay just yet. "We're gonna get through this."

"I wouldn't be so sure." Cathay stepped up. "We still don't know what Major James has planned or how he plans to do it. Whatever is inside that train car, on the other side of that door, it's gotta be dangerous as hell."

"It ain't like we're not careful," Jim Bob smarted off, garnering empty stares from both Cathay and Cannon.

"I might have an idea of what this is all about," said Cannon. "The sharpshooter who just abandoned the Major thought we were after what he called Thatháŋka Íyotake's curse."

"Who?"

"That's—"

"Sitting Bull," Cannon went ahead. "Thatháŋka Íyotake is his real name. They say that when Buffalo Bill was touring the world with his hundreds of horses, steers, and elk, alongside thousands of other Natives, performers, and people only looking to make a living, he gave Thatháŋka Íyotake a job."

"What does this have to do with anything?"

"Major James is a collector, a historian," said Cannon. "He is just the kind of person who would have heard the rumors about what Sitting Bull would do to kick off Buffalo Bill's Wild West Shows."

"I can't follow this for shit. I got booted out of

history class back in high school because I showed up smelling like this right here," Jim Bob admitted while holding up his handy flask one more time.

"Tȟatȟáŋka Íyotake was Lakota, and he spent most of his life in conflict one way or another. When Buffalo Bill gave him a job, he was a prisoner on his own land. They say that he was allowed to join the show as a popular attraction, tasked with the seemingly simple task of making a single lap around the arena on horseback. He gave speeches where he would speak of a different kind of future, but that isn't all he would say."

"The curse..." Cathay started to put the pieces together.

"That's right. Tȟatȟáŋka Íyotake has long been rumored to have cursed audiences beneath his breath in his own tongue. I ain't a betting man, but if I were, I'd damn sure put all my money on that being the same curse that J.R. was talking about."

"That don't even begin to make sense," said Jim Bob.

"Trust me," said Cannon. "I've seen much stranger things. We don't know for sure, but it's better to assume that anything is still on the table."

"What's the move then?" Cathay asked.

"If Major James really has found a way to control Tȟatȟáŋka Íyotake's curse, to somehow wield it against others—then we've gotta get it out of his hands."

CHAPTER 23

Stepping back through time is a dream often sought after, by romantics and realists alike, desperate to create and recreate the world in their own imaginations without end. It is a state of mind at best for most, a place they can visit in their own stories, perfectly content in the ability to come and go as they please. If given the chance, however, there aren't many who would value the chance to see time as it really was—unruly.

When Cannon, Cathay, and Jim Bob stepped beneath the steel archway and beyond the dented door showing signs of rust, they put themselves firmly in the embrace of a Wild West history, an era from long ago. It wasn't a dream, though, it was more like stepping into a crypt. A few paces in, the three were bathed in a warm yellow glow cast out from only a handful of bulbs swinging from the ceiling of the steel box they found themselves inside. The shadows that danced across the room gave each of them an inexplicably uneasy feeling. This was punctuated by the increasingly rough ride of the train that bounced and shook as it rushed down the tracks.

Despite there being a museum in every sense of the word stretching out before them, the group could only focus on the sign stretched out above their heads every bit as wide as the train car itself. Aged and worn, it featured a steam locomotive, dozens of military men clad in uniforms and weapons alike, cowboys perched on horses with lassos and six-shooters, stoic Native Americans tracing the border, and a single portrait of a mustachioed, long-bearded elderly man donning a politely rugged smile. Above his head was a string of unforgettable words.

BUFFALO BILL'S WILD WEST AND CONGRESS OF ROUGH RIDERS OF THE WORLD

"Would you look at that," said Cannon, his eyes tracing the banner only half-lit by the glow of the room.

"A bit on the nose, don't you think?" Cathay quipped.

The group took a step forward in unison before fanning out in separate paths winding through the maze of books, artifacts, artwork, and trophies—remnants of a lost age. Each person was more delicate than the last when they moved, trying to steady themselves against the swaying of the train. As Jim Bob and Cathay let their eyes wander in curiosity and confusion, Cannon stared straight ahead without wavering. The key to his own past would be found here somewhere.

A harsh cough breaking through the silence of the

train car from deep within the hoarder's nest of antiquities from the old West startled all three of them. In
the distance was the one who'd have the answers
Cannon was promised over a year ago. He was
beckoned toward the raspy gasps of life to find the
answers of his own.

The guttural hacking continued from a plump,
bearded elderly man with a single leg propped up on an
oversized wooden desk, buried in stacks of documents.
The twirls in his mustache pressed against his chubby
red cheeks. He wasn't focused on the three of them
barging onto his train or killing all of his staff, though.
In his lap was an old, inconspicuous leather bag. He
was hunched over in a coughing fit when the group had
barged in, completely consumed by his ailment.

"It's all over, Major James," Cannon hollered across
the train car, lifting his trusted .45 revolver up with his
hands pressed tight to the roughened wood grain
grips.

Despite finally being able to suppress his coughs,
the Major's eyes never left the bag. He didn't speak at
first, or even blink. He just stared.

"Ain't no one left for you to hide behind, you
coward crock of shit." Cathay couldn't help herself.

"You see this," said Cannon with a wag of the end
of his revolver. "This is the end of your so-called tour,
the end of the trail of bodies you've left behind this
train, and the end of you."

Jim Bob weaseled his way through the Major's
collection in an effort to get around to the other side of
the man in charge, just in case he needed to get the

jump. Against the back-and-forth swaying of the lights overhead, Jim Bob walked quietly up behind Major James.

The older man's eyes still remained locked on the leather bag resting in his lap.

"Go ahead and put that bag on the desk and stand up," Cannon continued, growing more uneasy by the second yet refusing to show it.

The Major's one good leg, unbeknownst to any of the three hell-bent on destroying what little remained in his life, was the one propped up onto his desk. He looked like he was comfortable, not at all riled up from their breaking in. In fact, he looked more content with what was happening than anything else in his life. There was even the faintest trace of a smile inching its way onto his face.

"It's so hard to find good help these days," Major James finally spoke softly. "It sure took you long enough, but I always knew you'd come. Your restless, roaming spirit would have never allowed you to stay at home too long, even after everything your family was given."

"We know what you're trying to do here," said Cannon, raising his voice as he spoke and ignoring the words slithering from the showman's lips. "I almost don't even believe it myself, but I've met assholes like you before. People willing to forsake anyone and anything in their path for something that isn't even real."

"Funny you would say such a thing," Major James said, refusing to raise his own. "Considering what brought you here, what you killed and maimed and hurt without end to find."

"I'm not the one planning on killing thousands of innocent people just for the simple fact that I'm able to."

"We're the same, you and I. Whether you want to admit it or not."

"Maybe we are. I ain't going to argue that with you after everything I've done," admitted Cannon. "I only want you to give me what's due, what you promised over a year ago."

"You'll have to remind me again what exactly that was," said Major James with a smirk as he looked to make eye contact with both Cathay and Jim Bob. "I *am* a feeble old man, you know."

"Tell me what you know about my father."

Before Cannon could even finish his sentence, Major James let out a hearty laugh that resonated from his bulging belly. It was deep and booming, and it mixed into the roar of the train still pounding its way down the tracks to a steel-clanging tune of its own making. All Cannon could do was watch and grow more furious by the second. The laugh that echoed out soon turned back into coughing, though, and the next few minutes were filled only with the wheezing of the Major catching his breath.

"You'll die sitting right there if you don't tell me what I want to know," Cannon told him, almost speaking through his teeth now.

"Don't let him get to you," Cathay warned. "He wants you not thinkin' straight."

"Listen to the girl," Major James said, only just

now taking his eyes off the leather bag in his lap for the first time. "She isn't quite as stupid as the one thinking he can sneak up on me in my own home."

"It's your choice, no one else's," said Cannon after a quick wave to Jim Bob to slow his pace. "I'll kill you where you sit if you don't tell me what you know. That'll put a stop to any plans you have to commit mass murder, I guarantee you that."

"Doesn't sound like much of a choice, tough guy," Major James commented.

"Or," Cannon continued without acknowledging the tour boss. "I can turn you over to the NHCP, maybe even put in a good word to some friends of mine to spare your life. Either way, whatever you had planned in Houston sure as shit ain't happening."

"You think you know what's happening, but you have no idea. None of you do."

"We're all ears."

Before he said anything else, the Major dragged his one good leg down from the table and forced himself to stand. With cracking knees and a sigh that lasted as long as it took to stand up straight, Major James brought himself eye level with those who had broken into his train. He didn't seem afraid or angry at their intrusion. With a deep breath, the Major once again pushed a handkerchief to his mouth and began another series of hard coughs that came from deep in his chest.

When Cannon looked at him, he didn't see the deadly mastermind Etta had painted a picture of. He saw only a man who was at the end of his rope. There was a mixture of restless exhaustion and dying ambition that emanated from his every move.

Cannon kept his six-shooter aimed at the old man's forehead as the distance between them grew shorter and shorter. A familiar clicking of the Major's cane echoed off the metal walls of the train car. His steps were broken, his breathing was noticeably labored, and his posture was haphazard. He came to stand no more than a couple of feet from Cannon's face but didn't say a word.

Still gripping the handle to the mysterious leather bag that hung by his side, the showman took a few seconds to enjoy a silent deep breath with his eyes squeezed shut as if he was savoring the sweetest of moments never to be had again. When he opened his eyes again, he spoke to Cannon as though he was the only other person on the train with him.

"You aren't in a position to make demands like you think you are. You come in here expecting the world to bend to your will, or the end of your gun, as it always has, but you're too late. You're all too late."

"What makes you think that?"

"Our little carriage tonight is not what it seems." The Major lifted his arms wide into the air. "It is a vessel for my salvation, one way or another."

"You're gonna have to be more clear than that, old man," Cannon told him without so much as a flinch from his revolver.

"It's a meat wagon now, and not just because of the bodies you left behind. You see, I will make my mark one way or another in the pages of history. It's supposed to happen, so there's nothing you could really do about it anyway. Why else would you think Tȟatȟáŋka Íyotake came to me?"

"I think you're doing what people like you always do," said Cannon. "You take what isn't yours, and if it isn't up for taking, you lie, cheat, swindle, and steal to make sure it ends up in those grubby little hands of yours anyway."

"Poor kid," said the Major, turning to stroll through his collection like a captain overseeing. "This train is getting to Houston one way or another. Either in one piece or about a million."

"Shit," Cathay blurted out.

"Wait, what?"

"I'll tell you later," Cannon told Jim Bob out of the corner of his mouth before turning his attention back to Major James who was walking through his collection. "You said I had a decision to make."

As the showman moved throughout his life's work, piled high in some places almost to the ceiling, the train rattled harder than it normally did. Just to his left, a stack of century-old letters with broken wax seals collapsed to the floor before a taxidermy trophy of a snarling wolf tucked away in the corner toppled over. The engine roared outside the steel walls and the floor shook more violently than it ever had, but Major James didn't stumble once.

"You can stop the train and save those poor, innocent, helpless souls," Major James cooed into a George Catlin tribal portrait of a stern-faced man with shapeless markings and a regalia that knew only how to evoke strength. "Or you can finally find the answer you've so desperately sought, the *truth* about who your dad really is."

Cannon's eyes widened at the words that had struck him like a ton of bricks. His chest sank, and both Cathay and Jim Bob knew immediately what was going through his mind. It was written all over his face. Without even giving himself a chance to think about what the answer should have been, he'd made up his mind.

"Don't risk it," said Cathay, trying her best to cut him off.

"It ain't worth it," Jim Bob chimed in.

"Maybe it's not," Major James interrupted with a smile finding its way onto his face that none of them could see. "Maybe I'm even lying to you. Who knows? That's a chance you're gonna have to take. Just think about this—what if I'm not?"

Cannon was ready to give his answer. It was on the tip of his tongue. Considering the choices he'd been given, it should've been an easy one. Before he had a chance to let the Major know what was about to happen, he was interrupted by yet another violent coughing fit. The old man was still perusing his own stash of priceless ancient artifacts and useless remembrances when he hunched over and lurched forward with every heave.

While waiting on the broken breathing of Major James trying to find air in his lungs, Cannon afforded himself the opportunity to steal a glance at both Cathay and Jim Bob once more. They were nudging him to make the right choice without saying a word, and they weren't doing a single thing to hide it. Their faces told the same story—stop the train.

He acknowledged each with a nod that assured them he was on the same page. The lights swaying more violently overhead caused shadows to drench them all before washing away in a harsh yellow light. Another jarring slam downward on the train sent stacks of books scattering to the ground and paintings falling from the walls.

The Major limped his way back toward his desk with an outstretched hand leaning on his cane. He rested his hip against the edge of the wooden desk and perched himself on it like a stool. Despite having just been nearly fighting for his life to catch his breath, he watched Cannon with a look on his face that was at an unnatural ease.

"I don't have as much time as you think," he told Cannon. "So, what'll it be?"

Cannon stared down Major James for two minutes straight. He let his eyes fall to his prosthetic leg hidden behind stained white pleated pants and noticed his tweed jacket that matched the stains more than the pants. His bushy beard and convincing eyes were nothing like the twisted words that came from his tongue.

"Tell me who my dad is," Cannon said.

"Cannon, no!" Cathay screamed out.

"What are you doing? You're bullshitting, right?" Jim Bob said.

"Tell me!" Cannon hollered over them both.

The laugh that started in Major James's gut was no more than a chuckle at first, but it soon grew into a boisterous howl that could've just as likely come from a thirty-year-old man in his prime.

"Come, come," he finally forced through his laughs. "This all started with my own great interest in the final American frontier. I have played in the medium of the Wild West for most of my life, and they always said my shows were built to shock, but even I couldn't have come up with an ending like this."

Cannon could hear the pleas of his friends on either side, but tunnel vision had completely settled in around him. He focused only the Major who was shuffling off behind the wooden desk at the center of the train car. Within a matter of seconds, Major James had the old, cracked and stained leather bag back in his hands. Cannon couldn't help but notice that the elderly man cradled it with reverence like nothing he would ever hold again could be as important.

The Major glanced up from the bag to motion Cannon over. "Come closer. Big Betty has us all, don't be afraid," he said.

"Cannon, he's lying to you," Cathay told him. "We're here to kill that son of a bitch, nothing else."

Cannon took a step forward, then another. He approached the Major like he was in a trance of his own making. Each delicate step carried him closer to the last missing piece in his life. He tried to consider contingencies to what he was doing, but his thoughts were scattered.

"I only want answers," he finally said. "You give me what I want and I'll spare your life."

"Answers you shall get, my boy, just come a bit closer."

"Don't listen to him!" Cathay called out.

Major James was hovering over the bag with shadows dancing across his face as the roar of the engine grew louder and louder. They were picking up speed and the train did everything it could to let them know. Each bump turned into a crater-sized hole that sent artifacts scattering across the floor in every direction. What was once a meticulously set up collection was now a frenzied, chaotic mess.

Cannon did as he was told, hoping to at long last reach anything other than a dead end to find who your dad was. His life had a cavity that was finally going to be filled. He reached the Major's side to the soundtrack of a screaming engine mixed with the cries of his friends for making an impossible decision. It had to be done. There was no other choice to be made.

"The things we want most in life are right here," said Major James with a gentle pat on top of the leather bag.

"I only want one thing," Cannon answered.

"Don't do it! Don't!"

The Major reached down to unfasten a single strap keeping the flap of the leather bag closed, shaking slightly with every movement. Now that he was up close, Cannon could smell the harsh musk that came from him. As he studied the man's face, Cannon noticed a slight drop of blood dripping from the corner of his mouth. Its crimson streak punctuated his deeply wrinkled face. It was a sign of the cost to be paid. It was a moment that he had obsessed over, fought and killed for, and he couldn't believe he'd finally found it after all this time. His stomach was flipping. His eyes strained to focus ahead. There was only one thing left to do—look inside the bag.

The next few seconds would be what determined the rest of his life, though he couldn't bring himself to understand the weight of it at the time. With a motion as simple as raising his hand, Major James unleashed a hell that no one else in the room could have imagined.

Bang.

Cannon darted his eyes over to the source of the gunfire only to see Cathay holding her lever action rifle pointed up into the sky. She slammed the lever down before yanking it back up to chamber another round and fired again.

Bang.

She repeated the motions once, jamming another shell into the barrel before firing off one more bullet.

Bang.

Cannon watched her without realizing she'd saved his life, but Major James had already succumbed.

The showman's eyes began to cry tears of blood as a serene smile washed gently across his face. He was beholden to the power he wielded for the final time. Experiencing his insides twisting and his brain melting to liquid, turning to sludge between his ears, Major James began to shake with violent convulsions. His fingers trembled, his knees knocked together, and his pupils rolled around inside his head.

"Just keep looking at me," said Cathay.

Before Cannon could answer, he was tackled to the ground, falling face first into the hardwood floor. His head slamming into the cracked boards was no different than having his own sense slapped back into him. When he finally skidded to a stop, he felt the weight of someone else lying on top of him and saw that it was Jim Bob.

"Close one there, buddy," he said with a smile. "You owe me one."

When he could finally roll over and get a look at Major James, his jaw fell open at what was happening. It was unlike anything he'd seen before.

The bag held his gaze like he'd been hypnotized. Blood poured from his ears, nose, mouth, and eyes in unison, covering his once-white clothes in a deep red stain that dripped to the floorboards. He sputtered and spat more blood out as the convulsions took over his entire body. Somehow, he managed to lift each of his hands out by his side, quivering and shuddering, and let out a wail that Cannon, Cathay, and Jim Bob would each take to their graves.

Without another word, the Major collapsed into a pool of his own blood, splashing it across the flying remnants of his collection still falling down around him. The train screamed forward as the three of them watched in silence as the last breath let loose from the showman's lungs.

"I screwed it all up," Cannon said, his eyes locked on the body of Major James. "I made the wrong choice y'all. This is all my fault."

Cathay and Jim Bob were standing over the top of him as he fell apart on the floor of the train. He was as broken as the Major in his own way, unable to come to terms with what he'd just done.

"I thought I could get what I wanted and still stop him," he admitted. "I thought I could do it *all*."

Cannon sank his face into his hands and started to cry. His shoulders heaved up and down, but no sounds escaped other than his panicked attempts at breathing.

"It's over," he let out.

Before he could say anything else, a hand rested on his shoulder. He pulled his face out to see Cathay leaned over him. She winked softly before she started to talk.

"We're still here," she said. "We'll figure this out together."

"I can't stop the train. That asshole is still going to get what he wanted, and all I got was another damned dead end! I just keep taking us backward."

"Well, I don't know about your dad or anything like that," Jim Bob said as he walked up behind them. "But I worked the railroad as a kid and these old 4-8-4s could hit 120 miles an hour in their heyday, but it ain't actually all that hard to stop an FEF steam locomotive."

Cathay turned to look at him with her eyebrow arched in intrigue. "You can stop it?"

"Sure can."

Jim Bob's answer was blunt, but he wasn't joking by any means. His placid response was contrasted by the unruly clutter thrashing around inside the train car as they reached uncontrollable speeds.

"How?"

"Funny enough, he just said how," Jim Bob told them both. "Don't you get it?"

The shrieking of the steel wheels against the rails pierced their ears. They could hear the wind rushing past through the bullet holes Cathay's newfound Winchester .30-30 lever action had just put into the ceiling. Cannon was lost in his own misery on the floor, and Cathay was doing everything she could to keep calm.

"You just go backward."

Cathay was the first to let out a booming laugh, and although Jim Bob couldn't exactly explain why, he joined in soon after. Cannon fought the urge at first—he truly did try not to laugh—but the irony was just too much to take.

CHAPTER 24

"I swear, I saw him peeping out from behind a stack of square bales. So, I scoot my ass over just a little bit more to break cover and I'll be damned if a shot doesn't graze right by my left ear. If there was any hair on it before, that bullet took it down to nothin' but peach fuzz."

"I thought I was the one who tagged him?"

"Are you kiddin' me? No way," Jim Bob waved his hand to brush Cathay's claims off.

"I'm pretty sure that one was me. Lanky guy with short hair wearing mostly black, right?"

"Come on, you know damned well that describes more than half of those goons."

Cannon just sat there, watching the two go back and forth like nothing had changed for them. Their bickering was a constant in a world always changing, always leaving him behind no matter how hard he fought. A smirk came across his face.

"So, who got the shot off exactly?" he asked both of them.

"It was—"

"Me," Cathay cut Jim Bob off with a side eye that could kill.

The trusty old stainless flask made its way back into Cannon's hand after a brief chuckle at their argument. He held the lukewarm whiskey and thought about the way it burned his tongue and warmed his belly after every drink. He was finally able to settle in for just a few moments and enjoy the company, and the fact that he wasn't being shot at too, so he decided not to take a swig this time and passed the flask on.

They'd made their way back to the NHCP headquarters in the historic city of Jefferson only a few hours before. The lobby was a mundane place to end up in after everything they'd gone through. Somehow, all three of them escaped the inevitable headlines when the train came to a stop and the authorities found the violence they'd left behind. Every news station in the area picked up on the story of the mad Major James and how he tried to kill everyone he came across. The only thing they didn't discover was the showman's prized collection.

Cannon watched as a continuous line of men carrying boxes stacked two, sometimes three high, containing just about everything they could get their hands on inside the Major's train car. Some were dragging in oversized paintings with canvas draped over them, others were hauling in statues and trophies that were too big to cover. He looked down instinctively at his side, checking to make sure the leather bag they'd recovered was still where he'd put it. With his left hand, he reached out and scooted it closer to him before turning his attention back to the banter at hand.

The flask only made the rotation between the two in front of him one more time before they were interrupted by the clicking of heels on outdated tile flooring headed their direction. A familiar voice soon followed. All three had to crane their necks to see Etta with a wide smile, shaking her head as she approached them.

"I can't even begin to describe the trove of information you just gave us," she said, still walking briskly. "It's going to take us years to work our way through all of this. It's going to change lives for people who thought their own history had been lost."

"Glad we could be of service," Cathay answered for everyone.

"We need to talk about this whole Thatȟáŋka Íyotake's curse, though," Etta told them.

Cannon patted the leather bag sitting next to him. "I already told you. It's real. That's all you need to know."

"I hear you, but I'll be the one to make the decision on what I need to know. As much as I want to take you for your word, we have to think about what we could learn from whatever is inside that bag."

"Well, ma'am, after what we seen that thing do to Major James, I'm not so sure you want to learn much else about it," Jim Bob answered.

"Trust us." Cannon felt the seriousness hit his voice and watched as Etta shifted uncomfortably. "This thing can't be trusted to anyone. We got lucky that the

Major wasn't able to use the way he wanted to. Next time, we may not be so lucky."

"What exactly is it you think we do here?" Etta crossed her arms as she asked them.

Men were still filing in and out of the headquarters location, causing the humid air to sweep in and replace the air conditioning every time the door swung open. Fluorescent lighting hummed above them, offsetting the mindless chatter of those tasked with unloading the Major's collection of antiquities. There was a musty odor that filtered in through the room, likely wafting from the old books and letters being hauled inside.

Cannon looked around at the commotion going on before he finally figured the question that Etta asked wasn't a rhetorical one. He'd worked for them long enough to know their mission. The NHCP existed to recover and restore the lost history of the Americas, preserve a stolen heritage that would otherwise be gone forever, and ensure the next generation can access their own culture. It was a mission he believed in, but he knew that Tȟatȟáŋka Íyotake's curse was something else entirely.

"The NHCP exists to recover and restore—"

"I know all that, Etta," Cannon cut her off. "This is different."

He watched as his boss let out a sigh that couldn't be ignored. She let it hang between them long enough for her to push her fingers into her eyes. After a few seconds of contemplating how to move forward, Etta finally spoke up.

"I trust you," she told them. "I trust all of you, but

you need to know that there are other forces at play. If what you told us about Tȟatȟáŋka Íyotake's curse turns out to be anything even remotely close to the truth, it could change everything for us. We don't live in a world where secrets are so easily kept anymore."

"This is one the entire NHCP needs to keep," Cannon implored her. "It is the voice of Tȟatȟáŋka Íyotake—not the curse—that is ours to protect. It ain't up to assholes like Major James, or whoever decides to take his place. It's up to us."

There wasn't much Etta could say in response to Cannon. Instead, everything he needed to know was written plainly across her face in the look she gave him. With an outstretched hand, she reached toward Cannon and gestured for the bag that was by his side. The leather was tacky and the deep wrinkles on its surface were easily felt. What was once a chestnut leather had turned almost black throughout its years of unknown hardships. Its strap was coiled loosely on top of the more structured frame of the bag, giving it the appearance of a gift neatly wrapped with a bow on top.

Cannon gripped the bag, feeling as though he'd made his case for what needed to happen, and gently held it up to place it in Etta's hand. She reached for the strap and wasted no time in slinging it over her shoulder. Instead of saying thank you, or even acknowledging Cannon for turning the leather bag over, she grabbed the closest employee in the lobby by the shoulder. A well-kempt man with speckled hair wearing a gray suit and black leather bolo tie turned to attention without saying a word.

"Warehouse fifteen, in the back lot," she told the man with a lower tone. "Go straight there."

Without another word, she shoved the leather bag into the chest of the employee who turned and disappeared into the swarm of people moving in every direction. Cannon watched it disappear as mysteriously as it entered into his life. In that moment, he knew he'd done the right thing, though he probably would never be able to understand why.

"I'm still trying to figure out how y'all got on the train to begin with." Etta's focus returned to the group, her hands now resting on her hips. "There isn't a ticket unaccounted for or an abandoned car in the area, it's like you just showed up onboard."

"Told you both the horses were a damn good idea," said Cathay.

"I never said they weren't," Cannon agreed.

Jim Bob scrunched his face. "For what it's worth, ma'am, I did actually disagree with using horses to rob that train. Mostly because they wouldn't get me my own damn horse to ride."

Cannon and Cathay shared one more hearty laugh at Jim Bob's expense as they fondly remembered the sight of him clung onto the back of a horse, complaining and cussing the whole time. It was a sight that neither were soon to forget, much less ever let him live down.

Etta had seen enough. "Forget I asked," she told them while waving her hands in the air and shaking her head. "Before I go, though," she added, looking to make eye contact with Cannon. "Did you ever have luck finding any leads on your dad?"

Cannon let the disappointment of coming up short fall on him again. The laughter that was in his eyes faded away and his shoulders sank just a bit lower. Risking the lives of both his new partners chasing down yet another rabbit hole wasn't something he'd ever be proud of. He anxiously rubbed at the back of his neck before finding the words to respond.

"Just another dead end," he told her.

"Not for lack of trying either, for what it's worth," Cathay threw in her two cents.

"He about gave us a heart attack going after all that," Jim Bob said, not to be outdone.

"You told them?"

Cannon eyed each of them, both grateful for their covering of his disastrous decision-making and wincing at just how much they really know about him. "Looks like it," he told Etta. "They got it out of me, if I'm being honest. Had to come clean if we were gonna see this thing through like we did."

"Good for you," said Etta. "I shouldn't be the only person who knows about this lonesome crusade of your own making."

"Well, you ain't. Not anymore at least."

"Since you're in such a sharing spirit, now might be a good time to tell you that someone else was waiting on you to get back."

Cannon scrunched his eyebrows as he thought about who she could mean. He relaxed them immediately when he saw who came around the corner next. His face was one of shock at first, but it soon passed, giving way to only a warm welcome. His knuckles whitened first above clenched fists before he found the strength in his knees to finally stand.

"Mom," he said as he got up from his seat in the lobby and held out his arms. "I'm sorry I never told you where I was."

Rose had hair that draped down her back, framing her face in a way that showed just how much she relished the new contentment in a blissful corner of the world she'd carved for herself. She looked happy and at peace. Her eyes glinted in the light like a colorful reflection from stained glass. When she scooped Cannon up, her embrace was as warm as ever.

There must've been a few minutes of silence between the two as they stood in each other's arms, refusing to say even a single word. It was a moment that Cannon had put off for far too long. When they finally took a step back, they stared at one another in a mutual understanding. He'd left without more than a few words over a year ago, and even though it was far from the first time they'd been out of contact, everything was different now. This time, Cannon realized it wasn't feelings of being alone that melted away when he was with his mom, it was only the joy to see her.

"I got a letter," he started to explain himself.

"Etta already told me everything," she said. "My adventuring days are long behind me, and I almost robbed them from you, so I'm not mad that you went off to find your own. Trust me, I understand."

Cannon nodded at her reassurance, never losing eye contact despite wanting to collapse in shame at his failures.

"Did she tell you I failed again?"

"You could've called me, you know. I've been trying to get in contact with you from the day you left."

"I know, I know," he brushed her off, trying not to feel so down in front of everyone.

"At first I couldn't quite track it down," Rose continued as she started to feel around her leather jacket with open palms. "I didn't make too much of an effort to stop you because of it. Once Etta here gave me a call and caught me up, I had Davy start digging around. Took a couple of months to finally find it, but we did."

"I have no idea what you're talking about."

"Here," said Rose with her hand awkwardly stuffed into the inside jacket pocket. "Been carrying it around for a few weeks now, hoping you would show up sooner or later on one of my runs."

Rose reached her hand out toward Cannon. Pinched in between her thumb and index finger was a small Polaroid picture that was creased and faded. There was a short scribble on the back that was facing up. Cannon watched her push it to him.

The picture felt familiar in size when he held it. Without reading the word that was hastily written on the back, he flipped it over to see a face that he recognized first as his own, before realizing that it was just a stranger looking back at him. The stranger had a short-brimmed cowboy hat tilted on his head and a wicked smile on half of his face. He wore a suit and tie that was too loose to be formal and his short hair was tucked up beneath his hat. His eyes were as piercing as he'd ever seen, blurred in the haze of the photo-graph, but as sharp as if he was standing right in front of him.

"That's him," Rose said with a smile. "That's all we got left of your dad."

"My…" Cannon let out.

"You never showed much interest in him when you were growing up. We talked about him when you were much younger, but I guess it sort of just stopped coming up."

"This is my dad?"

"His name was Will Garon, he was a good man," Rose told him.

"He's white?"

Rose couldn't stifle her laugh at his reaction. "Yes, good eye you got there," she said.

"What do you mean, he was a good man?"

"I think the movies always like to say the timing wasn't right. Just when we thought it finally was, he died a few weeks before you were born. You don't remember because I was too consumed with my own problems to ever remind you as you grew up. That's my burden to bear."

Cannon flipped the picture of his dad over in his hand to see the name "Will" written in barely legible letters across the back. Without thinking about it, he reached into his own pocket and pulled out an old picture of his own. This one had "Rose" written in the same handwriting on the back, and it was a picture he'd come to memorize every detail of through the years. The longer he looked at each of them, he came to see that they both had their picture taken in the same place. Not only that, the more he stared at them side-by-side, he came to understand they were even taken at the same time. His mom and dad were together when both pictures were taken. Holding them both in his hands at once, staring down endlessly into the proof of his lineage, of who he was, he sighed with relief.

Rose and Etta exchanged a glance that was almost identical to the one that Jim Bob and Cathay shared. Cannon paid them no attention as he lived in the unimaginable moment of realization for as long as he could. It was like putting the final piece of a puzzle in its rightful spot. He knew all too well what the bigger picture looked like, but to have the entirety completed was like nothing he'd ever felt before. It wasn't much, but something as small as the picture he'd been given made him feel whole again.

"Next time you hear about me trying to get in touch with you, please don't take a year to find me," Rose said as she moved forward to embrace Cannon one more time. "It might be important."

"No matter what," he let out. "I'll be there."

Cannon reached out to hug his mom one more time, this time only briefly. He stepped back and jammed both pictures into his pocket. He wiped the tears from his eyes, trying and failing miserably at hiding the emotions running through him. His thoughts were swirling. Looking around at those around him, he felt something that had escaped him for far too long, and he slowly began to understand that he'd never let it go.

He felt like he was right where he belonged.

CHAPTER 25

ONE DAY LATER

"My mom and dad were vagabonds, believe it or not. They'd go from one town to the next tryin' their damndest to strike it rich or at least put some food on the table for me and my sister. More often than not, they'd fail miserably at both," explained Jim Bob. "Once I got good at ridin', hunger pains were a thing of the past."

"That almost makes me want to cut you some slack every now and then," said Cathay.

"Not my fault my parents weren't famous."

"Now you know damned well mine weren't famous by any means."

"What do you call those people that follow you around everywhere you go with cameras and screaming questions nobody cares about?"

Cannon finally interjected into their back and forth. "Paparazzi."

"That's the word," said Jim Bob, turning his attention back to Cathay. "Anyone that has those paparazzi following them around when they go to buy groceries is famous. Don't care much at all what else you have to say about it."

All three were piled back inside a pickup together once again. The diesel engine hummed its familiar tune inside the cabin as they pushed eighty miles an hour down the highway headed southbound. It was the middle of summer, when temperatures get over ninety before noon. It made Cannon that much more thankful for the all-new dually with the turbo diesel that whirred when he stomped on the gas. It had cooled seats and an air conditioner that made you want to bring a jacket no matter what time of year.

The new pickup was nothing compared to the new picture that he had tucked away inside his pocket of the man named Will Garon, the man he now knew was his father. It was a weight off his shoulders, but sitting inside the truck with Cathay and Jim Bob by his side, he eventually came to realize that it wasn't the only answer he was looking for. He'd found a family of his own in their unexpected partnership together. He knew they'd never allow him to go out on his own ever again, and that was just fine by him.

The whole interior of the cabin began to ring with an incoming call. Cathay reached up and touched the answer button on the screen in the dash as Cannon kept his attention on the road, lost in his thoughts. Jim Bob was in his usual place in the middle of the back seat, his denim-clad legs spread wider than anyone's ever should in the back.

"Got the details, as promised." Etta's voice came through the truck speakers.

"Let's get to it," said Cannon.

"A Native American community council down in Jasper reached out to us a while back about some pretty wild threats they've been receiving," she began. "A few days later, we've got dozens of people talking about seeing spirits and hearing disembodied voices. Now, we're starting to hear the same old bullshit coming up about ancient burial grounds and this and that. We think someone broke into the council's offices and found more than they bargained for in the process."

Cannon shot Cathay a worried glance before speaking up.

"What do you need?"

"Y'all need to go to Jasper, meet up with the council, and find out who was threatening them before all this shit hit the fan," she told them, now speaking to everyone inside the pickup. "Once you figure out what they took, you go get it back. Simple as that."

"Not a lot to go on, Etta," Cannon said.

"More than we usually have, I thought you'd be excited about this one."

"We're fine," Cathay answered for him.

"You know, y'all don't have to be out on the road again so soon. We have other hands we can send out to let you rest. And I'm sure your mom wouldn't mind having more than a single afternoon to see you, Cannon."

"What Cathay said. There is too much to do. Mom knows that more than anybody on this call."

"You're right, as always."

"We'll check in when we know more," said Cannon

before reaching up this time himself and touching the screen to end the phone call.

Jim Bob wasted no time in trying to figure out what he'd just been roped into. "Did she say something about ghosts? I haven't told y'all this before, but that's probably where I draw the line on this whole thing."

"Don't be like that, I'll protect you," Cathay sneered at the back seat. "I've seen worse."

"I could tell you some stories that might change both of your minds," Cannon told them both with a smirk.

The group continued speeding down the highway with their new destination of Jasper, Texas guiding the way. Before Jim Bob could answer his prodding, Cathay went back to tapping the oversized screen to adjust their route to the closest bar.

"You can tell us some of them over a drink," she asked without looking.

Doing his best not to swerve into the shoulder and draw whatever smartass comments the two next to him were sure to have locked and loaded, Cannon did his best to look over at both of his new partners. His chest swelled as he acknowledged a couple of hard truths in this new life of his. The first was the hard-to-swallow fact that those two were as close to family as it gets, and the second, he just didn't care all that much to drink anymore.

"How about we finally go get that chopped beef sandwich instead?"

A LOOK AT BOOK THREE
ANOTHER DAY, ANOTHER BULLET

A FAMILY REUNITED. A LEGACY THREATENED.

Thomas Hunter has found untold success standing on the shoulders of his family's birthright. Thousands of acres of black gold have yielded more mailbox money than he could ever spend, putting him on the fast track to an easy life. Kaya Hunter has forsaken it all, instead choosing to advocate for those who have had their futures stolen by forces few dare to stand against.

When they each receive a letter warning them their family is under attack, Thomas and Kaya return home, only to find a mythical terror once lost to Caddo legend unleashed on the historic town of Jefferson. There is no money for repairs, much less time to chase things that go bump in the night— until an enigmatic man named Cassidy promises to save the city. He pledges unimaginable opportunities, and backed by millions of dollars and a deed to thousands of acres, he single-handedly leads the charge to revitalize the small East Texas town—by any means necessary.

Putting their history behind them to protect what matters most, Thomas and Kaya work to expose the would-be savior hellbent on using every trick in the book against them and fight to reunite their family in a desperate showdown for the final American frontier.

AVAILABLE APRIL 2025

ABOUT THE AUTHOR

Nicholas Osborn is a second-generation ranch owner and storyteller from the heart of deep East Texas. With a career encompassing everything from entertainment marketing to news journalism over the last decade, he has studied the craft of authentic storytelling and honed his writing throughout the years.

Nicholas's debut series aims to mythologize the pineywoods he grew up in and welcome readers to a new chapter of modern Westerns, born of the tall tales that helped shape the genre. His writing is inspired by the history of the Lone Star State, the greater United States, and the larger-than-life heroes, gunslingers, and "black hats" that gave us the myth of the west we know and love today.

Nicholas is an owner at his family's limousin cattle ranch and first-time father with his wife of over ten years. As one of multiple generations of his family working on the Red Rock Limousin Ranch, Nicholas has put his experience into words as an author with a passion to keep timeless Western culture alive and thriving for today's readers.